BILLY SIX GUN

BRADLEY VI

BALBOA.PRESS

A DIVISION OF HAY HOUSE

Balboa Press books may be ordered through booksellers or by contacting:

Balboa Press
A Division of Hay House
1663 Liberty Drive
Bloomington, IN 47403
www.balboapress.com
844-682-1282

Because of the dynamic nature of the Internet, any web addresses or
links contained in this book may have changed since publication and
may no longer be valid. The views expressed in this work are solely those
of the author and do not necessarily reflect the views of the publisher,
and the publisher hereby disclaims any responsibility for them.

The author of this book does not dispense medical advice or prescribe the use
of any technique as a form of treatment for physical, emotional, or medical
problems without the advice of a physician, either directly or indirectly. The
intent of the author is only to offer information of a general nature to help
you in your quest for emotional and spiritual well-being. In the event you use
any of the information in this book for yourself, which is your constitutional
right, the author and the publisher assume no responsibility for your actions.

Any people depicted in stock imagery provided by Getty Images are
models, and such images are being used for illustrative purposes only.
Certain stock imagery © Getty Images.

Editors:
Phil Blevins and Judianne Abramson

Print information available on the last page.

ISBN: 978-1-9822-7734-5 (sc)
ISBN: 978-1-9822-7735-2 (e)

Balboa Press rev. date: 07/27/2022

CONTENTS

CHAPTER ONE

———◇———

THE BEEPING

The beeping. That was the sound that he could never get used to. Beep. Beep. Beep. Not all at once, of course. Long and drawn out. Beep......(three seconds).....Beep......He lost count of how many beeps he heard over the past six months in this room. He started to think of a time before the beeps. The thought of the ocean came to mind. Yes, the trip with his wife to Santa Cruz, California. Not far from his own home in Hollister, California. That trip was memorable. The seagulls even seemed happy as they cawed from the pier and ate leftover clam chowder from the bread bowls made from one of the local shops. The sun shone on them, but it wasn't hot or unbearable, and tourists walked up and down the pier with joy as they spoke in all different languages from all over the world. Special, that was the word he was looking for. There were definitely no beeps then.

"Mr. Tunnicliff, that should do it for today. You did great!" Mary, his nurse, said as she removed the cap from his I.V. tube. Her smile was always radiant, even when the other chemotherapy patients in the rooms appeared miserable.

They tried to make it comfortable. The chairs were genuine leather and padded nicely. The televisions were always within view. William Tunnicliff estimated that he must have spent at least 6.1750 hours in each of the chairs. Numbers, he was good with those. After all, he was a Certified Public Accountant and worked as an independent contractor for big companies. Texaco, Walmart, and IBM were just a few. He liked to think of numbers as a key to the universe. One of his prized possessions that sat above his computer was a Nautilus shell. It had the Fibonacci sequence mathematically laying out each ring of the semi-circular shell as it grew with the formula.

Doxorubicin, the most potent form of chemotherapy available to him was brutal. Not at first. Always later, and at the worst times. Usually when he was about to try to work on something at his computer or just relax. Relaxing. That was something that felt like a distant memory.

"William, you're wife's here." Mary said, snapping him away from his thought for a moment.

William began to stand and did pretty well. That is until he stood all the way upright. Nausea hit him immediately, and it felt like his whole body was ready to pour out of his mouth. He wasn't about to let that happen. He closed his eyes, winced, and then with all his dignity, stood tall, pushing the feeling down into his stomach. He opened his eyes to look around the room. His eyes locked on a painting of a cactus hanging on the wall. He had seen it several times, hell, he had seen every painting in there a hundred times, but this time, the cactus stood out. It was in some type of desert setting with a red-tinged sunset in the background. He never noticed bees in the photo and flowers he had only noticed the cactus.

Interesting.....he thought to himself and tried to count the spikes on the cactus. As he began to count, the thunderous and distinct sound of a Harley Davidson motorcycle roared outside, causing him to look out the window. It was annoying. It reminded him of his annoying neighbor Steve.

"Baby, you're looking good!" his wife Rhonda said, holding out her hand as she did for every session. William smiled through the nausea and looked around the room once more. Fifteen patients were receiving chemotherapy today. Each of them six feet apart, wearing masks thanks to the COVID-19 pandemic. As if it mattered to a bunch of cancer patients. COVID might even be a step up from how the chemotherapy made you feel. At least before they could talk to each other and pretend there was some kind of hope. Now the governor took that away too.

He took Rhonda's hand and started to walk. Her blue dress clung to her body perfectly. She knew how to dress. Under any other circumstances, he'd probably go home and try to get her out of it as quickly as possible and practice making babies. That, however, was not in the stars for the Tunnicliffs. They had been married for 12 years and counting but had no children. Not for lack of trying. They did all they could. Neither of them had reproductive complications, and they tried everything the doctors recommended. They even consulted a fertility doctor. It was just not in the stars. Not in the stars then, and definitely not now.

William stopped briefly to catch himself, grasping Rhonda's hand tightly. She stopped and turned, but before she could speak, he said, "I'm fine." and continued walking. The motion of watching her dress must have made him dizzy. He concentrated, saying, *One more step. Just keep moving....*

"Mr. Tunnicliff, would you like to come in next Monday? Your treatment needs a little more time to leave your system." Mary said, popping up on his right side cheerfully. He never could understand how she was always so friendly when most of her patients faced certain death, albeit slowly. It must be daunting.

"Next Monday will be fine." he replied, continuing to walk. Mary nodded and disappeared as quickly as she appeared.

A woman in a wheelchair was wearing a robe and a headscarf, typical of cancer patients who lost their hair, wheeled by. He could see she felt the same misery he did. As sad as it sounds, he took comfort in it. Misery loves company.

The car ride back to the house was when he would have small talk with his wife, but not today. Rhonda was quiet as the car hummed down the road. He was grateful for that. The nausea was getting worse and came in waves. The hum of the engine seemed to make it worse. The passing blur of the scenery sped up the misery, so he closed his eyes. He felt at peace briefly until another loud motorcycle pulled up next to them at a stoplight. THUMP THUMP THUMP THUMP. The loud pipes woke him up. He looked over to see his neighbor Steve, his annoying nemesis, sitting on his black Harley Davidson stopped at the stoplight next to them. THUMP THUMP THUMP THUMP the pipes kept screaming.

"HEY WILLY!! GOOD TO SEE YOU!" he yelled over his pipes, waving at William. William waved back.

"It's William, you fucking Neanderthal!" William said. Still, it was Steve, and again, Steve was getting on his nerves. He had several run-ins with his neighbor asking him to turn down his music or stop revving his motorcycle at 7 a.m. The problem was that Steve was always so happy and friendly that he would respond happy, which shut down William's warpath.

"Oh, it's just Steve. You know how he is, honey. Besides, he can't hear you anyway." Rhonda said, looking straight ahead.

The light turned green and Steve gave William a peace sign before accelerating ahead of them. That fucker's always so God damn chipper.....William thought.

The motion aggravated his stomach as they pulled off, and he watched as the landscape buzzed by. Pulling up to his house he felt the dread of knowing he would have to move from his seat but was relieved that nothing was moving. The chemicals from the chemotherapy were horrible. It was like a cocktail of what felt like the flu coupled with diarrhea, amplified by a hundred. They forget to tell you that you'll feel like this and then be constipated at the same time because your body doesn't know what to do with itself.

It was a nice house, built only two years earlier. Tan with brown trim like many of the other newer homes. They called them "Earth Tones." They bought it when William was at the top of his career, making well over six figures. Now they could barely make the payment, and medical bills were piling up fast. The doctors at Kaiser had exhausted all efforts, so they switched to Blue Cross so William could go to Stanford Hospital for more aggressive treatment. Two months into the switch, they found out that the new insurance policy did not cover the latest treatments, and everything they had tried was only covered by twenty percent, leaving a hefty bill that was piling up. Today's treatment was estimated to cost around nine thousand dollars. They had depleted most of their savings but still had their 401K.

To make things worse, he wasn't able to perform his work. The treatments were so physically taxing that he could barely even move some days. He remembered back to his last pitch with Google for a contract that would have pushed his private accounting business into the mid-million dollar marker. Had he not passed out during his presentation, he might have landed that contract. That was the day they discovered he had colon cancer. Colorectal cancer to be exact. He had ignored blood in his stools dismissing it due to stress. He was only forty-one and in decent shape, didn't smoke, and worked out regularly. No reason for alarm.

"Need help, baby?" Rhonda asked, looking over at William slumped in the passenger seat. He sat there looking at Steve's motorcycle parked in his driveway. He heard her. He just didn't want to say he needed help. No matter she was used to this. She got out of the car, walked over to the passenger side, opened the door, and leaned in.

"I don't know why you're so stubborn." she said, reaching in and pushing the button, releasing his seat belt. He put his right arm around her neck, and she helped him out of the car. William stood up proudly and nodded as if to say, "I got it from here." Rhonda walked off to the front door. He could hear the keys jingling in her hand and then unlocking the door.

Steve's garage was open and he could see there was yet another motorcycle in his garage. This one was bigger and shiny. He remembered riding dirt bikes when he was a kid but couldn't understand why Steve insisted on having these bikes. They were just obnoxiously loud. Steve owned three companies and had twice as big a house. He couldn't figure out why he would waste money on those machines instead of a nice car or adding to his house. Nonetheless, that was the least of his worries.

William felt the all too familiar feeling of possible diarrhea but couldn't tell if it would happen or was it another false alarm? Either way, shitting himself in his driveway wasn't fun, and since he'd done it once already, he wasn't about to take that chance. He hurried as fast as he could, pushing through the front door, nearly bumping into Rhonda aiming for the downstairs bathroom. Too late. It wasn't a false alarm. He felt his pants soil as he got through the bathroom door. Fuck! He wanted to yell, but it only came out in his head. The smell from his pants immediately hit him, and he vomited into the toilet. At least he got that part in the toilet, he thought. The vomit scent and diarrhea instigated a chain reaction of vomit over and over again for the next few minutes. It felt like hours to him. Rhonda looked in and then left.

Rhonda returned with a fresh pair of sweats and underwear, holding her breath, as she put them on the counter and left the bathroom again. This incident wasn't their first rodeo. This type of thing happened at least three times a month, and it was increasing. Luckily, there was a shower in the downstairs bathroom and Rhonda had put baking powder on the counter, which they learned was suitable for covering up smells quickly. Rhonda left the room again and closed the door. She knew better than to try to help him. It just made it worse. When he finally got enough strength back, he got into the shower and started it, still wearing his clothes. He got undressed in the shower to let some of the mess get washed away. That way it didn't get all over the floor.

The water felt good as it cooled him off. He was exhausted. He kicked off his pants and washed himself off until everything was clean. Just a few months ago he was as fit as a horse. He could work all night and party with his wife when they had time. Now he could barely stand for more than a few minutes. He reached out with the shower running and put his wet clothes into the garbage can lined with a plastic bag. Another precaution they had learned was to put his clothes immediately in the washer, minimizing the smell. He refused to let Rhonda help with the process; he still had his pride.

The shower stopped, and he toweled off, put on his sweats, and grabbed his bag of soiled clothes. He walked over to the washer, dumped his clothes in, and started the machine. This type of thing seemed to feel like a regular thing now. He looked up to the stairs and dreaded going up the ten steps to his office. Ten long steps….Never used to notice them before, but now, they seemed like Mount Everest. He was no quitter, though. He made his way to the steps and could hear Rhonda come up behind him.

"Oh no. You know better than that. You need to sit down for a few minutes." she said, grabbing his hand. She guided him over to their living room and motioned for him to sit on the couch. He did so reluctantly. He knew she was right. After he sat for a minute, she put a glass of water on the table and went up the stairs to get ready for work. She had taken on several new jobs in addition to her regular job managing an office. He couldn't even remember which one she was going to this time. After about ten minutes, he felt his sickness begin to fade a little, and that was the signal that he could make it up the stairs. He got up and made his trek up Mount Everest, which didn't seem too bad this time. He got to the top of the stairs and felt light-headed but not nauseous, which was good. He knew the extra waves of sickness would come later and get worse, then taper off. You never actually feel better on these treatments, just less sick.

He managed to get to his office, his home. He spent a year getting his office just the way he liked it. Pictures of his family plastered on the right side, trophies, and nick-nacks from growing up on the left, and his computer with a big nice comfortable chair right in the center so he could look out the window.

He plopped into the chair and fired up his computer. This chair of misery is how he spent most of his days, even before he got sick. He quickly went to YouTube to find something to watch as he heard the clicking of Rhonda's heels as she walked around their bedroom. Hardwood floors, he was glad he got that upgrade. They felt really good on his feet when he was sick. Kind of soothing.

"I'm off to work Honey. Do you need anything? I made soup. When you're ready it's in the refrigerator. I'll be back around 8." she said, wearing her business attire. She must be working her regular job. For twelve years, they had been married. She was a good wife and she took good care of him. Both of them were busy, and the twelve years had flown by. 1 P.M. Funny how that worked out. He looked over to the wall and saw a picture, of them, with parrots all over them. He had balked at the thirty-dollar price tag to take a picture with the birds, but she convinced him to do it. Now he was glad she did. It was 1 P.M. in the photo. She didn't deserve this. She didn't ask to have a sick husband, and now he wasn't even a provider.

He logged onto his computer, hoping to salvage what was left of his clients by crunching some numbers before the next wave of sickness hit. He switched over to look at the spreadsheet he had created for his medical bills. Everything was in red. They don't tell you that every time the doctor looks at your chart they charge you. Every time they ask how you're doing they charge you. When they discuss a new treatment, you guessed it, they charge you. It adds up fast, and Kaiser wouldn't accept him back after leaving their coverage. Today's chemotherapy was the cheapest bill on the spreadsheet.

There comes the point when you're dying that you accept things. They call it the acceptance stage. Seeing the red, on this well-created spreadsheet that he was once paid thousands of dollars to create for clients, finally did it for William. He had gone from 200 lbs. to 120 lbs. The tax collectors and financial institutions, that he once navigated with ease, seemed to hit him at every turn. Depression started to set in as he looked at the different pages. He was good at balancing and making things work, that's why he so was highly paid. However, it seemed like he was plugging holes in a ship riddled with thousands of bullet holes and sinking fast. He only had so many fingers. They weren't completely broke and maybe had a year of finances left. Much less than he was used to having in the bank.

BRAP BRAP BRAP BRAP BRAP BRAP.... the sound of Steve's motorcycle outside seemed to thunder up to his office. "Asshole...." William muttered, still clicking through his documents. He tried not to dive into this because it always ended up spinning into a negative and depressing mood, but he couldn't stop. He always thought about Rhonda and how she was going to survive if he died. Now, after this last treatment, he felt mortality approaching quickly. One folder was left to click on, life insurance. He began clicking through the documents and the exclusions. Smoking negated the policy, suicide, murder by the beneficiary, and so forth. BRAP BRAP BRAP, the noise thundered into his office.

"FUCKING ASSHOLE!!" William yelled, getting up from his computer. The sickness seemed to dissipate in the anger, and he started marching down in a rage to tell Steve to turn that thing off. He had no reason to yell at Steve. It was before 10 p.m., and he wasn't bothering anyone. Still, this was a good distraction.

He marched down the ten steps in fury as he opened the front door heading straight to Steve's house. As he stomped closer, he saw both motorcycles out in front. BOTH were running in front of his house. The black bike he was riding at the stoplight was small compared to the massive red and orange bike next to it. Both of them thundering obnoxiously out of their altered pipes. Nothing from a factory came so loud that it rattled residential windows. As he got closer, he could see Steve tinkering around on the new bike, and he was bent down just out of his sight. William was going to let him have it this time when he noticed the sign on the smaller black bike that said: "FOR SALE $5,000". It caught him off guard since Steve was always messing with that thing. Before William could speak, he heard Steve say, "WILLY!!" as he popped his head up behind the new black and orange behemoth. He hated being called Willy. Only Steve did that and still did it even after telling him not to call him that.

"I see you got another one of those shit piles!" William said in an angry voice. The bikes were still running, and Steve made a gesture to his ear, holding it cupped as if he couldn't hear. He held out his pointer finger and turned off the new bike. Then he walked over to the black bike and turned it off as well.

"Willy! You're looking great, buddy! Fucking cancer finally met its match!" Steve said, holding both fists up in a boxing motion. William was annoyed, but after a statement like that, he seemed to loosen up. William pointed at the new bike.

"What's that thing?" William asked. Steve smiled and walked over, motioning his right hand in a fan-like motion over the bike.

"This, sir, is the new Milwaukee 8 from Harley Davidson. 114 cubic inches of sheer God-like beauty. Top-of-the-line Road Glide just came out. Just picked her up yesterday. Her name is Alice." Steve said proudly.

"For fucks sake, Steve, why do you insist on driving

me nuts with these things? With the money you make, you could-" he was interrupted.

"Buy anything I want? A Ferrari? A Lamborghini?" Steve interrupted.

"Yes!" William said, annoyed. Steve took a moment and looked William right in the eye for what felt like 20 seconds. It was probably two.

"Willy. When was the last time you felt free?" Steve asked him, throwing a rag down onto the seat of the new bike. He hadn't even noticed Steve was holding anything before.

"What do you mean?" he replied.

"I mean free, like nothing mattered. Free, like when you were a kid, and nothing bothered you. Like in the moment." Steve pressured. It took William a second to reach deep on that thought. He didn't remember.

"I...I don't remember. But that's beside the point. These things are driving me nuts up there, and you know I'm sick! What the fuck?!" William spat out angrily. Steve was taken aback for a second but then thought about it.

"I'm sorry, William. I didn't realize they were bothering you. I'll put them up and push them down the street when I start them up next time. Sound fair?" Steve said, picking up the rag.

"Yeah, you do that! Have some respect, man!" William said, still trying to remember the last time he felt free like Steve asked. He started to head back to his house but stopped. He was confused.

"What do you mean free? What did you mean by that?" William couldn't help but ask.

"You wouldn't get it, man. Just....head in, I promise I'll keep the noise down. I know your window is right there. I'll push it down the street next time." Steve said sadly. Now Steve sounded annoyed.

"I was 12." William said staunchly.

"What?" Steve asked.

"I was 12 the last time I remember feeling free. Dirt bikes. Remember I told you about that summer with my cousins and me in Idaho. They had dirt bikes, and we rode around the property and had a bonfire? We camped on my uncle's ranch. Don't you remember I told you about that? At your barbecue." William said, relieved that he remembered. What an odd question Steve asked.

"Why did you ask me that? You're not going to sell me into the afterlife bullshit, are you?" William finished.

"Willy, I was trying to get you to answer the question. Why do I do this? Why, with all the opportunities, do I choose these machines over the others? You're right, I can afford anything else, but yes, I choose the bikes. The answer is freedom. They make me feel free. You said dirt bikes, right? Have you ever ridden one of these?" Steve asked, pointing to the bikes.

"Hell no! You can keep those death machines! You know you'll kill yourself on those one day!" William barked back. Steve smiled at William, this time a little less friendly, and raised his left eyebrow.

"You think it matters at this point? I'm selling this one for five grand. I'll give it to you for four. You didn't come down here to yell at me for the noise. You always call me on the phone for that. No lower than four. Don't try to lowball me. It's already priced way below market value." Steve finished smiling sarcastically.

"Are you fucking crazy?! I'm not getting on that thing. I can barely stand half the time!" William barked again.

"Like I said. Does it matter now?" Steve finished and then started to polish his new bike.

"ASSHOLE!" William yelled and then stomped off towards his door.

"Four is the lowest I'll go, Willy!!" Steve yelled out, laughing. William held up his left hand with his middle finger up as he walked towards his door.

CHAPTER 2

FUCK THAT GUY!

"FUCK THAT GUY!" William said, storming up to his office.

"I'm going to call the fucking cops first; then I'll call the building inspector about that fucked up shed he has back there. THEN, I'll call parking enforcement about those junkers he has in the backyard! FUCK THAT GUY!" William said, pacing back and forth.

"Yeah, then I'll...." William noticed for the first time in several months that he didn't feel sick. Not at all. The blood was pumping through his veins as he thought of those bikes and his neighbor. He was clear in his head for the first time since he started treatment.

He thought about the trip with his cousins, the dirt bikes, the bonfire, and everything in between. He wanted to be an engineer, not an accountant. He was good with numbers. He used to recite Pythagoras for fun; he liked geometry and made things fit into the world. He loved those dirt bikes too, and the fire. Just him and his two cousins, Jim and Richard. He called Richard "Ricky." for short. It had been years since he thought of them. Years later, he didn't think of anything besides building his reputation as a consultant and attracting clients. Years since, numbers stopped being fun and became tools of the trade.

"FUCK THAT GUY!" he yelled out again. He stopped and looked outside as Steve began pushing his new bike down the street just like he said he would.

"When was the last time you felt free?" Steve's questions echoed in his mind. William sat down and began to reread his life insurance policy. At least when he died, Rhonda would be taken care of. He looked over each of the exclusions, and he was safe. Safe as he could get anyway.

The thoughts came back again from his time with his cousins, and when his mother found out he was riding dirt bikes, she said, "You'll kill yourself on those things!". He couldn't believe it. He was repeating what his mother told him. She also told him that accountants make money and consider accounting rather than engineering to make money. Engineering was risky, but you were almost guaranteed to make money as an accountant. She was right. However, he still wondered what his life would have been like as an engineer. Making the angles fit into a building or a machine, putting phi into a motor compressor ratio, or even making a coffee machine more effective. He chose safe rather than fulfilling.

"FUCK THAT GUY!" William said again. This time it was loud. Louder than he had been in a long time.

CHAPTER 3

SHUT UP AND TAKE THE MONEY!

I t didn't take Steve long to notice William storming up to him at a fast pace. He hadn't seen him move that fast. Even before he was sick, it looked like he was getting ready to fight or do something to him. Steve jumped up, held both hands up with his palms facing William, and said, "Dude! Willy! I'm pushing them down the street! I promise they won't bother you! Come on, man! Don't make me do something I might regret!" Steve said, backing up. He squared off into a fighting stance, feet shoulder-width apart with his hands still up in the air, palms facing William. It wasn't that Steve was weak or scared of William. William was sick, and Steve was NOT weak. He stood at 5'9", 200 lbs. and worked out regularly. He could easily level William with one punch. Before he could say anything, William held up a wad of cash.

"Fine. Four grand, I'll take it." William said calmly, holding up the money. Steve stepped back. He let his hands down.

"What?" He asked. He was genuinely confused.

"I said I'll take it. But I want a helmet, jacket, and gloves. That's the deal. I had some cash stashed away upstairs. You're right. I'm just sitting there dying in my window, taking it out on you. Here you go. Let's do this. I need to do something other than waiting to die." William gestured the money in an upward motion. Steve laughed.

"You're fucking kidding, right? I was just fucking with you. Dude, you can barely walk half the time. I can't sell you my bike, man. You'll kill yourself, and you won't even make it a...." William's eyes were deadlocked on Steve, and he didn't move, with the money still being held out. A long pause went by.

"What are you going to tell your wife? Huh? She's just going to march over and demand the money back, and there's going to be drama. My wife's going to come out and on and on. Come on, man. I appreciate the offer, but I'm going to have to say no, Willy. It was a bad joke. I shouldn't have done that." Steve said, looking down. William looked down at the ground for a second. He didn't even know why he wanted that bike now after yelling at Steve all this time. He used to joke about the bike being loud, and Steve was the Walmart neighbor. He just wanted to feel alive again. Hell, he'd even take tired, but he was sick of feeling like he was underwater all the time. Like death was a lake, and he was slowly sinking in it, but he could still breathe and watch the light fade away as he sunk.

In a much more civilized tone, William looked at Steve and held the money up again, "Steve....look. I need this. I've never asked you for anything before, and I know I've not been the best neighbor, but I need this.

I don't know if I'll have another chance." Steve looked up at William, seeing that William was genuine.

"I'm sorry, Willy. I can't. I just can't do it." Steve said, walking away towards his garage. William stood for a few seconds watching Steve walk away. He felt defeated. Another one of life's kicks to his balls. He walked over to the black bike. It was smaller than the big one Steve just bought. "Harley Davidson Forty-Eight" was painted over the black gloss paint on the tank. He put his left hand on the bike's grip and looked at the rest of the bike.

"Can I at least sit on it?" he asked Steve, still looking at the bike. He expected him to say no. These things were like Steve's children.

"Yeah, sure, whatever, Willy." Steve said from the garage. William grasped his left hand to balance himself and lifted his right leg. A small wave of sickness came over him, but he managed to throw his leg over the seat. He plopped onto the seat and sat up. He placed his other hand on the throttle. It was an amazing feeling sitting on this machine. Just a motor. Crazy, because it's JUST a motor. A man could die or fall at any second when this thing was moving. He pushed with his right hip as he did with the old dirt bikes when he was a kid. He was surprised at how quickly it was up straight.

He imagined being on the bike and riding like he did when he was a kid. Wind in his face, moving into the wind like the wind was an old friend. He loved riding those bikes, but never in a million years would he have got on one as an adult. Murdercycles, he heard them called. He also hated it when they flew by him when he was stuck in traffic. He sat there pretending to ride and must have got caught in the moment because he looked up to see Steve waving his hand in front of him.

"Yo! Willy! I've been talking to you for like five minutes from the garage! You've been on that thing for a half-hour already." Steve said. William looked up in surprise. It was like someone woke him up. He let the bike fall back onto the kickstand and slowly got off the bike.

"Sorry. I guess I just…. I don't know." William said, pulling his shirt down. Steve looked at him for a minute, and William realized that Steve had apparently already moved his other bike back into his garage. He didn't even notice.

"What kind of bike is this anyway?" William asked. Steve seemed to be waiting for that question.

"Well, Willy, this is a 2005 Harley Davidson 883. I bored it and put in a Hammer kit, so it's up to 1250. You see, the gearing ratio on the 883 makes it more powerful on the go. That means you can come off the line like a fucking rocket! Then I relocated the coil here…." and he kept on and on. William had no idea what he was talking about, but he listened out of respect. The first sentence was all he had asked for, but he could tell Steve was proud of his bike. After he finished, William nodded at him.

"Well, thanks for the time. Maybe I should've ridden one sooner, and maybe I wouldn't have been such an asshole to you." William said jokingly.

"Maybe!" Steve laughed. William started walking towards his house. He started thinking of his favorite YouTube programs. Maybe he'd watch some motorcycles on YouTube, get it out of him. He looked up at his two-story home, for a second, admiring it. It was a beautiful house, a newer model, and energy-efficient. He thought back to their first day in the house and all their landscaping plans. Rhonda spent hours decorating and planning out the color schemes. He guessed this would be an excellent place to die. Hell, he'd worked for it.

He shut the door behind him and took a deep breath looking at those damn ten stairs. He decided he'd get a drink of water instead to delay going up those stairs. He started to walk towards the kitchen when he heard a knock at the door. He turned around and looked in the peephole. He opened the door.

"What, did I scratch it or something?" William asked.

"Very fucking funny, Willy." Steve said, looking at him. Two or three seconds went by before anyone said anything.

"Well, then what?" William finally asked. Steve held up the wad of cash that William had left behind.

"You left it on the seat, jackass!" Steve said, holding it up. William went to grab it when Steve pulled it away. Steve took a step to the right and behind him was a helmet, gloves, and a jacket lying on the front porch bench. Steve pulled out a pink slip from his right rear pocket.

"Sign there." he pointed at a line on the pink slip holding a pen up to William. William signed it almost on command.

"I don't know if this is a make-a-wish fucked up adult foundation thing or what, but if Rhonda comes by my house later, I'm NOT opening the door!" Steve said, irritated.

"Come on. I'll show you how to start it. Do you even have a license?" Steve asked.

"I do. I had a client who was close to the executives at Honda. I got my license on a little Honda Rebel just to have it in case they wanted to, you know, wanted me to ride their bikes or whatever..." then he went on and on to Steve about all the different licenses he had for all the different clients. He had a class A license because he wanted to land a trucking company contract, and he had even started to learn to fly, but that client fell through. He did several different niche things to land his clients, but that was all they were for. That was also why he was so successful. When William was done rattling off everything, Steve rolled his eyes.

"Alright, overachiever." Steve said, walking back to his driveway. William quickly followed him, picking up the helmet and other items behind him. He grabbed his wallet, keys, and phone. He trotted behind Steve, putting the items in his pockets. He was excited for the first time in a very long time.

CHAPTER 4

GOING...GOING...GONE!

teve spent the next twenty minutes showing William how to start the bike, and how the turn signals worked and talked about all the different things he had done on the bike. William sat there wearing the helmet, jacket, and gloves while Steve went on and on. The sun didn't seem to bother him before, but wearing all that gear felt like he was in the African desert, especially since Steve had picked a nice big full-face helmet for him.

"Are we going to start this thing, or are you going to talk about it all day?" William finally asked. Steve stopped and raised his eyebrows.

"Well, alright, fire her up then." Steve replied.

William reached over and put the key in the ignition. Like Steve told him, he turned it to the right and watched as the gauges lit up. A slight hum could be heard as the electricity flowed through the system. He was grateful there was no kick-start like the other bikes he had ridden in the past. He admired the lights for a minute before pushing the ignition button with his right thumb.

"Chirka chirka BAM!" The bike fired up, and that

thunder from the tailpipe could be felt through the bike as it shook itself. The bike continued to rumble, and he felt the heat from the engine start to rise up against his body. The smell of the exhaust fumes surrounded the bike, and William tilted the bike upright and kicked up the kickstand with his left foot just like he was taught all those years ago. Very different than the tiny Honda Rebel he took his test on all those years ago.

"OKAY!" Steve yelled over the thundering of the pipes, "YOU HAVE TO BE CAREFUL WHEN YO-"

William had already pulled in the clutch with his left hand and dropped the bike into first gear with his left foot. He remembered. Before Steve could finish, he rotated the throttle twice, cranking the thunder so loud he couldn't hear anything, and then let go of the clutch slowly like he remembered being taught.

The bike sprang forward with enough force that William thought he might lose it for a second, but something kept him upright and his feet on the bike's pegs. He pointed the bike towards the end of the street and felt the wind again. That same wind from when he was a kid. He kept rotating the throttle, and the bike went faster, with the rumble getting even louder. It felt like the bike was going to explode, and it was SO loud. The bike screamed, going faster now.

"SHIFT!" He heard his motorcycle instructor yelling in his head from his class so long ago. He pulled in the clutch with his left hand and stumbled to find the shifter peg with his left foot. "TOE-UP!" He heard his instructor yell again from his memory. She was a tough 5'5" German lady with a very shrewd accent and liked to yell. She yelled at everyone, not just him, but they learned. Nobody in her two-day class failed. If you made a mistake, she would make you do it again ten times. Ten times. Not a single student failed, and he landed his contract without ever riding again.

He found the shifter peg and pulled in the clutch. He pulled his toe up, feeling the bike go into second gear. "ONE DOWN, FOUR UP, PEOPLE!" She yelled again from his head. Her heavy German accent seemed ingrained in him like a drill instructor. He released the clutch, and the bike let out a sigh of relief back to its regular rumble as the bike went faster. He did it again as the bike got faster and faster until he was in fourth gear now, going as fast as he could. He looked down to see the bike speedometer at 60 mph.

His initial terror and confusion began to subside as he looked ahead at the country road. He had been turning and shifting, then turning and shifting; he had no idea where he was now and could feel his heart racing. The wind thrashed against his body, and the wind was so strong, but he held his own. Now he could see the road as the bike cruised along steadily. "When was the last time you felt free....?" Steve's question echoed in his head.

He looked to the side to see cows grazing as he rode by. He seemed to be absorbing the road inch by inch with every second. The bike thundered under him, and he felt a kind of peace for the first time since.... well....ever. His life was always filled with the next big contract, then the next big project, and when he got sick, the subsequent treatments. He had never really had anything like this. He didn't even realize that it was unsafe to be on this machine, he just felt, well…free. There was no sickness here. He had to pay attention every second, or he could fall, and this machine wasn't like a car. It couldn't drive itself, and one false nudge and it was over. Yet, that didn't seem to bother him. He just kept riding, and with every moment came another. Then another. Moments. He had spent his whole life in these moments and never noticed them.

Just as he began to get lost in that moment, the car ahead of him slammed on its brakes. The lights lit up, and William heard, "GRAB THAT FRONT BRAKE AND STOMP THE PEDAL! THE BIKE WILL STOP FASTER THE MORE YOU PULL! THE FRONT BRAKE IS ALWAYS FIRST! YOU, STUPID, I SAID FRONT BRAKE!" The instructor's voice commanded him as he grabbed the front brake with his right hand and pushed the pedal on the right side with his right foot. The bike stopped fast and almost jolted him right off the bike. His cell phone flew out of his front pocket and went tumbling down the side of the road. William was so focused that the bike came to an abrupt stop. About six inches from the car in front of him.

William's heart was pounding from the close call. He was glad he took that safety course and tried to remember his instructor's name to thank her in his head, but he couldn't remember. He looked down to see the bike ignition lights were on, but the bike had stopped. It had stalled out. He had done what his German drill instructor said…. but he forgot to pull in the clutch like she had yelled out. Thank God this didn't happen in the class, or he would've had to repeat it ten times.

William remembered what to do. He pulled in the clutch, pushed the gears down with his left foot until it hit bottom, and then slowly pulled up just once to get it into neutral. Of course, that was what he remembered he was SUPPOSED to do, but he missed neutral three times before finally seeing the little green "N" light up on the bike's console. He pushed the ignition and again heard the "Chirka Chirka BAM!" The bike was running again.

Almost like he had been doing it for a while, he pulled the clutch in with his left hand, pushed the shifter peg down to first gear with his left foot, and slowly let out the clutch. It seemed like he belonged on the bike now. As unnatural as it once seemed to him on this foreign machine, now it seemed like home. He didn't feel like a victim for the first time since he could remember. A victim of his sickness, his life, and it was terrific….No stress. He did something he had not done in a long time; he laughed.

A memory came back to smoking Marijuana with his friends at a Scorpions concert back in the 1990s. He couldn't remember when, but the song "Send me an angel" played, and he felt like he belonged. Like he was meant to be right there, at that moment. Moment.

That word moment again. He was in the moment then, and he was there yet again.

Things they don't tell you about chemotherapy. It distorts your memory. You see, chemotherapy in and of itself is toxic. Unbeknownst to William before he got sick, cancer is a cell that refuses to die. It grows beyond its lifespan and takes up resources from the other cells as it grows bigger. These enlarged cells eventually become tumors as they collide together, sucking up even more resources from the body in a group. Once they get big enough, they are noticeable and can be tested. They are called "Malignant" or "Benign."

"Benign" means they will die off on their own, and they are not a threat. Cells just went a little haywire, but nothing to worry about; it won't spread. A malignant tumor consumes the resources to keep itself alive and grow other cancer cells. That hoarding of resources deprives the rest of the body of nutrients, and that is what kills you. That's cancer in a nutshell.

Chemotherapy is a strange but effective treatment. The doctors throw poison into the body, knowing that the tumors will suck in the resources first, meaning the poison. They send the poison into the body, hoping that the tumors suck in the poison and kill off the tumor. The problem is to do this; they send poison in and kill the rest of the body. This method means the rest of the body has to fight off the poison while it's killing the tumors. Hopefully, the body survives.

They don't tell you that your body is going into Mad Max territory. A desolate wasteland that kills off the passive cells that the body is used to having available. The cells that manage to survive also absorb the poison. Then, when the body uses those cells, you guessed it, they eat the poison. Hopefully, the tumors die first, and when the "treatment" stops, the body can recover without the cancer cells.

In William's case, the treatment was brutal. The colon-rectal organs are the last ones in the bunch to process waste. That meant the chemotherapy being put into him had to go through all the body before reaching the colon cells. Even then, the poison meant to kill the cancer cells was diluted. The chemicals used in this last round were so potent that the doctors were hesitant to try it, but what other choice did they have at this point?

William's attention went back to the road as he let out the clutch, again and again, shifting up and down, working the throttle as he rode down the road. He noticed things he had never noticed before. Birds would fly over him, and he could follow them by looking up. Other motorcycles would pass by in the opposite direction and wave. Only motorcycles, though. Nobody in the cars waved. It took him two or three bikes passing by before he started waving back. The warm air rushing over him felt like he was being swaddled, and as scary as it had been in the beginning, he felt safe. That was something else he hadn't felt in a long time. Safe. He was so weak from treatment most of the time; he worried about what would happen if someone broke into his home. He couldn't even defend himself or his wife in his condition. Another thing that he never thought of before he was sick.

There seemed to be a release on the bike, and he was flowing in the wind. A release that he'd been seeking and didn't even know it. Everything seemed to be standing still, even as he rode down the road at 70 mph. Everything seemed silent even though the wind was deafening, and the pipes were screaming underneath him. There was a certain stillness in the motion, but he couldn't explain it. He just wanted to keep that feeling as long as he could. So he did.

He kept riding the motorcycle on every road he could find. He got on the freeway several times, but he wasn't even paying attention to where he was going. It had been so long since he'd driven himself anywhere that it felt good just to be in control of something. That seemed to be another thing that was taken from him. Control. He had gone from controlling every movement in his life, and making decisions, to being controlled. The doctor's appointments, treatments, follow-ups to the pharmacy, and even grocery shopping. He realized that he had felt hopeless since he was sick but then thought more about his life as he continued riding. He wasn't just powerless or hopeless since he got sick. His life was filled with things that hijacked his freedom daily. He knew he had done it to himself but couldn't remember when it started. Chasing down the client and then after another client, spreadsheet to spreadsheet, meeting to meeting, and it went on and on.

He thought about it as a big fat bug hit his helmet

square on the visor. Even the bug was freer than he was before this. The bug flies where it wants to eats when it's hungry, mates, and just does its thing. The bug wakes up when it wants to, sleeps when it's tired, mates, and dies. The bug doesn't have to stay up until 3 a.m. putting out fires and doing spreadsheets. It doesn't have to get up at 4 a.m. and go to another state to get a contract, schmooze the company's bigwigs, or get useless licenses and certifications just to fit in and get the contract. Well, mostly useless, except for the motorcycle license.

He looked down to see the gas light on the handlebar console light up. He pulled over to the nearest gas station, pulled up to the pump, and flicked the engine switch off. He put the kickstand down and slowly let the bike's weight onto the kickstand. He looked at the gas tank and tried to figure out how to get the gas cap off. He stared at the black circle in the middle of the tank. The instructors showed them how to remove a gas cap in the class, but those you just twisted off. It took him ten minutes to figure out that he needed to push the cap in, and it popped up. He twisted the gas cap off and put his card in the machine. He learned that he had to pull the rubber sleeve back on the nozzle to get as much gas in as possible, different from a car. Then he twisted the cap back on and fired it up, heading right for the road. Three more gas stops, and he finally started to feel a little tired.

It was starting to get dark. He reached for his cell phone in his pocket and realized that he didn't have it.

He also realized he had been riding the bike for hours. Now he was lost. A shooting fear took over him for a second, and he felt a sense of panic. He looked around to see he was in the desert somewhere. He must've been riding for at least four hours and knew that because he had driven a car to the desert. Had he gone that far? He just wanted to keep that feeling. It wasn't just freedom; it was something different.

A second sense of panic came over him when he realized his phone was gone. His wife might have called him. He relied on GPS and map applications to get him from place to place, and worse off, he couldn't remember his wife's phone number. Nor any phone number for that matter. Modern technology. He locked it and forgot it. The smartphones meant he didn't have to remember. He remembered his childhood phone number to his house, his locker combination, but anything past 2010, he had no idea. He couldn't even use someone's phone. Then he thought of all the information on his phone, his clients, contracts, and all kinds of the things housed on our modern phones.

He tried to remember the path he took but couldn't. The darkness seemed to be falling faster than he could keep up with, and he was surrounded by it before long. Steve gave him the gloves and jacket, which were good quality, but the biting cold of the wind chill began to eat right through it, and he started to feel a different kind of cold he hadn't experienced before. He never really was an outdoors kind of guy. This biting cold from the wind seemed to go deep into his hands, making his body feel like frozen poison was lodged inside him. That was a good thing.

The second wave after his chemotherapy usually set in around this time. A volley of vomit and hellfire of diarrhea followed every week. Not this week though. The cold seemed unbearable, and the dark road he was on had no lights. The beautiful desert he was lost in before, which seemed like an endless escape, was closing like a demon's cloak waiting to devour him. In the distance, he could see the lights from a business. Miles away but visible. He hoped it was open. He didn't even know what time it was. Late. That's all he knew. The entire black sky had set in, and he kept the bike pointed towards the lights in the middle of the desert. The one good thing he took note of was the stars. He had never seen so many stars before, even when he was a kid camping. The sky seemed to be filled with them, and the darkness made them radiate as if they were right in front of him.

William's hands were so cold now he could barely move them. He finally knew what it meant when people said, "Bone-chilling cold." The lights were getting closer, and he could see a big sign. Something Saloon is all he could see. His eyes were tearing from the cold, and even with the full-face helmet, the wind was getting through. He was glad now that Steve had chosen it for him. The inside of the visor filled with fog, and he could barely see as he pulled into the parking lot. He had to stop for a second to gather himself and was grateful to see pickup trucks and motorcycles parked out in front. He pulled the bike around to the other motorcycles lined up and found a spot at the end. He put the kickstand down, dismounted the bike, and waited for the sickness to hit. Except, it didn't come. It remained frozen in him. He waited while listening to the music blasting from inside the Saloon. He could hear it beating through the walls, and he looked around the parking lot to see people coming in and out of the bar.

It was a place that he would run from if he were out with Rhonda. Trailer trash breeding grounds. Rebel flag and "Don't Tread on me" stickers on nearly every pickup. These were working pickup trucks, dirty and not fancy and raised like those he was used to seeing. These were straight.... redneck.

"HOLY SHIT! Is that a gun rack?!" William shouted in his head, looking at one of the trucks. Sure enough, it was. William had been anti-gun for the past few years, and he didn't understand why people needed guns.

His blood started coming back into his hands again, and he started to walk towards the front of the Saloon. It had a big red door, and he was surprised to see that there was no bouncer. With the crowd, he saw walking in he would've thought they would need one, but not here, and he just walked right in.

The Saloon looked like any other bar you would walk into anywhere else. Dark, smokey, a pool table in the right rear corner, and a big bar filled with people. The only thing different was that he thought he heard live music, and it wasn't. The music was coming from a giant jukebox with considerable speakers in the corner, and William could see couples dancing in front of it. The bar was packed, and he looked to the left and saw several different booths filled with people drinking and lost in conversation.

He had no idea what he would do. He just wanted to get home and get help getting there. As he was thinking, he was bumped so hard from his back that he shot forward into another person in front of him. The man caught him by his elbows and said, "Easy there, tiger!" and immediately from behind, he could hear, "Oh man, I'm so sorry! You okay? Here, let me get you a beer!" and the man hurried off from behind William before he could even see him.

The man was still holding William's elbows, and William felt like he would pass out. The warmth of the bar unfroze the poison in him, and he felt weak. He looked up to see a large man holding him by the elbows. He was at least 6'5" and must have weighed over 200 lbs. He had black hair, olive skin, probably Mexican, but he couldn't tell, and very strong. He thought he might be the bouncer for a second but looked at his clothes and saw he was wearing biker clothes just like he was. Except his jacket and pants looked much older. The man examined him closely, and William tried to speak but couldn't.

"Come on, my friend. Come sit with us." the man said, guiding him over to one of the booths. William plopped down into the booth and tried to gain his composure. He felt the sickness hit him and wanted to vomit, but he was too cold and tired.

"I'm Mo. What's your name?" Mo asked, sitting across from him. A blonde girl whispered something in his ear while sitting next to him, and she giggled and took a sip of beer.

"William." he responded, gulping down the sickness rising to his throat. "Mo, is there someone who can tell me how to get back to Hollister? I got a little lost and –",

"A little lost?!" Mo let out a huge laugh. It was a belly laugh that only a man his size could let go of. "Do you know where you are, Sir William? Dude, you're in Arizona, man!!!" Mo laughed again and then drank from his beer on the table.

"Ah man, sorry again. Here, I got you a Blue Moon; I hope that's what you were drinking. I didn't even see you, and I was talking to Lucy and totally…. didn't see you." the man said, putting a beer down in front of William.

The man was taller than Mo but thinner. About 6'7", with long brown hair and a full beard with a very light skin tone. He kind of looked like the pictures of Jesus you see in the church, except this Jesus had earrings in both ears, slender but strong-looking, and he realized both men were wearing leather vests. They must have motorcycles outside.

"Yo Jay! Where's my beer? What the fuck, man?!" Mo asked him. Jay made a slap to his forehead using his right hand and got up, heading back to the bar.

"That's Jay. Don't mind him. He's always like

that." Mo said, looking at William. The blonde girl started laughing, clearly intoxicated, and eventually, she stopped to light a cigarette.

"So, William. Fuck that. I'm not calling you William. Only the snobby English are called William; I'm calling you Billy. So, Billy, you're from Hollister. How'd you get out here on that little Sporty? Yo, that's a chick's bike, right?" Mo said, smiling. He drank from a glass of water.

"JUST KIDDING!" Mo laughed, putting the water down. The blonde girl whispered something else in his ear, and he held up his left hand, dismissing her while focusing on William.

"You're a long way from home, Billy. How'd you get out here?" Mo asked again. William began to speak when Jay sat back down next to him, causing William to scoot to his right.

"There you go, buddy." Jay said, plopping a beer in front of Mo. "He only likes these foo-foo O'Doul's. Non-alcoholic while sitting in a bar. I know, and I prefer red wine." Jay finished.

"SNOB!" Mo yelled out, laughing at Jay.

"I'll have you know that red wine has been around -"

"Since the beginning of time. We know Jay." Mo finished for him.

"You're an asshole; you know that, Mo? I was just about to talk about the tannins and how they-"

"Help the human heart. Yeah, we know that too" Mo finished before drinking the entire bottle Jay put before him.

"Jay, you know what they used to do in the Middle East when it came to wine?"

"Nothing because only pussies drink wine, and real men don't drink?" Jay uttered as if he had heard this before.

"Exactly!" Mo laughed. William couldn't believe what he was seeing. These men looked like these rough bikers, but they talked about things he didn't think bikers talked about.

"Next, you're going to tell me that sacred geometry trump's philosophy, right?" Jay asked Mo casually.

"Well, it does. The three primary shapes…. Hey Jay. I don't think Billy here is going to drink that. I think he needs….shit something else. Look at him." Mo said, motioning his beer in William's direction. William was slumped over now against what he hoped was a wooden post. He wasn't sure. He just felt the sickness setting in again.

"Do your miracle shit, you know…." Mo said to Jay.

"Why? He's just going to croak anyway eventually…." Jay stopped. Mo raised his eyebrows and pushed his forehead forward like he did when demanding something from him. Jay hesitated for a second, then rolled his eyes.

"Fine! Why though? Seriously? This guy?! Come on!" Jay protested, stepping back. Mo continued to look at him with that same deep stare. Jay eventually scoffed, reached into his vest, and pulled out a powder from his right inner pocket.

"HEY! BARTENDER! Yeah, you! I need a beer, at

least 12 ounces. NO, I don't fucking have a measuring cup; just get me a big fucking glass!!" Jay yelled at the bartender.

William could hear the conversation, but he was starting to fade off. The chemicals in his body seemed to all catch up at once. He seemed to have beat them back with the help of the motorcycle, but it was time to pay the piper. He tried to hold back the sickness but felt a dry heave come out.

"Whoa! Easy there, Infidel! Wouldn't want to disappoint now, would you?" Mo said before taking a big swig of whatever he was drinking. William looked at the glass and noticed that it wasn't a regular glass, but a massive stein like the Germans used. He could smell it too. It wasn't alcohol; it was something else. Black cumin. He had smelled it when he went to an Afghanistan restaurant with one of his clients. Very distinctive. Not just distinctive, but strong. People used it to relieve sinus congestion, if he remembered right. His client had told him that. He watched as Mo drank from the stein and looked closer at the cup. Intricate gold etching on the top of the border was all he could make out.

William looked around him, and it looked like a typical bar. A man was conversing with a petite blonde at one end, the other men were playing pool, and in the middle, the smoke hazed over the bar as people ordered their drinks. The dance floor looked normal with people dancing, but he noticed something else. He couldn't hear the music.

Jay returned promptly and pushed a giant stein in front of William. The stein was different than anything he saw in the bar. Everyone else had the standard bar mug and clear glass with flat siding or a clear round glass. This stein had a giant crucifix in the middle of it with what appeared to be pewter, and you had to push the thumb to lift the lever that revealed the essence inside the cup. William pushed his thumb down and looked inside. He took a smell and winced.

"Hey, look. I'm grateful for your help, guys, but this smells like…." William started.

"A monkey's asshole?" Mo finished, then kissed the brunette on his right side. William could have sworn she was blonde before. Jay made a dismissing motion with his right hand and walked away. Mo finished the kiss and let out a bellowing laugh.

"Fine! Don't drink it. Go ahead and walk right out that door, Sir William" Mo pointed at the door. "You're not a fucking prisoner. You came HERE and asked US to help you, did you not? So, here you go. Jay is giving you some medicine to help with that fucked up constitution you have, and you're throwing it back in our face like he's a freak trying to take something from you. Am I wrong here, "Sir Dick?" He laughed as he kissed the girl who was now ginger in front of him. He was sure before she was brunette before. Mo released his kiss and looked at William.

"No. No, that's not it…. I meant no disrespect." William plead.

"Then drink and shut the fuck up. I'm kind of tired

of listening to you anyway. Besides, you think you could get through that storm?" Mo finished. William looked outside to see a considerable rainstorm that he had not noticed before. This storm wasn't just a regular rainstorm. This rain sent water bullets down on the roof that drowned out the music. Lightning struck in the distance, and William looked outside the window into the desert.

"I…. I'm sorry." William said, picking up the stein. He held it up in a salutation looking for Jay to make sure he saw that he was not disrespecting the drink he had prepared. He looked across the bar to see Jay talking to a young girl in her twenties by the jukebox. She was a pretty girl, African American, and Jay whispered something in her ear, and she giggled. Mo caught on to this fast and bellowed out:

"Yo! Jay!" his voice seemed to thunder through the room. Jay looked up to see William holding up the stein. He nodded as if to agree, and Mo looked at William.

"That's probably the best you'll get." Mo said, drinking from his stein and holding it up as if to cheer. William held up the stein and rattled it to Mo's.

"To the best, we'll get!" he cheered.

"To the best, we'll get." Mo replied. William took a drink from the stein as Mo did the same. Mo held the stein back up after sipping it.

It didn't take long for Jay's potion to work. William seemed to be feeling woozy quickly. Thought, not like the sickness, this was different. Almost tranquil, but not drugged.

"Want another?" Mo said, laughing as he kissed the Latin girl that was for sure a redhead a minute ago. Or was he delusional? William looked up to see the woman, now a Middle Eastern woman with olive skin and precise black eyebrows that commanded respect.

"Can I get you another?" She asked, sitting on Mo's lap and reaching out to William's stein. At first, he was afraid but then remembered he was dying. When was the last time he had a drink of alcohol? He couldn't remember.

"Sure…" he replied, handing her the cup. He fell over and passed out as Mo grabbed the stein from William, and Jay was standing at his side now.

"Why?" Jay asked Mo.

"Why not? You know as well as I do not ask questions I don't want an answer to." Mo replied.

"This fucking guy? Really?!" Jay asked, pulling his stein out of William's hand. William was asleep. Passed out with his right hand extended out and using his right biceps as a pillow.

"This fucking guy?!? Jay repeated, gesturing towards the William passed-out. Mo, who usually had a rather aggressive demeanor, seemed to cave momentarily.

"You know, better than anyone, that people are sent into our lives to educate and not obliterate. Seriously, what's your problem with this one? Usually, it's the other way around, and I'm usually telling you not to let in the stray dog." Mo finished with a full gulp of his stein. The Middle Eastern girl on his side whispering in his ear. Mo stopped to contemplate what she said but then looked at Jay.

"I don't know." Jay said. He looked at William lying on the bar table. "I don't know where this guy starts or where he ends." Jay finished.

"Maybe that's what we're here to find out." Mo replied, staring at Jay. Jay took a second to absorb what Mo said and then seemed to light up.

"Fuck it! At least we get our vacation, right?" Jay laughed, holding up his stein.

"To vacation! But…. let's leave the jet skis out of this one, shall we?" Mo held up his stein.

"Agreed. Jet skis are kind of….for old married, middle-aged fat dudes. Not that there's anything wrong with that anyone who is listening….just not what we need right now!" Jay finished holding up his stein and looking around for listeners.

The two rattled their steins together, held them up in the air momentarily, then drank a long couple of gulps. They looked around the room to see the room alive with life. The timeless courtship of man to women in this tavern, the billiard table of judgment on whether a man loses or wins, and the best creation God gifted to man is music. Music could make a person rise to the clouds or drop into the pits of despair. The vibration of sound could make a person determine that their reality isn't set in stone. Music touches the soul, and right now, it was the Scorpions with "The winds of change."

"You know, Mo, they're right. The winds of change." Jay said, looking out at the crowd.

"You're smoking that shit again, aren't you??" Mo replied.

"No, dude...come on! You know it's legal in California, and if you think back, humankind made some real discoveries smoking that, but no, I'm not smoking anything. There's change coming." Jay rebuked.

"There's always change coming, bro. You know that, and we've seen it over and over. The more things change, the more things stay the same." Mo said, looking over at William.

"Not this time." Jay replied, looking out at the crowd.

"Really? Because it all looks the same to me. I mean, look, dude." Mo said, holding his stein up in an arch motion to the crowd.

"No. This guy's different." Jay said, shoving his stein towards William.

"How?" Mo asked, looking at William and looking back at Jay, confused.

"I don't know. I just know." He finished, then drank from the stein.

"Oh, now I KNOW you're smoking that shit!" Mo laughed with such a mighty bellow that even Jay started laughing. They laughed so hard that they both had tears in their eyes.

"Man, I've fucking missed you, bro!" Jay yelled out over the music.

"Me too, brother!" Mo held up his stein and clanged it against Jay's.

The night continued as the two talked over the passed-out William and the crowd playing out in the background. They talked about everything from politics to women until they looked around to see that most of the crowd was gone, and only a few of the employees remained.

A small Caucasian female approached their table, composed of William, Jay, Mo, and three random female patrons, several locals that the bartender recognized. Everyone at the table was drunk, passed out, or sleeping, and everyone but Jay and Mo remained sober and awake.

"Folks, it's closing time. You know, we appreciate your business, well, hell…." she looked at the bartender, who was also the owner.

"We appreciate the business, but we have to abide by the law, you know…." she said in a polite voice but also an assertive tone.

"Oh yeah...ABC right?" Mo said from the right side.

"What is ABC?" Jay asked, sipping from his stein.

"Alcohol, Beverage, Control." Mo said matter of factly.

"So? Are they here? Why can't we just…." Jay started, but Mo held up his right hand to Jay.

"We'll be leaving shortly, Miss." Mo said, looking at the barmaid.

"Just give us a few minutes. Our tab is settled, yes?" Mo asked. She nodded.

"Then just a few. I promise." Mo said, stroking his beard and nodding to Jay.

She looked back at the bartender and then back at Mo. She nodded and then went on about her business cleaning tables.

"Dude. That guy's passed out, and these two ain't movin'. How do you expect to get them out of here…." Jay started, but Mo had already slung William's left arm around his neck and started to pick him up.

"Just him. Leave the other two. The bartender will know who to call." Mo said, standing up with William.

Mo motioned for the barkeep to come over with his right hand. Instead, the owner walked over.

"Sir, can you call these ladies a ride home?" he asked, looking at the front door.

"This gentleman will come with us." Mo said, walking towards the front door. He looked around to see several men and women passed out on the floor.

"Yah….no problem. I'll add them to the list. You know, the Sheriff comes around at closing, so I hope you're not planning on driving." the man said from behind Mo.

"No….not tonight. We're across the street at the Starlight. Wonderful place. Very exquisite. You know, they even went as far as to place purple shag carpet in to distract from the stains on the walls? I mean, they went all out, buddy! They even give you three dollars of quarters for the massage bed! Sheriff won't have any trouble out of us. Well, maybe this fucker if he wakes up!" Mo laughed that same bellowing laugh that made the bartender laugh with him.

Jay opened the front door as the three walked across the street. It was Mo and Jay walking, with William being carried by Mo.

They walked across the street with the dust of the desert flowing behind them. The rains had dried quickly from the thunderstorm in the desert, but some moisture was leftover. The sweet smell of damp sand filled the air. The dust swirled in a random pattern behind the three from the topsoil that had dried out quickly. A few damp pockets could be seen remaining across the parking lot. The sands swirled as if in a dance with themselves as they faded off into the darkness. The three continued walking slowly, with William completely oblivious.

"Well. You picked a great place this year Mo!" Jay said, pulling out something from the inside of his right inside jacket pocket. They reached motel door number 3, and Mo said, "Yeah, baby! I know how to pick 'em!"

Jay placed a small tube up to his mouth, and it lit up. Jay inhaled deeply and then let out a huge puff of smoke that evaporated.

"What the hell is that?" Mo asked.

"It's called a vape. It's the new thing." Jay said, holding the pen-like object out to Mo.

"Uh, NO." Mo said, retrieving his room key from his right pocket.

"See that? A key. A REAL key." Mo said, sliding

the key into the lock. "Not one of those modern card thingies, or even worse, using your phone. An actual key that you put into the door. Imagine that." Mo finished. Jay let out a big smile and patted Mo on the back twice.

"A real key, and a real….well, whatever it is that you're going to do with this." He said, patting William.

"Wait a minute! I never said…."

"Said what? You're the one who wanted to keep this fish, remember? The stray dog? He's not staying with me." Jay said, walking away.

"HEY!" Mo yelled out, but Jay kept walking, letting out another plume of vape.

"Hay is for horses and cows like you!" Jay laughed.

Mo looked over at Jay, then the bar. It was a nice bar. The neon sign was still lit across the street. The Arizona sky lit up the night with stars. Out in the desert, there were very few homes and light pollution. The stars beamed through the dark like pinholes. It was like they were punched in a black piece of paper and put up to a light bulb. Mo looked up at the stars and let out a little laugh before lugging William inside the room.

He placed William onto the bed and then pulled William's feet up. He looked down at William for a minute. As a father looking at a child, he looked around the room. It was what you would imagine a dive motel to look like. Wood-paneled walls with tacky art. A velvet horse head was above the outdated television, and a random picture of a red barn with horses was on the other side of the room. The bathroom was to the right side of the room, and the quarter massage bed had three dollars worth of quarters by the bed. A room that had been frozen in time.

Mo looked a second time and then decided to go outside to look at the stars. After leaving the room, he sat on the curb and looked at the Starlight parking lot. Modern cars filled their spaces; one had a cord coming from where the gas tank would usually be. ECV was what was written on the stall. The electric vehicle was something Mo had seen before but didn't want to see it out here. He looked across the street to see the stragglers from the bar being picked up in taxis and random relatives coming to get them after the bartender had called them. Small town. Everyone knew everyone. He took comfort in this scene. He had seen it many times over, but he still took comfort in the remoteness.

"Feeling nostalgic, are we?" A female voice said from behind him. He looked up to see a beautiful redhead come from the shadows. As she approached, he recognized her immediately.

"Hey there, Lucy." Mo said, sitting on a planter box in front of his room.

"I guess I am." he continued.

"It's good to see you. Jay too." She said, puffing on a cigarette. The smell of tobacco bothered him regularly, but he let it go. They were outdoors.

"As is you." He replied, looking up at the stars. A long pause went by before Lucy sat down beside him. She looked at him, then at the sky.

"Of all the places you two could have gone, you chose my bar. Why?" She asked.

"Ask Jay. It was his idea; I didn't even know you'd be here, and I just showed up like I always do for our vacation. You own like fifteen of them anyway. It was his year to pick." Mo said, still looking up at the stars.

"I see…." she said, looking up with him.

"…and the meat sack in your room? I mean, come on, Mo, even you know that meat sack is filled with a chemical shitstorm that could take out a small village. What are you doing?" Lucy asked, puffing her cigarette. A few moments went by when Mo let out a sigh.

"I have no idea, and it just didn't seem right. You know, just leaving that guy in there like that." Mo said. Lucy laughed out loud after thinking about what he said, then she let out a second laugh and then stopped.

"You still have hope, don't you?" she said, looking at him. He didn't look at her. He just kept looking at the stars.

"Hope died a long time ago, Mo. Just like him, just like ALL of them!" Lucy said, pointing out in a semicircle.

"Why do you still cling to that useless rhetoric?!" Lucy spat out at Mo. Mo didn't budge.

"Yo! Lucy! Lighten the fuck up!" Jay said, walking up from behind them. He took a minute and stared at both of them before sitting next to Mo on the planter box. He held out his left hand and patted the box in a motion for Lucy to sit. She rolled her eyes and then eventually sat next to Jay.

"You two are fucking pathetic." She said, puffing on her cigarette. She blew the smoke in an upward motion. Jay took a hit of his vape pen and mimicked her smoke. His vape disappeared while her smoke lingered in the air.

"Yeah…... I guess we are." Jay replied.

"Speak for yourself, hippy!" Mo broke his silence. Jay giggled, and the three continued to look up at the stars.

"I guess we all are." Lucy said, looking up. There was a long silence as the three sat looking into the darkness with the pinholes of light reflecting at them.

"Kind of ironic…." Mo said, finally breaking the silence again.

"What? That you admit that you're pathetic?" Lucy said sarcastically.

"Deadlights." Mo replied.

"Dude….I thought I was the only one who liked to get high here." Jay said, taking another hit from his vape pen.

"Dumb ass! Dead….lights. Those stars we're looking at are probably dead. It takes thousands of light-years to reach the earth. By the time we see this, those stars are probably dead. Burnt out. We're looking at corpses." Mo said matter of factly.

After contemplating what Mo said, Lucy was the first to laugh.

"Isn't it all dead stars, Mo?" Lucy asked. She reached into her clutch purse and pulled out a small bottle of what Mo presumed was alcohol. A small flask. She

53

opened it by twisting the top and took a swig. She shuttered for a moment and then offered it to Mo. Mo shook his head side to side in an affirmative "No." She held it up to his nose, and he winced.

"What the fuck is that?!" He asked.

"Apple cider vinegar. It's supposed to support digestive health." Lucy said, taking another swig. Looking at her with a shocked face, Mo took the flask and gave her a long stare. He took a swig and let the putrid vinegar hit his throat, and winced as she did.

"That's fucking nasty!" Mo said, handing the flask back to her.

"Yes. Yes, It is!" Lucy laughed, twisting the cap back on and placing it back into her clutch. The three laughed for what seemed like five minutes before there was an awkward silence.

"Well…" Jay started. "At least we have tonight, and we have right now." Jay finished.

All three nodded in agreement as they watched the stars. That moment lingered, and all three held on to it as long as they could. The silence seemed more comforting than conversation amongst these old friends, and William slept silently behind them in room number three. The world seemed to pass them by as they just watched the sky in a world where doing such a thing was now forgotten.

Cell phones, jobs, politics, and the like all seemed to draw people away from this very thing. Not these three. Not now. They watched those stars with intent. A type of intent not known to most of the modern world of distracting technology. Then, after some time, they began to part ways. Back to their rooms, their lives, their futures. If anyone knew, it was them that the only thing in the world that was guaranteed was change, and the world was changing.

CHAPTER 5

FUCKTARD

"Hey, fucktard! You're drooling on my sheets! I'm not paying for that!" Mo yelled at William, who was waking up. The sickness hit him slightly, but it wasn't nearly as bad as usual. He didn't know what the man had said at first, but he was very clear when he said it a second time.

"Hey! Douchebag! Stop drooling on the sheets! They charge you for that shit!" Mo roared, this time pushing William off the bed onto the floor with his right foot.

"HEY!" William yelled out from the floor; he had pulled the sheets and bedding with him. He got up disoriented and tried to find the source of who was yelling at him.

It wasn't hard to find him, as Mo was already in his face. It took William a second to try to wake up when he got a good look at Mo. It was the man from the bar. He was olive-skinned, about 5'9", 190 lbs, and had a full beard. He seemed much bigger yesterday. William couldn't tell his race but knew he wasn't Caucasian. Mo stood over him with piercing eyes. Eyes that seemed the type that were kind and cruel at the same time. However, at the moment, they were not happy eyes.

"Get up, you jackass!" Mo yelled at him. William stood up and felt woozy. Mo looked at him for a second and followed up with, "Oh...are you feeling dizzy? Is your vagina giving you an....awry disposition? Well, get over it and get your shit! Check out is in 20 minutes, and I'm not paying for anything extra!" Mo finished throwing William's jacket at him. William caught it and held it to his chest, still confused.

Mo began to walk away, and William could see him clearer now. He had long black hair, neatly braided, that flowed down the back of his black leather vest. He wore jeans with a chain wallet that he had seen bikers wear in the movies. Jeans, boots, and a big knife on his right side.

"Get your shit. Let's go!" Mo said, grabbing a flannel shirt from the bed.

William looked around the room at the wood-paneled walls and the single bed. One side was disturbed, and a chair in the corner of the room resembled his grandparents' old velvet chairs. He started to examine the rest of the room when Jay came into the doorway.

"Yo! You coming or what?" Jay said, looking at William. He noticed Jay appeared to be Caucasian but wasn't sure. Just like Mo. He couldn't tell what either of their race was, but Jay seemed to have kind eyes and brown long hair. Jay was much thinner, and his demeanor seemed much more mellow. Still, even with a mellow demeanor, it was clear William needed to get moving. He looked around to ensure he had everything and then walked toward Jay.

"I need to call my wife. She's going to be worried." William said to Jay.

"Holy shit! No way, man! Do you need to call your wife? Shit! Well, what's the number, man? We'll square this shit away right here." Jay finished. William took a second and realized that he had already had this conversation with him and Mo the night prior. He looked up, embarrassed.

"I'm just fucking with you, man! I know. Hollister, right? California?" Jay asked, pointing both of his pointer fingers at him. William nodded.

"Don't worry. We got you. We're heading that way, anyway." Jay finished.

"HURRY UP, YOU FUCKS!" Mo could be heard yelling from the parking lot.

William walked out, following Jay to the parking lot to see Mo sitting on a motorcycle. It wasn't just any motorcycle though. This thing was even more obnoxious than anything his neighbor Steve had brought home. It was black with giant forks coming out, and it looked like it belonged in a cartoon. Parked next to it was an equally crazy-looking white motorcycle with a custom seat that looked like it was from the 1970s. Mo fired up his bike, and a massive explosion went off. Followed by the cadence of his pipes spewing out a loud thump after thump. William almost had to cover his ears. Jay walked over to the white bike and fired it up. It had almost the same ridiculous thunder that Mo's bike had but in a different rhythm.

"GO GET YOUR BITCH BIKE ACROSS THE STREET! WE'LL MEET YOU THERE TO GAS UP!" Mo yelled over the pipes pointing at the gas station. Before William could respond, both Mo and Jay were already in gear and fired past him. He could hear the thunder fading away as they went down the street. William looked up at the Starlight sign of the motel and then over at the bar. All of this seemed to be a disaster. He wanted to call his wife and felt stupid for not having her number memorized. He looked down the street to see the bikes disappearing and realized they were his only shot at getting home.

William walked across the street briskly to his bike parked in the same place he left it. He took the key out, put it in the ignition, and turned it. He pushed the ignition button and, "chirpa chirpa BAM!".

The bike was running again. William seemed to instinctively know how this bike responded after being on the road with it. It was part of him. Even for the short time he had it. William threw his right leg over onto the seat and felt the bike's vibration as it idled. He grasped the handlebars and pushed the bike upright, pulling the kickstand up with his left foot. He pushed the bike back, dropped it into first gear with his left foot, and released the clutch. What seemed foreign to him yesterday seemed to be second nature now. The bike leaped forward, and William guided it out of the parking lot. He turned left onto the street towards the gas station.

As he pulled into the Chevron gas station, where he saw Mo and Jay gassing up their bikes, he couldn't help but notice how outdated this particular Chevron was. It still had the old logo he hadn't seen since the 1970s. There appeared to be none of the modern conveniences, nor even a bathroom that William desperately needed. He pulled the bike up to the pumps behind Mo and Jay.

"Gas up. It's going to be a long ride." Mo said, walking towards the building.

"Shit! Even if this fucker gasses up, she's only got a buck in her! You better get a gas can!" Jay yelled out.

Jay finished gassing up his bike and handed the pump over to Wiliam. William took the pump and gassed up his Sportster. He looked over at Jay's bike, which looked massive compared to his. It was at least double the gas tank, but neither he nor Mo had a windshield or anything that looked modern on their bikes. Before looking at Mo's bike, he heard Mo yell at him.

"You looking at my bike is like trying to fuck my wife!" Mo yelled out. Jay laughed out loud and shook his head.

"He's just fucking with you." Jay said, smiling. For the first time, William noticed Jay's smile, and it was different than any other smile he had seen. He felt peace with his smile. When he smiled, a certain radiance about Jay made it feel like the world was alright, even if it wasn't. Kind of like a grandfather who puts you at ease just talking to you.

"What are you staring at each other for?!" Mo yelled out with his head peeping out of the gas station door. "Yo, Jay, you want beef jerky, or are you still doing the whole Vegan thing?" Mo finished.

"It's vegetarian, and no, I'm good." Jay yelled back.

"What about you, Billy? Jerky or no?" Mo asked. William thought for a second, and before he could answer, Mo replied, "I'll get one just in case for you." then disappeared back into the gas station.

The bikes were filled with gas when Mo came back from the gas station eating a beef stick.

"I thought you don't eat pork." Jay said. Mo rolled his eyes.

"It's turkey jerky, and I'm not eating that disgusting pig animal. You know it...."

"Yes, a pig eats its shit? Yeah....you've said it a hundred times." Jay finished. Mo laughed.

"Guys. Look, I appreciate all of your help, and I can pay you guys for your trouble." William interjected. Both Mo and Jay looked at each other for a second before they laughed out loud as if William had just said the funniest thing they had heard in years. After they finished laughing, Mo looked over at Jay and nodded.

"Sure. Here you go. Take my idiot box." Mo said, throwing William his cell phone.

"Call her up. You know how to use that thing." Mo finished.

"I....I don't know her number. I already told you that." William said, embarrassed.

"Ok. Well, Facebook, Twatter, Click Clock....I mean Tik Tok...find her." Mo said.

"We don't use any of those things. Well, I mean, I did for business, but we don't...." William started.

"But you don't remember your passwords, right?" Jay finished looking at Mo.

"Look, Sir William, the world's right there in your hand. With your fingertips, you can do whatever you want. Go ahead. We'll wait." Mo said, sipping water.

William looked at the two of them and then started trying to access his accounts. He started with Facebook, email, then his bank. He even tried to call his old house number and realized he did not remember anything, and it was all locked in his phone. Defeated, he handed the phone back up to Mo. Mo took the phone and looked over at Jay.

"Look, Billy, I don't know how you got out here or what your situation is, and I don't give a shit altogether. HOWEVER...." Mo pointed at Jay. "Jay and I are on vacation heading west through Arizona. We can at least get you halfway there, and you can find your way home from there. Or, you can stop at one of those cell phone shops on the way, and they can reinstall an idiot box for you, and you can get a hold of your wife. Sound fair? Or..you go old school and ask the attendant there for directions home and a map. I'm sure that would go over well." Mo said, looking over at the teenager working the counter inside the gas station.

"We're making a couple of stops along the way to see some old friends. You can tag along." Jay added. He nodded at Mo.

William took a second and figured he could stop at a nearby cell phone store to get a new phone. That would end all this. He nodded at Mo in agreement.

"Thank you, guys. Seriously, I know you don't have to help me. Thank you." William said sincerely.

"Oh...I feel a Golden Girls moment coming on... group hug everyone!" Jay said, putting his right arm around Mo. Mo quickly pushed him away. Mo looked over at William, staring at his bike. He smiled.

"It's a chopper with an S&S 121 motor kit. Don't worry about it; just try to keep up. Those little hamsters you got are going to be screeching!!" Mo said, starting up his bike. Jay's bike followed up in the cadence of thunder as he pulled up beside Mo. Jay's helmet had a giant crucifix on the side and a peace symbol on the back. ¾ helmet, so his face was exposed, but the sides covered. Mo's helmet was more Spartan. A black skull cap with no markings. Mo put on a pair of sunglasses as Jay pulled over a pair of old-school goggles that looked like they were worn in World War II. Mo put a cigar in his mouth, unlit, and moved it from side to side. William took the hint and ran over to his bike. He pulled on his full-face helmet, fired up the bike, and saddled up. He looked over to Mo and Jay. All three nodded as a go signal. Mo took the lead as they left the gas station, followed by Jay. The two seemed to move as one while William did his best to keep up clumsily.

As they left towards the highway, William looked out to see the beautiful desert rocks tinged red and weathered with time. They seemed timeless as the three of them hammered their throttles and passed the beautiful rocks. It turned into an endless landscape as they picked up speed on the highway. That same wind that William felt the day before comforted him. It welcomed him home, except this time with friends. The morning's heat faded away as the wind swept over them.

The three rode in tandem with William trailing behind, playing the accordion to match their speed. Jay and Mo took turns leading as the Arizona blue sky seemed to welcome them with every mile endlessly. The thunder of the pipes disappeared over time as the wind and the road took hold of them, moving in an effortless motion forward towards the emptiness of the desert.

William had no idea how he had come to be where he was. Nor did he care. In this landscape, there was peace. The sickness was gone; every time it would make an appearance, he realized he was falling behind Jay and Mo and would throttle forward to catch up. It seemed to be a series of endless moments. Each gas stop, followed by a quick lunch, coffee, and eventually, they came to another town. It seemed to be as if time froze.

Jay's bike broke down at one point, and the three of them had to fix it. William had no idea what he was doing, but he did as instructed, and they got Jay's bike back up and running. 108-degree sun, a small tool roll, and no help in sight. Usually, William would have been scared, but with these two, he felt confident. It felt like a miracle when it started again, but the three were cautious not to push it, so they kept the speeds down. That night, they camped under the stars in the desert.

"Yo, Jay. You got any of that vegan vagina shit that you had in Flagstaff? I'm hungry, and I know sickly boy over there is too." Mo said. Jay reached into his jacket pocket and pulled out two sticks of what William thought was beef jerky.

"These are made from a blend of eggplant, cucumber, and dried papaya...." Jay started as Mo grabbed them from him. He threw one to William, and he broke the other one in half and threw it back to Jay.

"Yes, and blessed by a Yak's ballsack under a full moon with a fairy. The man's about to pass out, for fuck's sake!" Mo barked, motioning with his right hand for William to eat it. William didn't hesitate. Mo was right he was starving. He quickly ate the stick, which tasted like a cardboard box. Mo waited for William to eat it before eating it himself, giggling.

The campfire that Jay made was in a full flame now with the darkness surrounding them. The reflection of the fire came back from the three bikes. They were positioned in a triangle behind them. Mo's idea was to cover them from the rear if anyone or anything came up behind them.

"Tastes' like shit, don't it, Billy?!" Mo laughed, ripping a piece of the jerky off and eating it. Jay sat silently eating his as if contemplating the food.

"Yeah." William responded, and all three laughed.

"Where do you think we are?" William asked, concerned.

"Judging by the cacti that Mo was sure to eat shit and face-plant on the next couple turns if he didn't get the jerky... probably somewhere in San Bernardino. California." Jay replied.

"So we're back in California! This is great news! Rhonda's going to be...." William started.

"Pissed." Mo finished.

"What do you mean?" William asked.

"Oh....I don't know. Her cancer-ridden husband jumps on a bike and is gone for days. Don't call or leave a note. Then he just mysteriously calls out of nowhere to say, Hi! I think that is going to raise some fucking questions." Mo said, taking another bite of the jerky and looking at the fire.

"Well, I know I'll be happy to talk to her." William replied.

"Yeah. Seems to be all about you, Billy." Mo said. William took a second and then became angry.

"What the fuck is that supposed to mean?" William asked.

"Guys. Let's just chill." Jay said, hitting his vape pen.

"No! What do you mean, Mo!" William said, clearly agitated.

"Nothing. There's just something I was taught, "You cannot guide the ones you love. God is the only one who guides following his will, and by his knowledge of those who deserve the guidance." Mo started.

"NO!" Jay yelled out, which startled William, having never heard Jay raise his voice.

"We're not quoting any books or scripture! How would you like me to start rattling off all the things in my head?" Jay yelled at Mo. Mo was taken aback and even slumped his usually strong posture at Jay's reaction. After a moment, he nodded at Jay and then looked at the fire, then at William.

"I'm sorry, William. We're on vacation, and I guess I kind of fell into some of my old ways." Mo finished and then stared blankly into the fire. William didn't know how to react. It wasn't just the words that Mo said, but that he was genuine with them in a piercing way that made William want to apologize even though he had not done anything wrong. Also, he called him William, not Billy. Everything he said was off-setting.

"Ok…..I don't know what just happened, but you said that for a reason. Right here is the first time I haven't felt like I was hopeless in a long time. It's pretty clear you guys know I'm sick, but I've never really had friends. Friends that tell you the truth about things. I've had clients, work friends, and colleagues, but not friends. Mo, what do you mean? Really….and I promise I won't judge you or be preachy." William pleaded.

"Like I give a shit about your opinion….Jay's right. Just let it go." Mo finished.

"No! What….Seriously guys, what the fuck?! You know I'm fucking lost out here in the middle of the desert! We've been riding, I don't know how many fucking miles now, broke down, hot as fuck, and not much time left. I know I'm not much, but I consider you friends, so what the fuck do you mean by that, Mo?!" William lashed out, and for the first time, there was no sickness in him. None. He looked Mo dead-on in his eyes and felt for the first time….even before he was sick…like a man. Mo took a second but then reacted fast before Jay could stop him.

Mo lept up from the sleepy campfire and grabbed William by the lapel using both of his hands, pulling him off his feet and locking eyes. Jay tried to break it up, but they were eye to eye.

"I'LL TELL YOU WHAT I THINK, BILLY! I THINK YOU RAN OUT ON YOUR WIFE, WHO WAS TRYING TO BE THERE FOR YOU! I THINK YOU LATCHED ON TO THE FIRST THING YOU SAW THAT MADE YOU FEEL ALIVE, AND YOU JUMPED ON IT! YOU DIDN'T GIVE A SHIT WHAT HAPPENED TO HER OR YOU, AND YOU SPED OFF! YOU JUMPED ON THAT LITTLE TWO-WHEEL CHICK BIKE, AND YOU KEPT GOING! YOU KEPT GOING HOPING YOU WOULDN'T MAKE IT BACK! YOU HOPED THAT IF YOU DIED, AT LEAST YOU'D GO OUT WITH A BANG!!" Mo pulled him up higher.

"MO! STOP IT!!!" Jay said and pulled Mo's shoulders, trying to get him to release his grip on William.

"TELL ME I'M WRONG, BILLY! TELL ME YOU DIDN'T LEAVE EVERYTHING BEHIND FOR JUST ONE MORE CHANCE TO FEEL

ALIVE! SAY IT, AND I'LL TAKE IT ALL BACK!"
Mo said, now pulling William even closer.

"YOU DON'T WANT TO GET BACK TO
HER. YOU DON'T WANT TO FULFILL YOUR
OBLIGATIONS. IF YOU CARED ABOUT HER,
YOU WOULDN'T HAVE LEFT TO BEGIN
WITH! WHAT DO YOU THINK SHE'S DOING
RIGHT NOW? HOW DO YOU THINK SHE
FEELS KNOWING HER CANCER RIDDEN
HUSBAND IS OUT ON A MOTORCYCLE AND
WAS ABOUT TO DIE ANYWAY, TOOK WHAT
LITTLE TIME SHE HAD AWAY FROM HER?
HUH?! NOW YOU JUST WANT TO CALL HER
AND SAY, "Hi baby, I'm here and uh...just went on
a little ride". IT DOESN'T WORK LIKE THAT –"
Mo wasn't ready for the full-out face punch from Jay.
Jay was a lot stronger than he looked as he knocked
Mo completely unconscious temporarily. William fell
back, coughing. Mo started to come back when Jay
began yelling.

"THIS IS NOT ABOUT HIM; THIS IS ABOUT
YOU! YOU AND KADIJHA! THIS HAS NOTHING
TO DO WITH HIM! YOU CAN'T TAKE IT
BACK. STOP YELLING AT HIM!!" Jay yelled out.
Mo looked over to see Jay was crying. A tense moment
went by before Mo nodded his head in agreement.
Whatever these two knew about each other, William
was in the dark. However, much of what Mo said was
true. Even if he didn't want to hear it, it was clear that
Mo was referring to something in his own life.

"You're....you're right." Mo said eventually. Jay looked down and then sat.

"Fucking drama. Every time." Jay said.

"You wouldn't have it any other way." Mo replied, rubbing his jaw.

"No....no, I wouldn't." Jay laughed.

Mo looked at him for a moment, and then they both started laughing. William had no idea what was so funny and he was just relieved to be out of Mo's grasp. Yet, as he lay down to sleep, Mo's words echoed through his head as he fell asleep. Not chemically induced, not exhaustion from vomiting....he fell asleep on his own.

CHAPTER 6

---◆---

BUD'S PLACE

The sight of the town gave William mixed emotions. For the first time in a long time, he hadn't felt sick or hopeless. Even though few words were exchanged while riding with Jay and Mo, these were his friends. A bond that seemed unbreakable when in the wind together. Seeing the town approaching with streetlights and billboards gave him a hallowing feeling knowing that he could contact Rhonda in this town.

He wasn't an idiot. One stop at a cell phone store, he could restore his account to a new phone for less than a hundred dollars. Complete with a list of contacts and all that a smartphone offers. As they approached the town, he saw a sign for T-Mobile. Why T-Mobile for an accountant with a multi-million dollar business? Easy. It was simple. He could go anywhere with it. T-Mobile piggybacked off several networks, never asked questions, and was as secure as they got. Plus, he owned stock in it. None of that mattered, though, as the thunder of the pipes now seemed to all be together in a cadence.

The fight with Mo from the previous night seemed to be forgotten as they thundered into the small California town that William missed the name of pulling in. All he knew was that he had just traveled across the desert and had no idea where he had been, but these two men with him made sure he got there safe just like they said they would.

They began to slow to a stoplight. They moved as one now. Before, William would struggle to keep up, but now, they seemed to move as one, a unit, a squad, a family. The light turned red, and they stopped. Mo nodded to the strip mall to the right, and Jay nodded back. They pulled into the gas station. Each took their position at a pump.

"Yo. Billy. We can get you a cell phone there." Mo said, pointing at the T-Mobile store. All three gassed up their bikes and pulled out of the station. Jay and Mo pulled up to the T-Mobile store and parked. William got off his bike and went to the restroom. He splashed his face with water and took a breath. As he exited the restroom he bumped into an attractive female. Blonde, petite, and before he could say sorry, she said, "It's okay, Sugar. I'm sure you washed your hands. Nice bike, hun." Then she winked at him with her left eye. She looked familiar, but he couldn't place where he had seen her.

The woman patted her hair and looked at her reflection in a compact mirror she was holding with her left hand. She closed the mirror and got into a big RV parked on the right side of the gas station. William shrugged and went back to his bike.

William filled up his tank while Jay and Mo were

in the store. Jay and Mo came out of the store and made their way to their bikes. He looked at them and then started his bike. It was running funny, like a misfire or something, where the bike seemed to cough a little. No matter, it was still running. He turned the bike around. He pointed towards the east, the opposite of where they were headed.

William hit the throttle and started east. Mo's words went through his head, and he knew he was right. He couldn't face Rhonda after abandoning her as he went on his last huh-rah! That's what this was. Now he was faced with the reality of facing his wife, whom he loved with all his heart and couldn't bear to think of the pain he caused her. Better to die in the desert alone, that's what he thought before being knocked off his bike by Jay, of all people. He thought it would've been Mo that would've kicked his ass, but it was Jay. Also, how the hell did he catch up to him so fast?

William got up, dazed from the impact. William hoped that being kicked off a motorcycle wasn't something most people experience. It hurt. Still, it was better than the sickness. Mo was the first person in his face, "Going somewhere, princess?" Mo asked, still wearing his glasses.

Jay walked up shortly after with the bike thundering behind him. He bent down face to face with William.

"Well?" Jay asked. William got up and started to pull his bike up. He got the bike to stand up and put the kickstand down. He looked over at Jay, standing with his arms crossed and goggles still on. William threw his right leg over the bike, switched it to "RUN." and tried to fire the bike up. Nothing. He tried again. The same. Four times, nothing. Out of nowhere, Jay was on his right side.

"Guess we better go see Bud, huh Billy?" Jay said calmly.

"Who is Bud?" William asked. Jay pulled out his phone and held his hand up to William as if to wait. Mo just stared at him. A disappointed stare, like a father looking at his kid that just screwed something up.

"What?" William asked, looking over at Mo. Mo just shook his head.

"Alright, he's on his way." Jay said, breaking up the staring contest between Mo and Wiliam.

"You can't run forever, Billy. We'll get your bike back up and running, but you can't run away. You got to face this at some point." Mo said.

Bud pulled up to the trio forty-five minutes later. He was driving a 1969 Ford F-100 pickup truck with a motorcycle trailer. The truck driver was very old. William guessed him to be in his 70s at least. The small Asian man jumped out of the driver's door with very thick glasses and overalls.

"MO!" The man said, looking at Mo.

"Bud!" Mo replied, hugging the man.

"Well….I ain't got much, but you know….we got the shop. Glad I do, or we wouldn't be here." Bud replied.

"Jay!!!" Bud screamed out, slowly waddling over to Jay looking like C3PO from Star Wars. Jay embraced

Bud as old friends do, and again, Jay let out some tears as if he had not seen Bud in many years.

William stood quietly watching this unfold, not knowing what he should be doing, and it was kind of awkward for him.

"Well, what do we have to deal with here?" Bud asked, looking around. He adjusted his glasses and locked on to William.

"Ha! We fixing him or the bike'?" Bud asked.

"Is there a difference?" Mo replied. Bud smirked and then let out a laugh.

"Mo, I missed you, man!!" Bud said, hugging him again. He let go and slowly shuffled over to William. The coke bottle glasses scanned him up and down. William felt the scan but, for some reason, did not feel judged. Bud, a small Asian man, seemed to have a calm about him that William had never seen. He couldn't describe it. Before he could speak, Bud spoke up.

"Let me guess. It sparks but doesn't fire." Bud asked, looking at him and blinking with enlarged coke bottle lenses.

"Yes, that's right. I tried to fix it, and these two did too; something's wrong." William replied.

"Nothing's wrong; it's about balance, you see? Without balance and equanimity, nothing exists. It can never exist if you can't bring your machine or the rider to homeostasis. It will be in a state of retardation...... oh dear....is that one of those words you said I'm not allowed to say anymore, Jay?" he asked, looking at Jay blinking through his lenses. Jay nodded at him.

"Ok, we won't call it retardation; we'll call it a state of unbalance. Anyway, if your machine or you are unbalanced, everything comes apart, and if one part goes, it all goes. You know that's all there is to life…."

"Balance. Yes, Mr. Miyagi, we got it." Mo said, smiling and pointing both fingers at Bud. Bud laughed internally and then smiled at William.

"Gentlemen, can you help me get this on the trailer. I'm afraid an old man like me has a little trouble with the heavy lifting, but I assure you, I can still troubleshoot and get her on the road." Bud said, pointing at William's motorcycle.

"Old man, I'd lift the fucking Empire State Building if you asked." Mo said as he pulled Williams's motorcycle up. He started to push it forward onto the motorcycle ramp, and he started to struggle when both William and Jay started to push the bike from behind. The three got the bike onto Bud's ramp, and Bud locked it into place with a lever. The loud metal thunk echoed slightly.

"Come on, boys. Let's get her back to the shop." Bud said, slowly making his way back to the truck. Mo and Jay pointed for William to get into the truck.

"Go ahead…..we'll follow you." Mo said, firing up his motorcycle. Jay's bike followed. William got into the truck's cab and looked over to Bud.

"No….I don't need you to drive. I'm not that fucking old youngster." Bud said, pushing the truck into gear. He looked over at William and then popped the clutch. The truck moved forward.

"Balance. It's all about balance." Bud said, and off they went. Bud's truck was towing William's bike, with Mo and Jay following, with William in the passenger seat looking bewildered out the window.

Balance. William remembered the last time he heard that word. His doctor told him that the anti-nausea medicine would balance his equilibrium so he wouldn't feel sick, and he was wrong.

As they pulled into Bud's tow yard, William noticed that it seemed odd for a tow yard. Sure, there were cars lined up, but they were stacked in even numbers, six to a row on one side, four to a row on another, and when they crossed the gate, even the gate seemed to hinge on a numerical system. A mathematical balance. Numbers, he knew those. There were four tires at the base on each side of a beveled sign that said, "Bud's Tow Yard and More." The sign was on the side of the gate, and you'd miss it if you were driving by.

They crossed the border, and William noticed Bud had several Doberman Pinschers. However, they did not bark as they arrived. Instead, they seemed to welcome everyone in. A lot different than what William would have imagined. The dogs followed the truck cutting in front of Jay and Mo as they crossed the gate. They expected this and had pulled back. William looked back, puzzled. Apparently, this was not their first time at Bud's Tow Yard.

The truck stopped in front of an old barn. Big, brown, wooden, just like you'd expect in the desert. Weather-beaten and old.

"Well." Bud said, turning off the truck. He opened the door greeting his dogs. William realized he had lost track of time. The silence was calming in the cab with Bud. He had no idea how long they were on the road. He had been in some kind of trance.

"What? What do you want, Shiva? Huh, you miss me or something?" Bud said playfully. He petted the first dog, then another. Then the other dogs William hadn't seen pulling in. Bud loved dogs. That was pretty clear. William counted at least twelve, ranging from big to small. No barking, though. Weird.

"Well, boys, let's get her on the rack." Bud motioned with his right hand. He adjusted his denim overalls and walked towards the barn. He pulled the doors open outward, and Jay had already started unhooking the tie-down straps on the bike. Apparently, William had missed that part too. Time seemed to be, well, distorted.

"You going to camp there or help? It's your bike." Mo said to William, still in the passenger seat. William snapped out of his daze and opened the door. He got out and looked around. Jay wrapped up a tie-down straps, and Mo was holding the handlebars. He didn't even remember tie-down straps when they mounted the bike.

"Alright, Billy, when I let her go, you just push from the back to make sure it doesn't come down too fast." Mo said.

William got behind the bike and started to push as the bike's weight started to go back. William pushed with all his might, but it seemed like too much. He gagged and felt a small amount of vomit hit the back of his throat. He was reminded that he was sick for the first time in a while. The chemotherapy chemicals had all but come out of him, but he still had it in his cells. The aftertaste. That was their job, after all, to kill off the cancer cells. It wouldn't be much good if it disappeared in a day or two. His doctor said prolonged exposure was needed to kill the cancer cells safely.

Right when he felt like he would drop the bike, Jay started to push, and the bike smoothly rolled off the ramp. Mo pushed the bike towards the barn, and William took a minute to compose himself. After a few breaths he noticed Jay looking at him.

"What?" William asked.

"How long?" Jay asked. "How long have you been sick?" He finished.

"Almost two years. Well, that's what the doctors think. I didn't know until about a year ago." William replied. Jay nodded. His long hair appeared smooth despite the riding. He said nothing, just stared at the barn. He pulled out his vape pen and took a drag from it, and the battery lit up the little light. After a few more drags, William broke the silence.

"Colon cancer." he said to Jay. Jay looked in his direction and nodded.

"They say it's one of the hardest to treat. How did you guys know I was sick anyway? I still have my hair." William asked. He always tried to appear healthy even if he wasn't. He hated people who felt sorry for him and would say random hopeful sayings. Oh, you'll be fine, just pray or whatever. Nobody seemed to like to face the ugly fact that it was deadly, and he was likely to die. More than likely. He WAS going to die, just sooner than he wanted. Not from Jay, though. He just shrugged his shoulders.

He watched Mo and Bud loading the bike onto the motorcycle lift.

"Who is Kadijha?" William asked. Jay shook his head.

"That shits complicated, man. Let it go" Jay smiled, taking another drag.

"That's the name you said the other night when Mo was about to take my head off. I still don't know why he was so mad; I didn't lose my phone on purpose. Who is she?" William pried further. Jay pushed his face within inches of William, and he instinctively backed away.

"She's his wife, from a long time ago, and you're never to repeat her name, especially in front of him." Jay nudged his head to the left in the direction of the barn.

"Unless you want to speed up that meeting with God." He finished looking William in the eyes with intensity, unlike Jay. Jay usually had a calm, almost peaceful gaze, but this was a piercing look. Intimidating, to say the least.

"Ok. I got it." William said.

"Come on. Let's go see what's wrong with your bike." Jay said, walking into the barn.

William walked into the old barn and looked around. Old Asian art was the only way he could describe it. Buddha statues, Terracotta warrior replicas, and various random exotic items mixed with tools and motorcycle parts. There was a second side to the barn with a car lift with an older Buick hoisted.

"If anyone can fix it, it's Bud. It's like magic." Mo said, watching Bud examine the bike. He was slow and methodical as the old man seemed almost to be speaking to the bike.

William looked down at his hands. They were black from trying to push the bike down the ramp.

Bud continued to examine the bike. Up and down, he looked, adjusting a lever here, pulling something there. He stopped for a second and took a step back. He held his right pointer finger to his lips and started to laugh. Bud walked over to the spark plug wire and pulled off the rubber boot. A loud pop could be heard as the rubber suction seal broke. He looked inside to see a small piece of cardboard fall out. He pulled the other one, and the same cardboard fell out. Bud let out a bellowing laugh. He put the plug wires back on and turned the ignition. The lights lit up the dashboard, and Bud slowly pushed the ignition button. "Chirpa chirpa POW." the bike fired up. Bud turned the ignition off and laughed again.

"Fucking Lucy!" Mo scoffed. "What is her fucking problem?!" Mo asked. Bud laughed while Jay looked at him stone-faced and shrugged his shoulders.

"Every fucking vacation! She fucks with us every time!" Mo said, angrily.

"Guess we should've checked. Lucy did that shit to

mine back in…. Shit, when was that? That trip down from Scotland to South Africa….” Jay said with Bud still laughing in the background.

“20 fucking 10! She knows we check our bikes, so she did that shit on purpose! She must’ve done it when we were in the store, knowing Billy wouldn’t check.” Mo said, shaking his head.

William looked at the three of them, confused.

Bud finally stopped laughing and wiped his tears. He let out a few more laughs and then looked at Mo.

“What?” William asked. “What just happened?” He followed up.

“That…..” Bud started by holding his pointer finger up as if to pass along some type of wisdom. William looked at him attentively. “Is what she said.” Bud said matter of factly. It took a second, but all three started laughing. Bud walked over to the plug wire and pointed at it. He hadn’t expected Bud to be funny.

“You see, someone put that cardboard in your plug wires with a rubber coat, and the spark wasn’t going through. It was just enough to start the bike and go for a little bit, but then the cardboard blocks the spark because of the coating.” Bud said, smiling.

“Come on, boys, it’s getting dark. I gotta feed my hungry angels out here.” Bud walked towards the door. Jay and Mo followed, and William strolled behind them. He looked around the shop and felt a certain calmness. A different kind of calm, almost as if right now was where he was supposed to be.

“Wait, who would do that to my bike? Why?”

William asked. Jay held his right hand up and swooshed it down in a *don't worry about it* motion.

William walked out of the barn and followed Jay and Mo. Bud went to the right, and the dogs followed him, jumping here and there. Still no barking. Bud had a way of bringing peace that spread to animals. Almost tranquil.

William watched as Mo and Jay went to the backyard and began putting logs into a fire pit. They talked and laughed here and there while William took a moment to look around.

The landscape seemed endless as the sky slowly lit on fire with a dazzling display of pinks and oranges against the clouds as the sun set. William could see mountains in the distance, but there was an openness about this place. He had lived for so long in suburbs and cities that he forgot what it was like to have space. It felt good.

"Billy. Over here." Mo said, patting a seat next to him. They had started the fire, and Jay was staring at the fire in his calm way. William sat next to Mo and heard Bud walk up behind him and patted him on the shoulder, dragging a cooler behind him.

"It could have been a lot worse, boys. You're lucky." Bud said, taking a seat.

"That bitch has always had a problem with us. I don't get it. What did we ever do to her?" Mo asked, pulling out a plastic bottle of water from the cooler.

"Now, now. You can't be for sure it was Lucy." Jay said.

"Seriously? Come on, man! Who else would do some stupid shit like that? If someone had a problem with Billy, they'd have slashed the tires or something. That shit took planning." Mo drank from his water.

"Besides, she's done that shit to us before." Mo said. Jay shrugged his shoulders, and he did not argue.

"Why do you still stick up for her anyway? After all the shit she's done to you?" Mo asked Jay. Jay took a few seconds and then replied, "Well, everyone deserves forgiveness. If I stay angry at her, what does that help?" Jay took a drag from his vape.

"It will help when you see her again and sock her in the face!" Mo barked.

"Sorry to cut in, guys, but where are we?" William asked.

"Well, I think that's pretty obvious." Bud said, staring at the fire. He poured himself a cup of something out of a thermos, took a sip, and said, "We are right here."

William couldn't tell if Bud was speaking sarcastically or not. He looked at Jay and Mo, who were still arguing over Lucy. He looked back at Bud.

"No, I mean, what state?" William asked. He was pretty sure they were in California from what he remembered, but he lost all direction out here.

"State?" Bud asked.

"Yeah, what state?" William asked again.

"Well, I guess we would be in an awake state." Bud replied calmly. He stared at the fire.

"Now you're just messing with me. You know what

I mean. California, Arizona, Nevada. What state are we in?" William said, irritated.

"We're on the border." Bud replied, sipping from his cup. William stared at Bud, who still had that calmness to him.

"Billy, you want some tea? A beer? Bud has everything in here." Mo said with the cooler open. He looked back at Bud and planned to say something but decided against it. Alcohol did not go well with chemotherapy, but tea did.

"Tea, please." William said, looking over at Bud, who remained motionless as if in a trance. Mo handed him a can of cold tea, and he looked at the label. Green tea. The kind you find in gas station refrigerators. His favorite. He looked back over at Bud, who was still motionless. He waved his hand in front of Bud's face to get his attention, but he didn't move.

"Eh, don't bother. He'll sit like that forever. He sat for days under a tree, and he didn't even move when a snake landed on his head. He'll be fine in the morning." Jay said to William.

"He's just going to sit like that? All night? Doesn't he go to bed or anything? He's like a million years old." William asked. Jay shrugged his shoulders.

"Sometimes. I don't know, man. He's just Bud. We've been friends a long time." Jay said, sipping from a glass.

"I thought bikers drank everything in sight and partied all night. You guys don't drink? I'd drink if I could." William said, remembering wine tasting with

Rhonda. They had such a good time when they went wine tasting. Rhonda. She must be worried sick.

"Yeah.... And we don't shower either because showering is for pussies. We roll into town, do a few wheelies, maybe a burnout, rape all the women, throw them on the back of our bikes, and go to the next town to do it all again." Mo said, annoyed.

William realized he irritated Mo.

"I'm sorry. I just know what I saw on tv. I haven't ridden a bike since I was a kid, well, I took the test to get my license, but I was trying to impress the executives at Honda. Turned out they don't even ride the bikes. I landed that contract, so I guess it was worth it.", William said, talking more to himself than to Mo. Mo looked at William.

"So, what made you get on that bike?" Mo asked.

"You're sick. That's pretty clear, and you look like you have at least some money. Why'd you get on that bike?" Mo asked.

William thought hard for a moment and then answered.

"I guess I just wanted to feel alive again. I was tired of feeling sick, and I figured the bike would distract me for a minute. My neighbor Steve was selling it and....I don't know. He asked me when the last time I felt free was and.... It was when I was a kid, riding dirt bikes with my cousins. I mean, don't get me wrong. My wife makes me feel free, but it's different." William stopped.

"Well, did you?" Jay asked.

"Did I what?" William asked, looking at Jay over the fire.

"Feel free." Jay said in more of a statement than a question.

"Fuck yes!" William said, surprising himself. He didn't use profanity often, but it just slipped out. Mo let out a laugh.

"That's why I kept going! I lost my phone somewhere on the road, and I know why you're mad at me, Mo, but I don't know what I did wrong. I get it. I should've memorized Rhonda's number, but man, I've been going through it. Some days I can't leave the bathroom because I shit, then I puke, then I'm so weak I can't even clean it up. Then when I do get the strength, the smell hits me, and it starts all over again. I don't know why my wife hasn't left me." William finished.

"Love." Jay replied. "It's the most powerful thing in the universe, and that's why she hasn't left you. All the religions in this world have tried to teach this, but it always gets misunderstood to mean what they want it to mean." Jay said.

"Yes." Bud replied, not moving from his trance.

"Couldn't have put that any better myself, brother." Mo said, smiling.

"Love is what you felt, William. That's why you kept going. Love, freedom, that feeling has had so many different words over the years. That's the reason we ride William. Well. That's why I ride. These old bones can speak for themselves. You asked why we don't drink. Drinking takes away the senses, the moment, and I can't have that. This moment is all I have." Mo finished. It was a pretty profound statement that William took in. He never really had friends like this, and the only person he could talk to like this was Rhonda. His other friends were work-related, or he had to filter what he said for one reason or another. Not here. Not now.

"Want to try it." Jay said, holding out his vape pen. At first, William held his hand up in objection but thought about it. Marijuana was supposed to help people like him. Supposedly, according to all the articles, it helped to relieve nausea. He would give anything for that. He flipped his hand from his palm facing Jay to now an open gesture of an open palm facing up. Jay placed the vape pen into William's hand. William took it and brought it to his lips. He had never used one of these before, but he assumed it was like smoking Marijuana when he was a kid. He puffed as hard as he could on the vape pen and then began coughing. "What the fuck is this?" William asked, handing the pen back.

"Green tea. I thought you would like it, and it's what you're drinking." Jay said, laughing at his reaction.

"You mean to tell me that you've been inhaling green tea this entire time? I thought this was Marijuana, CBD oil, anything, but I didn't think it would be green tea." William finished letting out a cough from the vapors.

Jay looked at him for a minute and then laughed. "You seriously think I could smoke that much weed and not fly into the sky? I'm puffing on this thing all day. You seriously thought this was Marijuana?" Jay finished laughing. He looked over at Mo, who was now laughing just as hard as Jay. Bud sat by the fire. He giggled.

"Dude. Nobody can smoke that much weed, or they'd be high as a kite! Come on, man!" Jay said to William.

"Well, I don't know, and I've never been around anybody who uses one of those things." William finished, looking confused.

"If the world would just take a second and take a puff of green tea, it would be a much different place. It changes your perspective when you just take a second and just be here." Jay finished taking back his vape pipe. William was genuinely surprised, and he was also disappointed. He wanted to try the vape pen for Marijuana, but he would not get that chance.

"Mo's right, you know. It's about this moment. There's no other moment other than now. Everyone is always caught in the future, the past, and always everywhere but the moment they're in. Well, except maybe for sex." Jay said, then took another vape drag.

"That's why the world's so fucked up" Mo started reading from something in his lap. He had pulled out an old leather-bound notebook. "It's always been like that. Ever since I could remember, I guess that's why so many people use drugs. That's probably why they can't get off the internet. Hell, they can't even communicate anymore without that Faceplant and Twatter." Mo finished making fun of modern-day social media. He looked up at the stars and then back to William.

"You know, I never asked you guys. What do you do for a living?" William broke the silence.

Mo smiled, "See? It's hard to be in the moment, isn't it? Ever try just looking at the stars, being right here and now?" Mo pointed at the ground. His beard reflected the fire, and his face was tinted with orange. William took a moment and then almost responded instinctively but then paused. Mo was right. He hadn't even noticed the stars or the fire. The silence was awkward at first, but then calmness surrounded him. The awkwardness of the silence gave way to a peaceful crackle of the fire. William began to understand what Mo was talking about. This moment.

"Well, my last paid job was as a carpenter, but that was a long time ago." Jay said softly. William winced as he was shaken from his newfound peace.

"I was a prince." Bud said, remaining still. William waited for a laugh, but it didn't come.

"No, really, he was. It was a long time ago, and Bud here is a bonafide prince in Southeast Asia. He even had his statues and everything." Mo finished. A slight giggle came out of Bud, but he stayed steady for the most part. William laughed.

"You don't believe him? That's ok. Nobody ever does, but it's true." Jay cut in after seeing William laugh.

"What about you Mo?" William asked.

"Me? Well, not a tradesman or anything. Well, I

know you probably wouldn't believe it, but I was born into a good family. We were pretty well off, so I didn't have to work. I was very fortunate." Mo said, looking at the fire. He picked up a stick and started poking it into the fire logs.

For the first time in a long time, William had been away from a computer screen at night, and it was liberating.

"Were you rich? What did your parents do?" William asked. Mo continued poking the fire.

"Well…. My father died when I was six, and then I lived with my grandfather until he died. Then my uncle. Rich? Not really. I grew up in the middle east with my mom. We had money, but things were different then. We weren't obnoxiously rich, but we had enough that I could go to school and such. That was a big thing back then. I've had several jobs, but my favorite was as a teacher. Jay was a teacher too. That's how we met. That's how all three of us met." Mo pointed the stick, motioning at Bud.

"Oh, so you're teachers? What grade did you teach?" William asked. Mo looked over at Jay, and they both burst into laughter. They continued to laugh as William stared at them, confused. Was it something he said? What was so funny? He looked at Bud, who was giggling with them but stayed staring at the fire.

"What? What's so funny?" William asked. The two continued to laugh until Jay finally stopped.

"Ah, man Billy if you only knew the history. Anyway, it was a long time ago, and that didn't work out so well for any of us. But we're here now; that's all that matters." Jay finished.

"Well, that's not true. It worked out for me; I'm in heaven here. Look. How can it be any better?" Bud said, still deadlocked on the fire. William looked over to see several of his dogs lying down beside him. Wait….

"What is that?" William said, pointing at Bud's feet. William jumped up and backed up. Jay looked over and responded calmly.

"That's a dog, and that's a snake. That's a rabbit… And I'm not sure what that thing is." Jay said, pointing his stick at the various animals.

"What? What the hell is he like Doctor Doolittle or something?!" William protested. He was scared of snakes, but that was beside the point. How were these animals sleeping at his feet?

"Eh, don't worry, man. You'll get used to it. Bud's got all kinds of animals out here, and there's an Emu somewhere out there." Jay pointed out into the darkness.

"Only one lion, though." Mo said calmly.

"Wait! Did you say a lion?! Out in the open?! I gotta get out of here." William started to walk towards his bike, and Mo pulled him back by his waistband.

"Relax, Billy. I was just kidding. Don't worry. They won't hurt you; they probably won't even leave his side; they run off and do their thing if they do. They don't bother people." Mo finished.

"How is he doing that? I mean…. Is he a zoo trainer or something?" William asked.

"You know I'm right here. I can hear you, I'm old,

not deaf." Bud said from the other side. Both Jay and Mo laughed.

"He's always been like that since we've known him. Animals just feel safe with him. People too." Jay said, looking at the dogs lying next to Bud. He reached down and petted the dog. The dog raised his head momentarily and then returned to his comfortable posture crossing his front legs in front of him and placing his chin on his legs.

William thought about it and realized he was right. He remembered being next to him in the garage and having a safe and peaceful feeling. He felt safe with Bud.

"That's amazing." William let out after letting everything settle in.

"Did you want another tea?" Mo asked, seeing that William had knocked over his tea when he jumped up. He hadn't even noticed. William looked down for a second and then back up at Mo.

"You know what, I'll take a beer." William replied. It had been a long time since he had any alcohol, and he was feeling pretty good.

"How do you do that?" William asked Bud, accepting the beer from Mo. The dark brown bottle was cold to the touch, just like he remembered. He took a swig and looked over at Bud. Bud shrugged his shoulders and continued staring at the fire.

"I think it has something to do with his teaching days." Mo said to William.

"You see, back when Bud used to teach, he was teaching in Southeast Asia, and there was a lot of wars going on. People out there were rough. I don't mean rough as you think here. I mean ROUGH. You know Bud once got a murderer to turn his life around completely. He intended to kill Bud, but he eventually became one of his greatest students because Bud is so calm and peaceful. A long time ago, mind you, but I think that has something to do with why the animals are so calm around him. Anyway, that's what I gathered." Mo said.

"I think it's cause he's so damn handsome!" Jay cut in. Bud broke from the fire and looked at Jay. He took off his beanie hat and rubbed his fingers over his bald head soothingly.

"Can't argue there." Bud laughed, causing the others to laugh with him.

It wasn't long before William's condition set in. Half a beer hit him fast. He started to feel fatigued. As much as he was laughing, laughter took a lot out of a cancer patient. As much as he wanted to continue, he felt the ever-heavy eyelids coming down. His body needed to rest. He laid down and looked up at the stars. He faded off to sleep as Jay and Mo laughed and talked about things. Things that he did not think people like the two of them talked about. Politics, art, history, and most of all, ethics.

Jay began to quote Aristotle when he fell off to sleep. He wanted to stay awake for that conversation, but he couldn't. He dozed off next to the fire as the conversation continued in the background.

CHAPTER 7

BILLY SIX GUN

The gunshot rang out, and William sat up. He looked over, and Bud remained in his chair with the same gaze and unbreakable concentration as the night before. The fire was out, and smoke bellowed up slowly.

A second gunshot went off behind him, and William started to back away, looking for a direction to run.

"Don't step there." Bud said, still staring into the log. William looked down to see some type of trap that Bud must have set up.

"I keep it there for the coyotes. They eat my dogs' food. It won't kill them, it's just really loud. Too loud for this morning." Bud said, still not breaking his gaze.

The third gunshot went off, and glass could be heard breaking.

"Louder than that?!" William protested.

"Finally! You've gotten rusty old man!" Jay yelled out from behind the barn. William walked around the barn to see Jay and Mo. Mo was loading a black revolver with bullets. Billy looked to see glass bottles and tin cans standing on a stump about 10 yards down from them. Mo noticed William and yelled out, "Morning, Billy!!". Jay waved his right hand up to say hi and took the pistol from Mo. He lined up the sites of the gun and....BANG! He missed. BANG! The sixth shot, he finally hit the tin can he was aiming at.

"I'm rusty?" Mo laughed. Jay shrugged his shoulders.

"Yo, Billy, you want to shoot a couple of rounds?" Mo asked.

"Me? Oh no. Those things make me nervous." William replied.

"You ever shot one?" Jay asked.

"No way, man. I don't like violence." William said.

"Who said anything about violence?" Mo asked.

"Well, that's what they're for, right? Killing?" William said, pointing at the gun.

"Well. The gun could be used for killing, but I've never killed anyone with one, and I've never even had to point it at anyone." Mo said.

"Well. If you think about it, it's kind of like a knife Billy,. You can argue guns are made for killing. Or even a bow and arrow. It's just a gun. It's who is shooting it that makes it a killing tool. I've never shot anything or anyone other than targets. Come on, try it. Maybe you'll think differently. Besides, what do you have to lose at this point?" Jay finished waving a gesture for William to come over to him.

"I don't know, man. Don't I need a safety class?" William asked, hesitating.

"A safety class?" Mo said.

"Luckily, you have two former teachers right here. It's straightforward. There are only four rules. Number one, you always treat all guns as if they are loaded. Even if you know it's not loaded, you still treat it as if it's loaded. Rule number two, you never put your finger on the trigger until you have made a conscious decision to fire that weapon. Rule number three, always keep your weapon pointed down range away from people. The last rule is to know your target and what is behind it. There is nothing behind those cans and bottles but a dirt mound. There you go. You're certified." Mo finished walking over to William. He nudged William's right shoulder gently, and William walked over to Jay.

"Okay, Billy. This is pretty easy. You hold it just like this but don't put your finger anywhere near the trigger. I'm assuming you're right-handed because your throttle is on the right" Jay placed the gun into William's right hand. William grasped the gun and put his finger above the trigger on the frame as Mo showed him.

Jay helped William get into a firing position by lining up his shoulders and pushing the gun out in front of him towards the targets.

"Now, the rules of marksmanship are pretty simple, but they are also tough to master. It's your breath, your stance, how slowly you pull the trigger back, and how you align the sites up here. The front site goes in between the back two sites. Then whenever you're ready, you slowly pull the trigger, but not until you have made that decision to fire that gun." Jay said, pointing at the sites on the gun. He stepped back and let William have some space. Jay stayed on his left, and Mo was on his right.

William was nervous but had always wanted to

try shooting a gun despite his current liberal views of them. He liked how it felt in his hands but was afraid of the noise. He lined up the sites as Jay said and slowly squeezed. "BANG!" followed by a glass bottle exploding. William let his breath out in excitement and turned to his right. He felt Mo push his right hand back to the center away from people; that's why they stood so close.

"Holy shit! Did you see that?? Holy shit!" William shouted out.

"Not bad, kid! Go ahead; you got five more in there. Just make sure you keep it pointed that way." Mo said, letting go of his hand. William smiled and nodded. Jay and Mo took a step back. William looked through the sights again, and "BANG" followed by five more, each hitting the target.

"Kids a natural." Jay said.

"Nah. Probably had good teachers." Mo started laughing. William stood looking at them with a huge smile.

Mo looked down at the gun.

"You know Jay. I got a good road name for Billy. Ready?" He paused dramatically.

"Billy Six-Gun." Mo announced.

"Yeah, that's pretty good." Jay responded.

"What's a road name?" William asked.

"It's a name bikers get on the road with their friends. You don't get to pick your road name; only your buddies get to pick it. You know…. Like a nickname? Not your real name. That's boring." Jay explained.

"Oh. So what's your road names?" William asked.

"Jay." Jay replied.

"Mo." Mo replied, both staring at him.

"Oh, I thought those were your real names." William responded.

"They are. Kind of." Jay said, shrugging. "Like it matters. Billy Six Gun....I like it"

Mo started to walk towards the front.

"You can keep that, Billy. I got like five." Mo said, continuing to walk. Jay took a minute to show him how to open the cylinder and load it. He explained that it was a Smith and Wesson .357 and could take two types of bullets, the .357 and the .38. William was confused, then Jay told him the .357 was a cannon round, BIG boom, and the .38 was like a car backfire. William got that analogy.

"Wait, I can't keep this on me. I'll get arrested." William said, closing the cylinder with the new bullets.

"Only if you get caught." Jay replied and winked at him.

They walked to the front of the barn where Bud had opened up the shop doors. Bud had moved out Williams' bike, and all three bikes were in front.

"So, what's her name?" Bud asked William holding a rag and polishing something.

"Name?" William asked.

"Yeah. What's your bike's name? Everyone names their bike. Thought you knew that. Young people." Bud said, shaking his head.

"I don't know. Jay, what's your bike's name?" He asked.

"Mary. She's named after my mom." he replied.

"What about your bike, Mo?" William asked.

"Fatima after my daughter. Jay calls her Fatty. He thinks it's hilarious." Mo patted the tank. Jay laughed.

William thought for a second.

"Well. Can I name my bike Rhonda after my wife?" He asked.

"Name her whatever you want. It's your bike, Billy. Sorry, sir, Billy-six-gun as you've now been anointed." Mo said. Both Jay and he bowed in a gesture of royalty. William laughed.

"I guess I'll name her Rhonda. That way, I'm riding Rhonda, get it?" William smiled. All three laughed.

Bud held up his right hand, "Rhonda, it is." he said and walked into the shop. He returned with a paintbrush and a plastic container.

"Every lady that comes to Bud's gets to leave with a gift. Where do you want me to put her name?" Bud asked.

"Right rear fender." Jay answered for him. "That way, she's always got your back." Mo shouted out.

"Right rear fender it is." William said. Bud nodded and went to the bike's rear, and he started painting slowly.

"You should feel honored, kid. Very few bikes have one of those." Mo said, loading up his bike. They had saddlebags on their bikes, big-box-looking ones with a flap that folded over from the top. William wished he had a set of those.

"Yeah. Maybe four. Well, five now bikes have one." Jay said, checking various things on his bike.

"I thought this was a full-time repair place. There's a sign and everything." William said, pointing to the big sign above the barn.

"Yeah, well, he doesn't get much business. We're off the beaten path. Besides, he's super picky on who he lets in here. Wants to protect his animals and all. There are evil people out there that would take advantage of an old man in the middle of nowhere." Jay said.

"Oh. I didn't think of that." William said.

"The world is not what it used to be, I guess." William added.

"The world is how it is and how it always will be. Nothing's changed." Mo said.

Bud finished, and the three of them went to the back fender. The word "Rhonda" flowed over the rear fender. The lettering was perfect, almost like a work of art in gold lettering.

"Hey, how come he got gold, and I got silver?" Jay asked.

"Yeah, and I got black." Mo chimed in.

"He smells better." Bud answered and laughed. The two old friends embraced Bud with hugs. Bud turned to William, and William reached into his pocket.

"How much do I owe you?" He asked, holding up his wallet.

Bud smiled, "I never touch money. It's never done anyone any good." Bud replied.

"But… You have to take something. You fixed my bike, let me stay here…. You even gave me your beer. You have to take something. Nothing's free." William protested.

Bud looked at him, then back at the other two sitting on their bikes.

"Oh, here we go." Mo said, slapping his gas tank. Bud looked back at William.

"What's this word, Free?" He asked.

"Free. You know. Getting something for nothing." William replied.

"What is nothing?" Bud asked.

"Nothing. You know…." William held out both his hands in a begging-type gesture. He looked over to Jay, who shrugged back at him.

"No. What is nothing?" Bud asked.

"Something of value, okay?" William struggled to answer.

"So, nothing is something without value?" Bud asked.

"Well…. Yeah, you got to take something to balance things out. You know. Keep the lights on." William said.

"So, what is value?" Bud asked. William thought for a second.

"Value is something that can…." William started, and he couldn't think of it. What was value?

"Ok. Money. Money has value, right? That's how

you could buy this place, and it has something you can trade." William was proud of his answer.

"So the only thing of value is something that can be traded?" Bud asked, and William answered quickly.

"Well. No. You can value your relationship, and you can value something important, and it's not always something that can be traded." William finished.

"So, then, if I value everything and I value nothing, what happens then? What if I value nothing on the same level as something?" Bud asked, and William was confused.

"Well....I don't know, but you have to let me compensate you for your time." William said, trying to end the conversation and get Bud to allow him to pay him.

"Time. Gentleman, Billy wants to compensate me for my time." Bud said, looking at Jay and Mo, who were now giggling like schoolgirls sitting on their bikes.

"What is Time, Billy? Isn't now a time?" Bud asked.

"Look, I don't mean to be disrespectful, but-"

"Then you'll answer the question. What is Time?" Bud pressed on.

"Time is a way to measure... Well, time. Twenty-four hours in a day. You know what the time is. Stop messing with me." William was getting frustrated. Not because of the questions, but that the questions could only lead to more questions.

"24 hours. That little machine in your wrist. Is that the way to measure Time? How can you prove Time existed 10 seconds ago?" Bud asked. William laughed.

"Come on, Bud! You know I can't! But you know it's been ten seconds!" William laughed.

"Prove it." Bud responded very calmly. William tried to laugh it off.

"I can't." William said.

"That little machine, what time will it be in an hour?" Bud asked. William looked at his watch.

"9 a.m." William responded.

"If an asteroid hits right now and wipes out the planet with your watch, aka, wrist machine, is it still 9 a.m.?" Bud asked. William looked at him, confused.

"Well, yeah. We'd be dead, but it would still be 9 a.m." William said, knowing another question was coming.

"Prove it." Bud said. William shook his head.

"I can't and wouldn't be able to because we'd be wiped out." He responded.

"Ok, then at least prove to me there are 24 hours in a day." Bud said.

"That's easy. You just watch the clock, and it will count 24 hours." William said proudly. Finally, something he could answer.

"No, that means your device can count what appears to be Time by its mechanisms, but that doesn't prove what Time is. What is Time you can measure and compensate for? So what is Time, Billy?" Bud asked.

William had never thought about time like this. Bud was right, but time was backed up by science. Man, if he only had a smartphone, he'd jump on the internet and give that old man a run for his money. He thought about the question, this time longer.

"I guess the only time I can measure if you throw out all clocks is now." William responded. Bud smiled.

"Well, if now is the only Time, how do you place value on it?" Bud asked.

"Wait. What? I'm so confused." William said, blinking quickly.

"Well, I'm going to give you a freebie. I value, that's the word you said, moments. The now as you just said. So would you like to compensate me with what you said holds value to you, which is money? Would you like to pay me for my moment in time at the rate I believe I should be paid?" Bud asked.

William looked confused, but then he took out his cash. Now Jay and Mo were in full laughter behind him. Bud stared at him like a frog behind his glasses.

"So, how much do I owe you for the repair?" William asked.

"Oh, that's the past. I don't hold value in the past, remember? I value now, so I'll take 20." Bud said, holding out his hand palm up. William raised his eyebrows and placed a twenty in his hand.

"I value this moment. Another." Bud said. He repeated the process until all of William's cash was gone. William shrugged.

"I value this moment too. You said I needed to be compensated, your words. So what's in your wallet?" Bud asked. William got nervous.

"Nothing. It's empty, and all I have is credit cards." William said.

"Do those hold value to you?" Bud asked.

"Well yeah. I have to pay them back, but yeah, they're worth…."

"I'll take those too. As a matter of fact." Bud reached over and took the whole wallet.

William was confused. Surely the old man wasn't going to take all his money. Anger and panic took over for a second. Did they bring him here to set him up? If that were the case, they could have just robbed him in the desert. They gave him a gun, for God's sake. He was angry at himself for even thinking that. Bud started to walk into the shop.

"Wait, can I keep at least one card? I just need to buy a phone when we get to town." William plead.

Bud stopped. "Well, you just purchased several moments in time. Can't you just take those?" Bud asked.

"No, those are free." William said.

"Really? Free? They just cost you plenty, your whole wallet. Maybe you can trade them." Bud replied.

William sighed. He could probably call his bank when he got to town and say he lost his card. Everything was so instant now. Except here, apparently.

"So let me ask you now, Billy. How are you going to pay me?" Bud asked.

"What do you mean? You have all I have." William replied.

"Do I? I have ALL you have…." Bud asked. Faster than any human he'd ever seen move, Bud snatched the pistol Mo gave him out of the front of his waistband and had it to William's forehead. He forced the barrel hard into William's forehead. William winced and felt his heart race and his sphincter muscle tighten. He had never had a gun pointed at him, nor had he ever been in this much danger. The closest he came before was a near miss on the freeway.

"HOLY SHIT! JUST TAKE IT! I'M SORRY! TAKE WHATEVER YOU WANT!" William yelled out. He remembered the blast of the gun, and the fear swallowed him.

Bud cocked the trigger back, and William heard a click, click. He wasn't shown how to do that by Jay, which made this even more terrifying. He thought about Rhonda, his house, his life, and everything all at once.

"Well...so it appears you do place value at this moment. Anything you say? Take anything? Everything you got? I heard you correctly, right?" Bud asked. William nodded frantically, and Bud pulled the gun back.

"Interesting. A moment ago, before this moment here, of course, you placed value on these." Bud said, holding up William's wallet and cash. "These were so important to you a moment ago, and now, they're.... what?" Bud asked. William stared terrified at the gun.

"Billy, don't be rude. Answer the man." Mo said from his bike. William looked over at the two, who watched nonchalantly. They could have been eating popcorn and watching a movie.

"They're yours! Take them. I don't want them. Go ahead. You can have my bike too!" William said.

"Oh, now that's too far." Mo said, shaking his head.

"Dude, strap on a pair Billy. If Bud were going to kill you, he'd have done it already. I think he's just tired of being indirect and passive, so consider yourself lucky. He's direct, but to give up your bike. Man. I'm disappointed." Jay said.

"You NEVER let anyone take your bike, Billy. That's like....sacrilegious or something." Mo said, shaking his head.

Bud let the gun drop to his side. He took a deep breath and let out a sigh. William was relieved to see the gun drop to his side. His heart started to calm down, and he was still breathing heavily. He felt like he was going to die a second ago.

"You see, Billy. In the end, everyone wants this moment. How many seconds was that, Billy? How many minutes? Hmmm? How much was that moment worth or this one here? It isn't until it's taken away that you realize the value of this moment. There is no compensation for increments of moments. If I point this gun at your head and threaten to take that moment, you'd give anything. That moment becomes priceless. So, why wasn't the moment before? Since when did this" Bud held up the wallet "outweigh this?" Bud held up the gun. William shrugged his shoulders and shook his head. Bud tilted his head down and giggled. He handed William the gun back, pushing it to his chest. William clasped it with both hands, relieved that it was no longer pointed at his head. Then Bud held up the wallet and cash. He waved it in front of William and then pushed it on top of William's hands. William moved his right hand and caught the wallet, clasping the gun and his wallet to his chest. William was breathing heavily when Bud let out another loud laugh.

"That's why I don't touch money, and I encourage others not to either, Billy. For all of my students, I told them not to touch money. Not until they understand the moment. Now you understand the moment, and maybe you'll understand a little more now. When you started to value that object in your hand or those numbers on your screen more than your moment, you lost the meaning of that word "value" that I asked you to define. Hell, not too long ago, a cow was worth more than a bar of gold, and even then, it wasn't until that moment was taken that they knew how much that moment meant." Bud said, walking back towards the shop. "Go on now, Billy. Go home. It was nice sharing those moments with you." Bud said, walking into the shop and closing the door.

It took William a second to compose himself. After several seconds, he looked up to see Jay staring at him.

"Well? Do you need to change your tampon or something? I'd like to get on the road at some point." Jay said.

"What...what are you fucking serious? Jesus fucking Christ! Did you not see what just happened? I mean,

he was all nice old man yoda last night, and then…."
Mo cut him off.

"Maybe he's tired of waiting for fuckers to get the message and chose a more direct teaching approach. Leave poor Jesus out of this. He had nothing to do with it….man. Bud's a bad motherfucker Billy if you only knew. But you won't. So, as Jay said, you need to change your tampon, or are we going? You're barely going to make it to the next gas station with your Barbie bike, and I'm not pushing. That's your bitch you push her." Mo finished. He fired up his bike. The thunder of his pipes bounced off the barn, making them echo into the valley.

Jay's bike followed, and the dual rumbled a cadence of thundering pipes. This gave William a sense of urgency. He quickly pushed his wallet into his right front pants pocket. He looked at the pistol and then put it in his waistband in the front. He sat on his bike and then realized he better move the gun. He switched it pushing it into the rear of his waistband. He turned the key, saw the familiar green "N" for neutral, and then pushed the ignition. "Chirpa chirpa POW!" and his bike was thundering next to Jay and Mo. The three bikes thundered against the barn in a harmonic symphony as they idled together. Jay nodded to Mo, who dropped his bike into gear and started to move forward. William followed Jay in the back. Jay and Mo held up two fingers to Bud in the garage. William looked back. Still a little shook up, he did the same. Bud was working on some random vehicle, and he saw Bud salute with a wrench to his forehead and then down.

The wrench came down when he did this, and William saw a snake curled up and wrapped around Bud's head. Coiled repeatedly in a round motion covering Bud's head to the top. The head of the snake looked directly at him. William blinked and looked back. He must be going crazy. Maybe it was the chemotherapy and the stress; he didn't see a snake anymore. It was a beanie hat, like the one Bud had worn earlier. In any case, he was just happy Bud didn't have a gun to his head anymore, and he was grateful that he fixed his bike.

As they pulled out of Bud's driveway, William was still surprised that of all those dogs, none of them were barking. Despite the loud pipes and that they were strangers. They kept down the country road with William eating the dust of Jay and Mo, who were in the lead. Luckily, the road had less dust as they came closer to the pavement. For some reason, William had not remembered this road being so long. He wiped the dust from his visor and watched as Jay and Mo turned right onto the pavement. He followed behind them, happy that the dirt clouds were over.

As they continued down the road, Jay was on the right, Mo on the left, and William in the rear center. They began to move as a team. A group, and now all of what Bud said, started to settle in with William. What would he pay for THIS moment right here? Two new friends, REAL friends that he had never experienced before. How much would he pay to meet Bud and live in that moment? What value can you place on this moment right here? Thundering down the road with his friends in the middle of a desert. Hot. Uncomfortable, and wind shooting into his face. Yet, still loving every second of it. How much was that worth? A kiss from his wife, a hug, a smile from a stranger, and the list went on. They were all....he thought of the word. Priceless.

Even with sweat and chemicals from his chemotherapy dripping out of him, how much would he pay for this moment versus the moment he was married to Rhonda? How was one moment measured? You couldn't. Each moment was just that. It was a moment. They had no value, and yet they were priceless. Each moment was priceless and worthless at the same time because they were gone as quickly as they came. Once they were gone, they were gone, just a memory. A memory that may or may not even be accurately remembered. What's to say that the mind didn't contort things to what it wanted rather than what happened? Could that be guaranteed? What if the thing he remembered happened differently, and he just remembered them the way he WANTED to remember them? Sure they may be close, but the mind is a powerful mechanism. The mind William knew had an entire doctoral field of psychologists with Ph.D.'s who could not yet understand it.

They picked up speed to around 70 mph or something close. He was at a point now where he didn't look at his speedometer. He just kept up with

Jay and Mo. Jay and Mo were his next thought. What happened with these two? He felt like these were his best friends, and he barely knew them. Less than two days, one of which was spent with him sleeping. Yet, even during this short period, he felt closer to these two men than any of his friends. He shared things with them, and Bud, for that matter, that seemed to be authentic. Nothing superficial. It was almost like these guys cut him down to his core and made it, so he wasn't scared to be himself. He wasn't about to blow a contract or make one friend look better or worse. No politics, no agendas. No social nuances or corporate culture.

Just being. Being. That was a word he seemed never to be able to isolate. That word had to be in a sentence with something else. Just like the word "Moment" that would now be drilled in his head forever thanks to Bud. What happened? How did he get so close to these two guys so quickly, and where the fuck were they going? He noticed signs here and there, white with a green backing, but he had no idea where he was or where they were going.

Nonetheless, if he was honest with himself, he didn't care. He knew he had to contact his wife when they found a town with a cell phone store, but there weren't any so far. Another weird anomaly he noticed. The remoteness almost beckoned for the banning of cell phones, and there were no stores that sold them. Hell, even the local liquor store sold cell phones. Not here, though.

They continued into the desert with what seemed

like endless asphalt and hot wind. The jacket Steve gave him seemed ridiculously hot, and then he felt something new with his bike. A sputter. At first, it was every couple miles, and now it seemed to be every mile. He remembered he had to push his girl. He looked up at the right time to see "Newman Exit 2 miles" with a gas station symbol next to it. He felt relief but then felt a sputter. Then another. "Newman Exit 1 mile." the sign said before he heard "sputter sputter…..cuchoo….." and the bike stopped. He pulled in the clutch and came to the side of the road. Jay and Mo went down the road for a minute and realized William was gone. They turned around and eventually and found him. William tried to start the bike several times but had no luck.

"Well, shit. I think you're out of gas." Jay said. His bike was still running.

"Yeah, that sucks. We'll go down the road and see what we can do. You start pushing her in the meantime." Mo said.

They sped off onto the highway asphalt, and William got off the bike. He started pushing the bike in the hot sun and realized fast that the leather jacket he was wearing had to go. He took it off and put it over the handlebars. It was fine in the wind but became a human oven when they stopped. He could hear Mo and Jay's pipes disappear. He started to push the bike, and it felt good. He pushed and pushed, listening to something he was not used to. Silence. He continued to push the bike down the road and heard birds above him cawing. He looked up to see birds swirling around him and got caught in the beauty of the moment. He could hear the pipes of Jay and Mo coming back towards him and looked back down from the birds. Jay's bike thundered up next to him, and he came to a stop after killing his engine and coasting to William's location.

"Beautiful, aren't they?" Jay asked, looking up.

"Yes. I was just looking at them." William said, still pushing.

"Yeah....people think they're hawks all the time or eagles, but they're not. They're vultures. They're waiting for you to die so they can eat you." Jay finished, still looking up at the birds.

"Still. They're beautiful birds, and they got a eat." he finished.

"Oh. I almost forgot." Jay said looking at Wiliam. "They didn't have a gas can, but I thought you might want this." he said as he threw a small box at William. He fired up his bike and then rode off down the street. William looked at the box. "Summer's Eve Douche" the title read with an attractive brunette on the front of the box. He threw it to the side.

"ASSHOLE!!" William yelled as Jay's bike came cruising by him. He kept pushing but laughed. He couldn't help but laugh at that one.

He was close, less than a quarter-mile away, when Mo came riding up. As expected, he threw a bottle of sex lubricant at him, telling him that it might help smooth things along, then rode off. William couldn't help but laugh again at the moment. He thought about what Bud had said about the value of a moment. Jay and Mo were bullying him while he pushed a 400 lb bike down the road while battling cancer and the after-effects of chemotherapy, yet, instead of feeling sorry for him, they chose to razz him. Mo did warn him that if he ran out of gas, he'd have to push it himself. He wasn't bluffing. When William thought about it, he was pretty sure that he probably would have told them not to help even if they did try. He realized that this was one of the first times in a very long time that he felt..... Empowered. That was the word. Sure, it wasn't sealing a multi-million dollar contract for accounting, but he controlled these bars. He controlled the bike's speed when he pushed it, and the physical exertion of pushing made him feel less sick. HE controlled the moment.

"Oh, I forgot. In case you need to spice things up with Rhonda...." Jay said, coming back a third time to bully him. He threw a vending machine condom at him that said, "French Tickler" on it. William was already halfway up the exit incline now. Jay and Mo rode up behind him. This time they both got off their bikes and ran up behind William. The three pushed the bike up the overpass ramp and then towards the gas station. William jumped on and coasted to the pumps, which felt like an Oasis. Shade. William was so grateful for the shade. Jay and Mo ran back to their bikes and joined William. Mo walked over and handed William a bottle of water.

"Billy Six-Gun needs to learn to carry a fuel can." Mo said, drinking from his water bottle.

"Yeah, if you're going to have a bitch bike, you

better get a few of those bottles." Jay said, drinking from his water bottle. A few seconds went by, and William looked at Jay.

"Wait. You had these water bottles the whole time? What the fuck, man?! You could've filled one of those up with gas, and it would've got me here, you dick!" William said, shaking his head.

"Oh, and it's not a bitch bike; it's Rhonda. It's an 883. Bud said it has better gearing than both of your bikes, plus it has the most reliable motor that Harley Davidson has ever made. The Evolution." he started.

"See...you think I'm just some cancer boy that has given up on life and latching on to your tits like some lost soul lucky to find you fucks. But I'm not.

See, while you three were playing grab-ass with my spark plug wires, I took the time to listen to what Bud was saying under his breath. All that talk about the year, make, and model of my bike and everything good and bad. He said all that. Did you hear it? No, because you fuckers were too busy staring at the bike and bullshitting.

Then I noticed all the numbers on the manuals he had in the shop. I guess you guys missed me going through the 2005 Harley Davidson 883 Sportster manual right in front of you while you two just watched Bud like a couple of groupies at a Poison concert. Well, guess what fuckers?! I learned a thing or two. Yeah, it's not a 1200; I know it's an 883, the smallest in the line, but the engine is still the same. It's been bored to a 1250. The displacement and the ratios are all spelled out in the manual, a very detailed manual, by the way, which says that my bike, even though smaller, given the right components, will be faster off the line using torque than both of your monster gas guzzlers. Also, the manual to the right was the Big Twin, which I believe you have, right Mo?" he asked, looking at Mo. Mo looked a little shocked but nodded.

"Well, by the looks of your bike, you've upgraded to at least a 121. That is clear by the S&S 121 emblems on your heads, also known as the top cylinder. Did you replace the compensator when you upgraded? If not, the last thing you'll have to worry about is running out of gas with your "bitch bike" third wheel friend here. Oh no…..you're going to blow your shit right up. That primary side compensator sprocket will blow like a fat girl on prom night. Books and numbers. That's what I do." William paused. He looked over at Jay smiling in almost a smug smile towards Mo. He looked surprised at William's rant.

"Oh, and as for you. A knucklehead, I believe it was called in Bud's manuals. Am I right? It looks like a knuckle when you look at it. Well…." he started, and Jay's expression quickly changed. A look of concern now came over Jay, and he zeroed in on William.

"Well, I hope you sealed that up like a boat because apparently, they leak from the side valves. So, yeah. I get it. I'm a rookie. I'm new. I haven't ridden bikes like you guys. I haven't run around the desert-like some fucking snake sucking and fucking everything that moved. I'm not the toughest guy around, and yeah, I get it. I'm out of my depth here. I get it!" William was conceding his physical status.

"Whoa, man, who said anything about sucking and fucking? You know how hot it is out here? That's some serious ball sweat, Billy." Mo scoffed.

"I wasn't always like this, you know." William started. Jay and Mo looked at each other and then back at him. William pulled the pump from the stall and started pumping gas into his tank.

"At one point, I was somebody, you know. I.....I had everything. I landed multi-million dollar contracts. Shit, that NOBODY can land. I could calculate and land reports and projections for companies like Honda, Google, and the like. I...." he stopped as the fuel tank lever clicked.

"What exactly is somebody, Billy?" Mo asked, lighting a cigarette.

"You know we're at a gas pump, right?" Jay asked him.

"Yup. I'm hoping we blow up so Billy will finally shut up." Mo replied, taking a drag from the freshly lit cigarette. "Tell me, Billy, why are you so pissed off?" Mo finished.

"Because you guys are assholes! You know I'm sick! You could've helped me!" William burst out. Even though he probably would've stubbornly held on to the bike, still, they could've offered to help. Mo laughed.

"Hey, Billy. Nothing worth it is ever easy, and nothing easy is ever worth it. That gas right there you're pumping. You earned it. How many of those whatever a million companies….how much of that money you made did you ever really earn?" Mo asked. William pulled the pump nozzle from his tank and put it back on the stand. He thought about it for a second.

"What do you mean?" he asked.

"I mean…well shit. Do you feel like you earned that gas right there? Or did Jay and I give it to you?" Mo asked. William looked over at him.

"What? It's a simple question. Did you earn it, or was it given?" Mo asked.

"I earned it!" William replied. His weary body lunged forward.

"I still don't understand what you're getting at. I just want to get to a cell phone store." William started. Before he knew it, Mo was right in his face. A second ago, he was on his bike smoking a cigarette, and now he was inches from William's face. Again.

"No. Tell me now, what did you earn and what was given to you just by you fucking existing. Huh? What, now I'm the bad guy and the bully? If I remember right, it was YOU who came up to both of us in that bar and asked us to get you back home. Now I'm the bad guy? So, tell me, Billy, how much of your life was earned and how much was manipulated or just given to you by existing?" Mo asked.

"Yo, Mo, maybe you should cut him a little slack. Just a little." Jay said.

"Why? Because he's dying? OH, WELL, let's stop the world for that shit. Holy shit, everyone, Billy's dying! Let's start a GoFundMe page! Fuck that! Billy, answer the fucking question. You were dying the second you were born. How much of your life was earned? Hold on, let me rephrase that, how much do you THINK you earned?" Mo finished.

William looked over at Jay, feeling defeated. He had tried to bark at the two of them, and now he felt shut down by what it must feel like to be barked at by the Alpha dog in a wolf pack. Mo shoved his right shoulder with his right hand.

"WELL? How much? How much did you earn?" Mo pressed.

"All of it. I earned ALL of it!" William barked back.

"Well, then where is it? Mo asked.

"What do you mean where is it? It's in my house, my car, and my 401K. You know. That's beside the point." William said.

"Well, then I guess I'm just a dick then." Mo laughed. A long pause went by while William pouted to himself.

"What were you getting at?" William finally asked. Mo shrugged.

"Don't know, but seems to me like pushing your bike, holding your weight, and filling your tank. That means you earned your spot right here, right now. Not down the road in the future, and not in some bank account, but right here and now. But what do I know? You're the one with the fancy title." Mo threw his cigarette down and crushed it with his right foot. He blew smoke in William's direction. It wasn't tobacco, something else. Not Marijuana. Cloves. He remembered the smell. William put his gloves on and thought about Mo's words.

"Well, I guess you're right. You're still assholes." William said. Mo pointed at Jay.

"No, HE'S the asshole. It was his idea!" Mo laughed.

"What?" Jay responded, "You never know when you're going to need a French Tickler. Those things come in handy, I'm telling you!" Jay finished.

William wiped the sweat from his brow and couldn't help but laugh. He noticed that he wasn't feeling as sick, and he felt almost like his first two appointments, mainly because it was so damn hot. The sun seemed to beat down on him like heat lasers no matter where he went, even in the shade.

"Hey, where did you guys get those vests? I want one. At least until I get to the next town. I won't need one for very long. Can I get a cheap one somewhere? This jacket's a little too much right now." William asked.

"Hell, Billy. They're expensive, and you're only about a day's ride out. Maybe you want to keep it. It gets cold out here." Mo said.

"No, I want a vest like you guys. Not like I can take it with me, right?" William laughed after he said it. He stopped for a second, and it was the first time he acknowledged it out loud. He was dying. He looked around for a second, and then it settled in. Before things got uncomfortable, Jay said, "Yeah. Alright. Next town over, there's a spot."

The ride out of the gas station seemed to be almost

automatic now. William knew to let Jay or Mo go first, whoever was in the lead, and then catch up into formation. Even in this short time, he figured out who was faster and slower. Jay seemed to cruise while Mo seemed to throttle up and down quickly. Sometimes Jay would put his right hand back on his seat to relax. Mo did some kind of surfing in the wind with his right hand every so often. William found himself swerving back and forth playfully on the bike behind the two of them.

As the miles fell under his feet, he began to feel empowered again. This moment that Bud had so graciously pointed out seemed to be the only thing that mattered now. One small mistake, and he could crash into both of his friends or vice versa. He wasn't just responsible for his riding but also for them. A forced trust seemed to be imposed on each person in the party that thundered down the road. Not that any of them would look at it like that, but that's what it was. Before William had time to think of it any further, Mo's turn signal was on, and they were turning right into another small desert town. Still, no cell phone stores. How did these guys know about all these spots? Where did they live? Out here, maybe? Is that how they knew where to go? They must have ridden out here before...multiple times.

Before any more questions came to mind, they pulled into a small strip mall with two buildings. It was the typical strip mall you'd see out in the southwest. Wooden side panels with glass doors that swung both ways. On top of the roof was a model horse made out of iron and "Western Supply" across the banner. Jay and Mo stopped their bikes and William followed as Jay and Mo entered the building.

The inside of the building looked like a throwback to Old-Time America. A Chevrolet Stepside, restored, was in the middle with hay bales around it as a display, and the whole store was decked out in a cowboy theme. The smell of leather was potent. Jay and Mo began walking right past the saddles proudly on display. William had never been in a place like this. He curiously looked at the price tag on one of the saddles. It was ornately decorated, and he gasped when he saw the price tag was $4000.00 on sale. He dropped the tag like it was a dangerous snake and followed behind Jay and Mo.

"Well, where have you two been?" an old man asked from their left. William looked over to see an older man, possibly in his sixties, decked out in full cowboy gear, including the Texas necktie. Salt and pepper hair, medium build, and standinhg upright.

"Paul!" Jay said, walking over and hugging the man. Mo hugged the man as well.

"Billy, come over here and meet one of my old students, Paul. Paul, this is Billy, he wants a vest like we got." Jay said.

"Yeah, a former student. Man. You know what's funny? We didn't get along well at first, did we?" Paul asked.

"No, sir, we most certainly did not, but it all worked out in the end. Considering you became the teacher!

He took over my teaching and taught for a long time." Jay responded. The man looked over at William, and he held his hands up to form a box with his thumbs and pointer fingers like two guns.

"This way, young man. What kind of leather do you want? We got every kind, even alligator, and we got denim too." Paul asked. The old man moved pretty quickly for someone his age.

William followed him. Jay and Mo veered off to look at the latest western wear.

Paul walked over to a section with a vast selection of vests. He was right. Every kind William could think of, from leather to ones with rhinestones and frills. He thought Elvis Presley would have even been impressed at the selection.

"You know, when I took over Jay's teaching it was a little rough. Tried to write about it, but that went a little off course. Good times though. Very good times. Anyway, what did you have in mind?" Paul asked.

"Careful there, Billy. Your vest says a lot about you as a biker." Mo said from about ten feet to his right.

"I'm not a biker, I'm just riding that bike until we get to the next town with a cellphone store." William scoffed.

"Really? Well, then why didn't you drive your fancy car out here? Why'd you buy your neighbor's bike? You know....when was the last time you felt free and all that shit?" Jay chimed in. William had forgotten that he had told them the whole story.

"Fine. I guess I am trying to be a biker, but not a

real biker like these guys. It is kind of fun." William said to Paul. Paul raised an eyebrow.

"Oh yes. A real biker rides all year long in the rain and snow, doesn't EVER take off their leather suit of armor, and ALWAYS takes the bike no matter what. Even if he has to haul a couch, it's on a bike. Plus, you need to eat your dinner on the side of the road and fight everyone who looks sideways at your bike! That's a real biker! Sorry kid, I can't sell a vest to you unless you're a REAL biker. Just pick one. Stop being all dramatic." Paul finished pointing at the vests. "We get people in here all the time who just started riding and even the ones who want to look the part and don't ride. We don't care." Paul finished.

"Give him the pink one with the rhinestones. We can bedazzle his bike to match. It will be cute." Mo said, holding up a very American-looking red and blue denim shirt with white stars.

William looked over the display and found one that looked like the old wild west gunfighter type. It was brown with a V cut coming down from the sides. It had concho stars on the buttons and lace-up leather on the sides to tighten the vest. It looked new but had a black tint on the leather. It wasn't too flashy, but it did stand out. William tried on the vest and it made him feel good looking at it in the mirror. Paul held his hand out, and William took off the vest for him to hold. He pulled another off the rack and put it on. Too big. He had lost so much weight since the treatments. He sighed momentarily and then began to take it off.

"Hold on there, youngster. You like this one?" Paul asked. William nodded.

"He should. It even has an inside pocket he can keep all his hurt feelings in." Mo laughed. Jay laughed with him.

"Well, let's look at you." Jay said, walking over to William. William liked the vest, and it fit him perfectly once Paul had used the side laces to snug in the slack. There was something about wearing a leather vest that he liked. He had never worn one before, and now he understood why the bikers wore them. It allowed your arms to be free but kept the wind off the chest. Well, at least that's what he imagined it would be.

Jay looked him over with Mo standing behind him. They nodded in agreement.

"It suits you Billy." Mo said.

"Not too Liberachi, but you don't look like a character out of Sons of Anarchy either." Mo said, walking around him.

"Keep in mind that the vest has to be functional. You want to be able to move the stuff from your pants to your vest so it's more comfortable." Jay added.

"Well, it's just temporary." William replied.

"Well, isn't everything? Meh. Don't get it. Just wait it out. We'll be approaching Flagstaff soon." Mo said.

William looked down at the price tag. $150.00. He thought about taking it off, but it seemed to mold on him.

"Well, I can always use it when I ride horses. You know, ride off into the sunset with all this time left on my hands." William laughed. Then Mo's sentence set in.

"Wait….Flagstaff? I thought we were in California already." William barked.

"Well…..we were, but then Bud had to come to get us because of your bitch bike, and he's right there at the crossroads, so we had to backtrack to his place, then you said you wanted a vest, so we stopped here." Jay said.

"Wait, that's like three hours away. We went three hours backward to get this?" William asked, thinking of the distance.

"Yeah, time flies when you're in the desert, Billy." Jay said. William looked around for a minute.

"It didn't seem that long of a ride." William replied.

"You know Billy. Bikers are pretty particular about their vests and jackets. They say it's a reflection of who you are. You know… it helps you feel more confident when you ride. You sure you like that vest, or do you want to try on some other ones?" Jay said, pointing to the other vests. William thought for a minute and then decided to try on the other vests. They were either too tight or loose and just didn't seem to fit him right. He put on his original vest and looked in the mirror. He looked like a cowboy from the old west days, maybe even a gunfighter. He liked it. He puffed his chest out.

"I'll take it." William said, still looking in the mirror.

"You sure about that, Billy? It's not cheap." Mo said.

"What am I going to take it with me?" William said, twisting side to side. He used to make fun of his neighbor Steve for wearing a leather vest. Now here he stood, modeling it like he was buying a suit.

"Well, that's the last one, and it's been on the rack for a while. I'll knock off 25 bucks if you promise to buy Mo a toothbrush." Paul said with a serious look. Mo looked at him and then covered his mouth.

"Just kidding. Seriously though, I like to sell things that people appreciate. I think you'll appreciate this vest. Plus, it comes treated already." Paul said, walking over to the counter. William pulled out his wallet and gave him his card. Paul began to ring it up on the register.

"You boys are heading to Mexico again?" Paul asked.

"Yup. Our favorite place." Jay replied.

"Not many places like that left." Paul said, punching numbers into the machine.

"No, sir. One of the last of its kind. If not THE last of its kind. It's a long ride but worth it." Jay replied.

"You remember we used to say it's a long way when we traveled way back when. Now it takes a half-hour in a car. Less on one of those." Paul said, pointing the motorcycles outside. Jay nodded.

"How, exactly, do you two know each other?" William asked.

"Well, Jay and I have known each other a LONG time. He's a great teacher, even got me on board. We used to go town to town talking about-"

"That was a long time ago." Jay interrupted. "Paul meant to say we used to teach together back in the day. You know, back then, teachers traveled a lot." Jay finished. Paul looked at him, confused, and paused. He figured out that he was talking too much and then nodded in agreement.

"So, all of you were teachers?" William asked. The three of them looked at each other.

"Yes, I guess you can say that. Anyway, the daylights a' burning, and I'm starving. Hurry up." Mo said, waving at Paul, "I'll see you next time, P!" Mo continued walking towards the front door. Jay remained behind. Paul finished the transaction and had William sign.

"Jay, I can't tell you how good it is to see you, old friend." Paul said, holding his arms out to hug Jay. Jay gave him a big hug, followed by pats on the back.

"You too, my friend. You take care now." Jay said, turning to walk outside. William took a few more moments to realize Jay was gone because he was too busy playing with all the pockets on his new vest. He looked back and forth for Jay and then hurried to catch up. They exited the store and approached the bikes.

"Hey Jay, I don't know if I asked, but what did you use to teach?" William asked. Jay shrugged, "You know. I taught a little about everything, I guess. Mainly philosophy, I guess you would call it." Jay said, throwing his leg over his bike. Mo was already on his bike with his helmet on. Jay put on his helmet and started to buckle it. William did the same and then looked at his seat. The jacket was slung over the seat.

"Hey guys, can I put this in one of your bags?"

William asked, picking up the jacket. Mo and Jay looked at each other and laughed. They simultaneously held up their middle finger, commonly known as the bird, and then started their bikes.

William followed two miles down the road with his leather jacket tied around his waist by the sleeves and the wind hitting his new vest. He was happy with his new vest and liked how the wind felt on his arms, and he felt free again. The road turned into a blur for a second, but William felt good like time was frozen, and he could just keep riding like this and never look back. The road was long with no stops, making it seem like it would go on forever. After about 20 minutes, he lost track of time. He lost track of his speed, where he was, or what direction he was going. He was almost in a trance as the bikes moved together. Almost like they were supposed to be right then and there at that moment for some unknown reason. This peace that he felt was new, and he didn't want it to go away. He understood even more why people were so passionate about their motorcycles. Now he was right there with them.

As the mile marker showed "Flagstaff 10 miles" mixed emotions hit William. That's where he would find his phone store. He was looking at right here and now and had to choose.

He would call his wife, maybe catch a flight back to California and go back to his life. That life now seemed so far away. It had only been a few days, but it seemed like months when he thought about it. It was almost like night and day. However, he wanted to talk to his wife and felt a little relieved yet disappointed as they approached Flagstaff. The scenery changed. Cars were now passing by them in a steady stream, streetlights appeared, and strip malls appeared on the outskirts of town along with billboards. He had not realized how these everyday things we see become so noticeable once they are removed from our lives.

They crossed a sign that said, "Flagstaff city limits, elevation 6906, founded 1882". It didn't take long to find a cell phone store. They pulled into a strip mall, and he could see the store with all the big cell phone company logos. Next to it was a bar called the Whisk Whiskey. The strip mall was a newer mall with Whole Foods as an anchor. As the three biked pulled up in front of the store, they put the kickstands down. William's ears rang from the wind as Jay and Mo dismounted their bikes and took off their helmets.

"Alright, Buddy, we're here. Just like we promised." Mo said, taking off his sunglasses. William just sat on his bike, staring down. Jay and Mo looked at each other, then back at William.

"Yo, Billy! We're here." Jay said.

"I know." William replied but still didn't move. A long pause went by before he spoke again.

"I...I can't go in there. I've...I've had an accident." William said. Mo looked at him and then looked down to see diarrhea running down William's left leg. William stared at the ground. He didn't feel sick, but it just came out when they stopped.

"They told me this would happen. The doctors

wanted to give me a colostomy bag a few months ago, but I said no. Guess I'm paying the price now. You guys can go ahead. I'll figure it out from here." William said, still staring at the ground.

"Fuck you, Billy." Mo replied. "What size pants are you?" Mo asked.

"No. It's ok. I'm grateful that you guys got me here, but I can manage." William replied.

"That's not what I asked you, Billy. What size pants are you?" Mo reiterated.

"Don't piss him off, Billy. He'll knock that shit right off of you." Jay laughed. William was glad they weren't disgusted by the sight of his feces and grateful that he had friends right now.

"26." William replied.

"26. Got it." Mo said. He put his helmet on and fired up his bike. He looked back as he backed out his bike, looking for cars. He dropped his bike into gear and sped off. Jay stayed behind. There was a long silence before William spoke.

"Jay, thank you. I don't think I would've made it here if it weren't for you guys. That was stupid of me to get this bike. I don't know what I was thinking. I can barely stand most days, and the genius that I am jumped on this thing. I was going to take it around the block or two. Just wanted to be…"

"Free? You already said that." Jay interrupted.

"No. I think I just wanted to be distracted. At least for a minute. There was only so much YouTube and T.V. I could watch. I can't get any work done and I don't know I guess I just wanted to stop feeling sorry for myself. I guess God has a funny way of making shit like this happen." William said.

"God has nothing to do with anything, Billy. The choices that we make that end up in unexpected results are always blamed on God or Satan, but in the end, it's our choices that make things happen. You chose to get on that bike. God didn't put you on it. Just own it. That was your decision. I don't blame you, though. I think I would rather go out on two wheels than have a disease eat through me until I couldn't move. I get it." Jay said, taking a drag from his vape pipe.

"Well, thanks for putting that delicately." William said, almost laughing. He liked how neither Jay nor Mo seemed to hold back what they thought. Jay gave him a thumbs up and watched the people as they walked by.

"Where are you guys going on vacation? It sounds like you two travel a lot together." William asked. Jay took a breath and looked at William.

"It's a cool little town in Mexico. Probably boring to most people, but we like it. Yeah, we've been friends for a long time, but we only get to travel together every so often. We're pretty busy. This year is good, though. We're meeting up with a few more friends; it will be fun." Jay said.

"How far is it?" William asked. The fluids on his leg had started cooling, and he felt gross as it dried on his legs. He was mainly talking now to stay distracted.

"I don't know. A week's ride, maybe? I don't keep track of time all that much. We just ride. It's funny, though, what happens when you cross the border. The ride can be beautiful with untouched landscaped for hours, or you can run into bandits or Federales who want your bike, or even an occasional Senorita who needs a ride. That's where the real adventure begins. A lot of unknowns over there. Luckily Mo and I know some people there. Still, it's always something down south." Jay said, and he could hear Mo's bike pulling up. Mo cut the engine and drifted into his original parking space next to Jay. A plastic bag with clothes hung from the left handlebar and swayed as the bike came to a stop.

"You're lucky. Walmart's right there. You owe me forty bucks, Billy." Mo said, getting off the bike. "Jay, let's go talk to the bar owner there." Mo said, pointing to the Whisk Whiskey. The two walked off, and for the first time, William felt alone. He knew they were right there in the bar next door, but he felt alone and didn't like it. He looked around, feeling helpless. He didn't want to get off the bike. The rest of the feces in his pants would run out of his pant leg if he got off. At least now, nobody could tell unless they got close, but if he stood up, there would be a puddle.

William watched as the people walked by. Couples, families, and a few solo people. They walked with such energy that William felt jealous. He thought back to when he was healthy and remembered running and working out. He didn't like it then but would give anything to be able to have that option again. He focused on his breathing. He began feeling a little sick because he could smell diarrhea coming from his pants.

Jay and Mo appeared from the bar and waved William over to them. William nodded and slowly got off the bike. He felt the rest of the fluids go down his left leg onto the ground. He looked around and was glad that nobody was around him. He slowly started to walk over to Jay and Mo.

"Come on, man, the owner said we could use the bathroom. Lucky nobody is here yet. Go ahead." Mo said, holding up a plastic bag. William looked at his bike and was glad to see that his seat was not smeared with his feces. He walked over slowly, feeling the liquid seeping out of his leg. Embarrassed was an understatement. He was used to wearing Armani suits tailored to his body and meeting with executives, and now he was dragging his feces through a strip mall to a bar called the Whisk Whiskey.

He expected Jay and Mo to make fun of him as he entered the door, but they didn't. Mo guided him over to the restroom and handed him the bag. William took the bag and thanked him. The bathroom was nice, well beyond what William had thought would be in a place called the Whisk Whiskey. It had nice tile, and the urinals were made out of beer kegs cut out and mounted on the walls.

William removed his soiled clothing and used the paper towels to help clean himself off. He felt relieved to be out of his clothes that he threw into the trash can. He opened the bag to find a package of underwear and a pair of jeans. He put them on, and a wave of sickness hit him. He immediately threw up in the sink; luckily, he had not eaten anything, so it was mainly bile. He waited until he felt the blood come back into his face and started the faucet to clean up. He realized that he was missing socks and looked in the bag. Sure enough, there was a package of socks that he missed. He looked over at his shoes which had feces on them. The sight of it made him sick again, so he grabbed a paper towel and threw them in the trash. Then he realized that he didn't have another pair and pulled them back out. He cleaned them up in the sink the best he could and put them on. *Things they don't tell you about cancer...*he thought.

He walked out to the bar to find Jay and Mo talking to the bartender. He walked up, carrying the plastic bag with his clothes in it, and he wasn't about to let someone have to clean that up.

"Is there somewhere I can throw this away?" William asked. The bartender was a tall African American male, 6'5" and big. He must have weighed at least 250 pounds, by William's estimate.

"You can throw it here." the man said with a heavy Caribbean accent opening a large garbage can.

"Oh, I don't know. It might smell." William replied. The man laughed and then pointed outside to the dumpster.

"Out there then, my friend." the man said. William nodded and went outside and found the dumpster. He threw his clothes in, making sure he still had his wallet, and he did. He turned and walked back inside. The three were still talking when he walked up. The bar was nice. Trendy with a lot of old woodwork but lots of antique road signs and nick-nacks. The one that caught his eye was a sign that looked like it was from World War II with a pin-up girl on a bomber.

"Looks like you had a rough day." The bartender said smiling. He had the type of smile that probably never left his face, even if he was angry.

"Billy, meet Sammy. Sammy is one of the strongest men in history!" Mo said, pointing at the bartender.

"Wait, you two know each other? Is there anyone you guys DON'T know out here?" William asked. Jay and Mo laughed.

"Hey, we didn't even know Sammy worked here, and we haven't seen him in many, many years. Mo just came in to see if we could use the bathroom and realized it was Sammy. So, yeah, we know a lot of people, and we've been around." Jay said.

"A long time." Sammy finished. The more he talked, the more William thought it was different than a Caribbean accent but couldn't quite place it.

"My friend, I have a flat upstairs. Would you like to use it for a shower? They did not tell me that you had that type of accident. You can use my shower if you like." Sammy said, pointing up with his right hand. Sammy was wearing a white polo shirt and tan pants. *A strange thing to wear as a bartender...* William thought.

"Oh, thank you, but I don't want to intrude. I'll be ok." William replied.

"Nonsense! If my friend Jay has taught me anything, it's that we must help each other when we can." Sammy said, walking over to William. He wrapped his arm around William, and he felt the immense density of Sammy's arm even though he was gentle. Mo was right; Sammy was powerful. Sammy shook William a little and then started walking, beckoning with his right hand for William to follow. William looked over at Jay and Mo.

"Better follow him, Billy. I wouldn't want to make that man mad." Mo said, drinking from a cup. William hesitated, then followed Sammy up a set of stairs. William followed, and Sammy pointed at the bathroom. Sammy pulled out his keys and opened the door, then walked in.

"I just did laundry, and the towels are fresh, my friend. I'll wait here for you. I have some business to attend to anyway." Sammy said. William walked into the small bathroom, which seemed very clean for a single man. He remembered when he lived in an apartment with roommates in college, it looked like a barn, but this bathroom looked like it could be in a hotel. William closed the door behind him and started the shower. The shower had glass sliding doors as he had in his house. Except, there were no hard water marks on Sammy's doors. He must clean them all the time because William's shower was marred with stains. William started the hot water and then got undressed. He was very grateful for this shower. He felt filthy and embarrassed. He got into the shower and felt the hot water hit him. It felt like heaven. He had not had a shower for days, and then the accident made things even worse. The shower continued to feel amazing, and William didn't want to get out. However, he didn't want to be rude either. He shut off the shower and got out, toweling off and then using the towel to dry the doors.

It was the kind of tiles you see in hotels, the kind you would see in something like a movie. William didn't know how an apartment way out in the middle of Arizona might have had these style tiles, but he was intrigued. He looked around and then decided it would be rude to linger. So he put on his clothes, cleaned up the best he could, and then walked to the front room. When he got to the front room, he was amazed. He had not taken the time to look around when he first came in because he was so embarrassed. However, now that he had a little bit more time, he looked around. This apartment was not one of an average person. Sammy had been around the world and then some. He looked as if he was a child in a museum. There were artifacts, tiny little things here and there, that stood out. A statue here, a portrait there. This apartment was not an apartment of a typical bartender either.

Sammy had books and books everywhere. Some were on bookshelves, others on the floor. Old books mixed with new ones, but all organized and seemed to have their place in the apartment. William began to walk around the residence from the hallway. Behind Sammy's wall, he noticed several pictures of multiple people, people of different races, creeds, and religions. White people, black people, Hispanics, Asians, and so forth. There were pictures of Sammy at the pyramids and the temples of Thailand; clearly, Sammy had been around the world. He walked out to the living room. He looked to the left and saw what looked like an ancient statute. It looked like it was made out of salt; it was very primitive. A male and a female embraced in a hug. William had seen things like this before in museums, but never in a person's home. He continued to look around when Sammy appeared on his right side. Sammy did not notice him. He was captive in some type of journal that he was writing. But once he noticed that William was out of the shower and in his living room, he closed the journal quickly and then looked up at him. He smiled.

"Do you feel better, my friend?" Sammy asked.

"Yes." William said, looking around. He continued to look around. But there was something about Sammy's smile that caught him off-guard, and he didn't know what it was.

"You like the artifacts?" Sammy asked.

"Yes. I don't know what they mean, but clearly, you have been around. This was not what I was expecting from a bartender working at a place called the Whisk Whiskey." William said.

William continued to look around the room, and every inch seemed to tell a new story. Before he could get through the room, Sammy interrupted.

"It's amazing what happens over time. You become a different person, my friend. Everything from birth to death. You think it is supposed to go one way, but it goes another, and you have no control over it. However, if you look at history itself like I do, you get a new meaning." Sammy said, gesturing with his right hand around the room for William to look at.

William looked around the room, and this time he continued to scan. It was almost like he was in another world, another time. He couldn't quite place it.

"It's okay, my friend. You're here for a reason." Sammy said.

"What do you mean?" William asked.

"Well, if you weren't meant to be here, you would not be here." Sammy said.

William was perplexed now. He was grateful that he let him use the shower. However, he didn't know what he meant.

"Here's what I mean. Everything seems to be one way, but it's another. Am I right? Think about your journey so far. Is it, Billy? I can't remember if you like Billy or William. Your journey has taken so many different turns you don't even know where you are or how you got here. Am I right?"

"I prefer William, and yes, you're right. It has." William said. Looking around.

William nodded, thinking about what Sammy was saying. Sammy was right on every point. And that's what worried him.

Sammy looked around the room, different objects here and there randomly.

"Do you see what these are, William? These are artifacts. Pieces of time. These are things that you don't get back. And that's why I keep them. Reminders of the fact that the world gives you a small amount of time, though, in your case, it probably seems minuscule, given the fact you're dying. Life itself will only give you a certain amount and only the amount you can handle. Did you ever think about that?" Sammy asked William.

"No. I did not think of things like that. I didn't think of anything until I got sick. Then all I had to do was think. Even then, I didn't think of that. So what you're telling me is that life only gave you or me the amount of time we could handle?" William asked.

"Yes. Then some people live curses with an extra life. Did you ever think of that? Have you ever noticed the people who complain the most live the longest?" Sammy asked.

"Shit, you're right." William said, thinking about it. William looked at the statue he could not seem to let go of, the very primitive one amongst all of the beautiful artifacts in the room. William pointed at the statue and asked, "What is this?"

Sammy looked at the statue for a second, and he shook his head.

"That's a picture of time. A time when things were a lot different. A time when things did not always equal what you think they meant. Suppose you take a look at that statue over there. Do you know what it is? If you study the Bible, you would. That is Samson and Delilah. They are very well known in the Bible. But as always, things get twisted. Just like them." Sammy said, looking at the statue. He seemed to gaze at it with remnants.

"No, I don't know what you mean. As far as I know, Samson was defeated because Sorry-Ass-Delilah, cut off his hair in his sleep. Am I wrong? Are you telling me that this represents Samson and Delilah?" William asked. Sammy looked at the statue for a moment, then looked over at William.

"Yes. That's what that statue is. What you are not seeing is what the actual story is, William. I know the other guys call you Billy, but I think you prefer to be called William. Is that correct?" Sammy asked. William nodded. Sammy continued.

"Well, William, you're partially correct. Samson and Delilah are actual figures of history. However, Delilah did not cut off his hair to make him lose power. Delilah cut off his hair as a sacrifice. I know it's hard to explain. Samson was so powerful that he could have destroyed anything in his path. And I mean ANYTHING. When something is that powerful, there has to be a counterbalance. That's what she was trying to do. It had nothing to do with taking a side here and there. It had to do with balance. Took me many years to figure that out. These statues here helped me figure that out." Sammy said, looking at the statue intently.

"So, you're telling me that the Bible has it wrong?" William asked. Sammy looked at the statue for a little bit longer, then looked over at William.

"Yes. But I'm not the one who tells the world that. I'm sure you would think of things differently if you were there. Like anything else, it is the beholder who sees it, and the writer who forms it." Sammy said, looking over at William. William felt slightly intimidated for a second but then looked at Sammy again.

"Well, I suppose if I were, there would be a different outcome altogether. Things always get mixed up in the storyline." William said.

"Sir William, as Jay calls you; you are wise beyond your years, my friend. Yes, things get mixed up in the story for sure. Anyway, that's not why we're here. I wanted to make sure that you were cleaned up and felt good. One time, I remember I went through kind of the same thing. I had lost everything, everything that I thought was dignifying, and someone helped me as well. So I'm kind of returning the favor. You have some good people downstairs you are riding with. I hope you understand and appreciate that from the bottom of my heart. I sincerely hope you understand they are GOOD people." Sammy said, looking intently at William. William looked back at him and then replied, "Yes. I do. Anyone else would have left me behind. They didn't, and I'm forever grateful to them. They even helped me fix my bike when it was, well, sabotaged, but they helped me. And they got me here. They could've left me." William finished.

"Well, my friend, there's something about you that they like. That means there's something about you I like. Let's go back downstairs." Sammy said, gesturing towards the door.

William exited the apartment and walked down the stairs.

"Wow, you have a long commute." William said,

joking. Sammy politely giggled as they entered the bar. Jay and Mo were in the same place at the bar talking.

"All better?" Jay asked. William nodded.

"Thank you, guys. It's embarrassing." William said, looking at Mo.

"Ah hell, Billy, we've seen worse. Trust me. Well, the cell phone place is next door. We're going to wait here for you and catch up with Sammy." Mo said, pointing next door.

"So, Sammy, how did you get here of all places? The last time I saw you was in the homeland." Jay asked. The three began conversing as William left out the door and walked into the glass doors of the cell phone store. It didn't take long for William to get a phone and everything set up with the sales associate. She was an olive-skinned girl; William guessed she was in her 20's.

"There you go, sir. You're all set. All your account information will load up in about 10 minutes and restore itself.." she said, handing him a new black iPhone. He almost upgraded to the newest model like he always used to but decided against it. He looked at her name tag. Her name was Sarah. William looked at the phone that said "Updating" on the screen, and he began to look around.

It was a typical cell phone store like any other. It had pink walls, plastered ads, and cell phones on display. He looked outside at the bikes and realized that this was it. He was going to call Rhonda, and the journey ended. He would go back and live what was left of his life at his home. He wondered how long he had left. It couldn't have been very long, judging by what just happened and the physical exertion. Probably knocked down a lot of time, but it was worth it. The good news was that they said he'd be constipated in the last days or months of his life. Clearly, not there yet. A sudden sadness and feeling of doom came over him, thinking of being in front of his computer watching YouTube videos. He thought about this unintentional adventure he had just had and the good friends he had found. Close friends, friends he hadn't had before. He wished they could be there when he finally left. He looked down at his phone and then back at Sarah.

"Sarah. Let me ask you a question. When was the last time you felt free?" William asked. She looked at him, confused.

"What do you mean?" Sarah asked.

"I mean, when was the last time you felt free? You know, like everything was good and just….free?" William responded.

"I don't know. I feel pretty free right now. I mean, I have to work, but other than that I think I'm free. I can tell you what we have for free here. If you buy…." Sarah started on a sales pitch, but William looked away as she went through her spiel.

"It's ok, Miss. I was just asking. I'm good with the service. I'll be going now." William interrupted. Sarah looked at him bluntly, slightly offset by the interruption, then smiled and handed him his receipt. She thanked him for his purchase and turned to the next customer.

William took a moment and looked around the store at the people. It seemed like everyone was preoccupied with their devices that they hardly even noticed the interaction between Sarah and William. William looked at the phone that read 80%. Sometimes, he wished these devices had never been invented, but then realized how they have helped connect people, even if it wasn't convenient, and realized they were unique and useful devices. Connecting people at the push of a button. Information previously only allowed to the elite was now available to everyone. Still, most people only use their phones for garbage social media and porn. William was no different, even if he wanted to be. Before he got sick, he was the same. Now, however, this 80% marker was the difference between the two opposites. His life with Jay and Mo, and his old life. 100% the meter read and the phone powered on.

Fifty-seven text messages, 23 voicemails, and 84 missed calls. The majority from Rhonda, but 11 from the Hollister Police Department and several others from "Private Party" callers.

"Oh shit." William said out loud.

"Sorry, sir, what was that?" Sarah asked, diverting from her current customer.

"Nothing.….just….you're looking at a dead man." William joked, forgetting about his condition for a minute. Sarah gasped and began to tear up. Clearly, she didn't think it was funny.

"No...No, I didn't mean that. I meant my wife…. anyway. She's going to KILL me. Thank you, Sarah."

William said, walking out of the store. He began to dial Rhonda's number with a sense of urgency, and his heart raced as the phone rang. One ring. He stepped outside next to his bike.

"You stay right there, Mister." Rhonda answered, surprising William.

"Baby! Look, I can explain...." William started but was quickly countered.

"Explain?! Explain that my husband took off on a motorcycle after months of cancer treatments while I was at work? Hijacked, well...no, you BOUGHT Steve's bike and took off? Oh, you didn't think Steve would rat you out, but he did!" Rhonda's wrath was like a harpy driving a pitchfork into his ear.

Mo and Jay watched from the Whisk Whiskey and widened their eyes, looking at William from the bar. Even Sammy could feel the wrath behind the bar, and none of them were even in hearing range.

"Five calls to the police, two private investigators, and you know how I found you?! Yeah, that's right, you used your fucking ATM card, and I know right where you are! Flagstaff! Fucking Arizona! I already called in sick after you used your card at some Western Wear place, and I'm twenty minutes away. Where are you exactly, and don't try to dupe me! I want answers, William! I'll be there in 10 minutes!" Rhonda shouted through the phone.

Jay and Mo watched as William was taking a beating on the phone. They could see the conversation as William occasionally held the phone away from his ear and eventually gave the universal symbol of a husband in trouble with his shoulders shrugged and pushing the phone in the center. He put the phone in his right rear pants pocket and then sat on his bike. He crossed his arms and looked down at the ground. Mo nudged Jay with his left arm and nodded towards William. Jay nodded at Sammy, and Sammy held up both hands and flapped them in a palms-down motion to shoo them away. Mo smiled, and they walked out of the bar over to William.

A slow walk but deliberate. Mo walked up behind William and grabbed his shoulder.

"Preparing for battle, are we?" Mo asked.

"More like a beating." Jay responded. William was relieved they came out. He thought they had left or were done with him.

"She's going to divorce me for this. I know it." William responded. Mo looked around for a second, then looked back at William.

"I'm sorry, Billy, but I might have missed it." Mo said.

"Missed what?" William asked.

"Ok. So, maybe I missed the part where you hit your wife? Hurt her? Lied to her? Did all that shit. Shit. Jay, I missed it. When did he do that?" Mo asked, looking at Jay. Jay shrugged and took a hit from his vape pen.

"I didn't do any of that shit, Mo, and you know it!" William responded.

"Then, my friend, maybe it's time you cut the

bullshit and talk to her. Have you even talked about the fact that you're dying?" Mo asked.

Jay chimed in, "Yeah, man. Not like just a treatment option or what comes up next, but talked about what happens when you die? That's what you're avoiding is what it sounds like, that you're going to die. Everyone worthy dies, you know, and only the cursed live forever."

"Hey, shut up, Jay! The man has enough to deal with outside your philosophical bullshit." Mo barked. Jay looked over at Mo with an initial look of anger but that quickly changed to acceptance.

"He's right, Billy. What I meant to say was that I don't' think you guys have talked. Just kind of gone on day by day, hoping that things turn out alright. Like they have always turned out for you guys. Except, this time, it hasn't. As humans, we just cling on to hope, and when tragedy hits, we keep clinging to it and hope it repeats itself, but it doesn't. So maybe it's time you two had that talk." Jay finished. His words were relieving to William, and they rang true to the core. Still, he felt hesitation.

"Look, Billy, you're not the only one in history who has had to face the wrath of an angry wife." Mo said, looking him directly in the eye. "However, at the end of the day, it's not the wife or anyone else that is going to choose your destiny. It is YOU. She'll be here fast. Your wife is smarter and more resourceful than most I've seen, but she's a wife. All she wants is answers. She's scared, Billy. If you think you're scared, you need to think of her. What happens when you're gone? It's not money she's worried about. You guys have plenty of that. She's been working two jobs to keep from facing the same thing you're avoiding. It is that you are facing death and facing it fast! What do you think she's feeling every day seeing you deteriorate before her, and she's healthy? Do you think she married you for money? She has been throwing money into the bank account left and right with her jobs and still trying to take care of you. She's scared, Billy, scared of losing YOU!" Mo said.

"DUDE! Would you please shut the fuck up?!" Jay said, looking at Mo intently as though he had said something at a dinner party he shouldn't have.

"Wait…..how did you know Rhonda's working two jobs?" William asked.

Jay looked over at Mo with wide eyes.

"Well. I just assumed." Mo said.

"No. You said two jobs. We have money in the bank, and I have life insurance that sets her up for life, so she doesn't have to be working two jobs, but you specifically said TWO jobs, and we just met. How did you know that?" William asked Mo. Mo winced back and for the first time looked off guard. He had always come off as confident and almost arrogant, but now he looked confused.

"He just picked that up from our fireside chats." Jay chimed in.

"No, that's pretty fucking specific for a fireside chat! How did you know that, Mo?!" William barked. As he said that, the grey Nissan Sentra with the Enterprise Rent-a-car logo appeared in the lot with a furious Rhonda at the helm. She zeroed in on William, and Mo and Jay quickly picked up on it. They raised an eyebrow at William and then quickly retreated into the Whisk Whiskey, a sage move on their part. The grey rental vehicle came to a stop in front of the bikes with a furious wife nearly flying out of the driver's side door, rushing over to hug William, followed by several slaps to his vest and tears coming from her face.

"WHAT WERE YOU THINKING?!" Rhonda shouted as Mo and Jay hid behind the bar window, still watching.

"A fucking motorcycle! In your condition! You know I damn near had to threaten to kill Steve before he told me what you did?! I came home from work and thought everything was fine, and I even heard your FUCKING YouTube going and thought you were upstairs! It wasn't until bedtime that I found you missing!" Rhonda yelled.

"EXACTLY!" William said, which seemed to take Rhonda off guard. The two stared at each other for a minute.

"What the fuck is that supposed to mean?!" Rhonda asked. William looked at the bike, then at his vest, and finally at Jay and Mo cowering inside the Whisk Whiskey. He let out a short sigh.

"It wasn't until you looked up at that pathetic office that you realized I was gone. That SAME fucking office I've been working out of for our whole life in that house.

Tell me I'm wrong. Would you have even noticed if I shut that door as I do during a client meeting?" William interrupted. Rhonda looked at him for a few seconds.

"Yeah….that's what I thought. Look at me, Rhonda! Look at US! When was the last time you felt free? Huh? Tell me. That question was asked to me, and it fucked me up. Yeah, we've been free a couple of times, like in Hawaii with those birds and snorkeling, but really, were we free? No! We were on a time constraint for our honeymoon. Remember? We had to be back because I had a meeting. Two weeks. That's all we got. A week here. There were a couple of days there, but we weren't free. We were on borrowed time to be made up later. When was the last time you were free, baby? I mean free. Not the made-up version of an extended break that Americans call a vacation or a sabbatical; when did you feel FREE? Well, for me, it was when I was a kid on my cousin's farm, and we rode dirt bikes. So, when I got the chance, I jumped on it. I bought Steve's bike and thought I might get one more shot to have that feeling. That feeling of being free! I didn't mean to wind up here. I lost my fucking phone! I don't know where."

Rhonda interrupted.

"You lost it on Pacheco Pass. The private investigator found it." Rhonda said dryly.

"Yay." William said in a sarcastic voice. He was annoyed, and it seemed like nothing he said penetrated. A pause went by before she responded.

"I'm still listening." she replied. William looked at his bike and then back at her.

"Are you?" he asked.

"I didn't come out here on vacation now, did I, William? Go ahead! I might be mad, but I'm listening!" she replied.

Mo looked at Jay and said, "Maybe we should go out there and kind of help?"

"Not yet." Jay replied, staring intently, taking a drag from his vape pen. Mo nodded and looked back at the two.

Rhonda's body language couldn't have been more transparent. Her arms were crossed and her left shoulder faced away from William. Mo couldn't hear what they were saying but wanted to help, and he decided against it and took Jay's advice.

"Look, baby." William started. "We've never really talked about it. We've scheduled appointments, moved forward with treatments, but we've never talked about it." William said.

Rhonda's body language changed. Her arms dropped to her sides, and she faced him.

"Talked about what?" she asked.

"That I'm dying." William said bluntly.

"Don't say that. We have the best doctors, and we're going to…" she was interrupted.

"Beat this. Yes. I know. This doctor is the fourth doctor to tell us this." William finished. It didn't take long before Rhonda's eyes swelled up with tears which caused William to do the same. He loved his wife more than anything and avoiding pain was the entire reason why this had never been discussed. No words were said for a brief time. It was not until William felt that connection to his wife that he had felt before he got sick that he began to speak.

"I'm dying, Rhonda. There's no way around it. Look at me. I just shit my pants pulling into this lot trying to get a phone to call you. Luckily, I found some friends that got me here, but I don't have much time left." William said as if stating the sky was blue on a clear day. Everyone knew the sky was blue, but nobody said it. In William and Rhonda's case, nobody wanted to say it. Saying it meant there was a reality. It would happen. Reality, that was something neither of them wanted to bring into this world.

Rhonda took a second to absorb it.

"We can beat...." Rhonda started.

"We can beat this. Yes, that's also something we've said before." William finished.

"Well, what the fuck William?! You're my husband! You don't think I'm scared?! You don't think I haven't thought about what happens next?! We built a life together! Now it's disappearing, and I don't know what to do!" Rhonda yelled as the tears began to roll down.

"I'm scared, William! What am I supposed to do?! My whole life is built around you because I love you! Fuck the money! Fuck the house! I don't know what I'm supposed to do! What happens when you go, huh? Where do I go?! Half of me just wants to trade places with you! I would if I could! Do you think it's easy to see the man I've spent my whole life with in pain and dying in front of me?! It's NOT William! It's NOT easy!" Rhonda shouted. She was about to start again when William interrupted.

"Is that why you are working two jobs? Avoiding all this? Maybe a distraction or two? Think I overlooked that? I don't blame you for that. I'd probably do the same." William finished. It had bothered him that she had been working so much, and now he finally said it. He knew he had limited time before, but now it was all cards on the table. Rhonda looked over at him with the tears still flowing. She nodded.

"It's not the money, William. I….just can't lose you." Rhonda said. The tears flowing from her just added to his pain, and William nodded as his tears added to her pain. Each of them seeing the pain in each other hurt even worse than their own pain. Tears flowed for some time before William broke the silence.

"Baby. We can't help the cards we've been dealt, but we can play our hand and go out like Kenny Rogers in that Gambler song." William said, looking at her intently.

"What do you mean?" Rhonda asked.

"I mean, I'm dying, but I'm not dead yet." William said, still looking at her. Rhonda looked confused.

"Look, baby, I'm saying that I'm not dead yet. It's not how we die, but how we live that makes the difference." William finished. Rhonda's tears stopped for a second, and she laughed.

"Are you seriously quoting The Last Samurai right now?" she asked. William laughed and nodded.

"Yeah, baby. My favorite movie. Katsumoto had

it right. I haven't really lived as I wanted, but now we can." he said.

"How?" she asked. William looked over at the motorcycle.

"Oh no. We need to get back. The doctors said they could get you back into chemotherapy…" she started.

"No. I'm done with that. I'm done with all that, and I'm done putting you through that. I met a guy recently who talked about the moment. THIS moment. Looking at you right here, right now, I wouldn't trade for any moment. I'm done wasting what little moments I have left with you. I want to live, baby…..even if it's for a short time, but I want to live with you. I don't want to be sick and fucked up in our million-dollar house on the bathroom floor for a couple more minutes, and I want to live for this moment. Right here, right now. That machine over there gives us that. Those friends staring at us from that window, they give us that." William said, pointing over at the Whisk Whiskey. Jay and Mo saw him pointing and instinctively ducked.

Rhonda took a minute to absorb what William had said. Then she looked over at the bar and asked, "What friends?".

CHAPTER 8

WE AIN'T A FUCKING CIRCUS!

Jay and Mo tried their best to duck and peek over.

"DUDE! They're walking over! Hide!" Jay said to Mo as William and Rhonda opened the bar door. Sammy continued to clean the glasses behind his bar and nodded at William as he came through the door.

"What can I get you, my friends?" Sammy asked as William locked eyes with him.

"Whiskey. Neat." William said, winking at Sammy as if he had ordered it before. He hadn't.

"Just to give you a little warning. Jay is the lighter-skinned guy, he's mellow, but Mo is kind of animated." William said, walking through the bar and searching for Jay and Mo. They were easy to find. Nobody else was in the bar.

Mo was the first to stand up and open his palms in a welcoming gesture, and Jay followed with both palms spread out.

"Billy! Good to see you, my friend! I thought you were going home." Jay said, stepping in front to shield Mo. He had dealt with situations like this before, and he was either going to get slapped or hugged. Mo's pride wasn't having it as he stepped to the side of Jay and made the same gesture.

"Billy! Glad to see you brought someone to offset that ugly mug! How you landed this beautiful lady, I have no idea!" Mo said. Both now stood waiting to see Rhonda's reaction.

Rhonda took a minute, then placed her hands on her elbows, staring at them. She didn't know if she was enraged at them or highly grateful. The stare-down was intense, and it broke with a sudden hug to Mo that he certainly thought was a punch and winced before being embraced. The second hug to Jay followed.

"Thank you for bringing my husband to safety." Rhonda said after letting go of Jay.

"Oh...no problem Mrs. Tunnicliff. He was never really in any danger. If anything, he brought us to safety." Jay replied.

William thought for a second but did not say anything. He had never told Jay his last name. Nor had he told Mo. Even during their most intense discussions.

"Well, nonetheless, thank you." Rhonda said.

"This is Jay, and this is Mo. The bartender back there is Sammy." William said, pointing to each person as he introduced them. Rhonda shook hands with each person and then walked over to Sammy for the final handshake.

"So. Where did you guys meet my husband?" she asked.

"Well, that's a funny story. We were a little lost, believe it or not, and…." Mo told her the story. A few laughs were exchanged as William sat back and listened to the three banter. It was good to have this conversation with her. Over the past years, it was mainly the two of them in their home, but having others made it more communal and comfortable.

"Well, Billy. I'm glad he finally found you, Missus. I suppose you got it from here." Mo said, pushing his glass to the side. He looked over at Jay.

"We should get going, Jay. Daylight's burnin'. We gotta be in at least border territory by tomorrow if we're going to make it." Mo said, then looked over at William and Rhonda.

"As for you two, have a safe trip back." Mo finished. He nodded at Jay, and they stood up.

"I'm going with you." William said dryly. Rhonda looked over at him. Jay and Mo immediately rebuked.

"What?! No, Billy, look, it's been fun hanging out and all, but it's time for you to go with your wife like you said you wanted. You got your ride in. Go home." Jay said, turning to leave.

"No. I said I'm going with you." William said sternly. Mo seemed to lose patience fast. He turned and slammed both hands on the table.

"Do we look like the fucking circus Billy?! Besides, who said you're even invited? OUR vacation, not yours. You don't even know where we're going, and you might not even survive the…"

"I DON'T CARE!" William shouted, standing up. Rhonda winced as he splayed out both hands.

"I'm going…." William pushed both hands in a

downward motion. Mo looked over at Jay, confused. Jay just shrugged his shoulders, confused, then shook his head.

"Rhonda! Do you want to chime in here? You know, the voice of reason?" Mo plead with her. Rhonda looked over at Mo, then at Jay, then a very long pause as she looked at William.

"You...you ever watch someone you love die?" Rhonda started. Mo just looked at her. "You ever watch them throw up so hard that they break their ribs? Do you know what that's like? Have you ever watched someone you love go from being at the top of their lives, having everything, and begging for just a little bit of their time because they're so busy and successful, then watch them turn into everything they've feared. Watch them fall into a spiral of depression, then repeat it over and over again, taking them to get poisoned, hoping for just a few more days with them?" Rhonda asked very sternly before she continued.

"Well, I do. William was right. I took up jobs just to escape things. It's not easy. It never is. We have money, yes, and he's right. I resented him, and I was so....so angry. It wasn't his fault, but he was right. I was avoiding this. I took him to all of his appointments; I watched as he withered away. Day by day, I watched him in front of his computer, then later helping him to bed, hoping that he wouldn't have to get up in the middle of the night, but he always would. He'd need my help to get to the bathroom. Then, yes, I don't want to say it, but I began to resent him. Not so much him, but the sickness. I wanted to escape, and then I found a couple of jobs. I told him it was to help us out, but it wasn't. He knew it. I knew it. We just kept going on day by day until now." Rhonda looked down at the table and then up at Mo.

"When he first went missing, I won't lie to you. I felt a sense of relief." She looked over at William, ashamed but then continued.

"Then, panic set in. When I realized he was missing, it was like my life had collapsed. The thought of him not being here….I freaked out. I called the police. I questioned the neighbors, and when I found out he bought a bike, I was SO….Angry. I don't know how to explain what happened next. Hell, I don't even know what happened next. I just know my life focused on finding William. Then, we talked out there in that parking lot when I did. A talk that we should have had a long time ago, and yes, he's dying. My William is dying. I'm going to be alone. As scary as that is, it's real. I'll face it when it happens. I didn't think about him during this whole thing, only me and us. Our life. Our trips. Our friends. Everything is connected between us, but I never thought about William, my husband. The person who I've spent all these years with. I didn't think about him, and how he was feeling, I just plugged along every day.

Now. We're here. In Arizona, somewhere I'd NEVER think we'd be, but my husband says he needs this. He doesn't want to go on getting poisoned and feeling like hell, and I don't blame him. Demanding he go back after hearing him say that would make me the most selfish wife on earth.

So, if he says he wants to go with you, I support it. The truth is, I haven't heard him say he wanted anything since he got sick. He went from being driven, focused, and nearly unstoppable when he put his mind to things; into a shell of who he was and just went by day by day. I watched his spirit wither away every day, and I couldn't stand it. I hated even being around it. Then, he jumps on a motorcycle and winds up going nuts down in Arizona with a couple of rowdy bikers; THAT sounds more like my William. So, you might not be the circus, but this happened for a reason. You two are the LAST people I'd have thought my William would be buddies with, but my grief counselor said that sometimes things happen when we don't expect it and to follow it."

"Grief counselor? Have you been seeing a grief counselor? I'm not dead, Rhonda" William butted it.

"Yes, William, I've been seeing a counselor, and no, you're not dead, but you sure acted like it. I didn't have anyone to talk to, so yes, I went to a counselor. Now, to finish what I was saying before being rudely interrupted by my husband, I don't understand why I'm here right now or why William found you two, but I know that this is better than what we had before. It's better than watching my husband convulse into a ball and have to help him to the shower to stop the dry heaves. If he wants to follow you and die out there, then that's what we'll do.

I was so scared when it set in that he was gone. I felt horrible guilt and pain. So many things unsaid, I....I didn't know. Anyway. We're here now. William and I talked. I get it now. He knows he's dying. I know he's dying. There's no more dancing around it, no more ignoring it. I hate it, I don't want it, and I just want things to go back to what they were, but they won't, and they never will. I love that man right there." Rhonda said, looking over at William.

"I'll support what he wants. If he wants to join the fucking circus, then I'm in. He goes out how he wants to go out, but I'm going with you." Rhonda finished with a direct stare at William, and Mo threw up his hands and stepped back.

"Whoa! Wait a fucking minute here! What are you two talking about?! First, YOU nor Billy were invited to OUR vacation. Jay, did you invite them? I don't remember inviting them. Where we're going is fucking remote, Billy! It's not like an easy ride down as we've had so far. It's not..." Mo started.

"I don't care! Just...just let me follow as long as I can. Fair enough?" William asked, looking at Mo and then over at Jay. "Just let me follow long enough to live until I can't go on. Then Rhonda can take over. I....I just need this, guys. I don't know what else to say. It just feels like this is the last of my.....free will. Choice. Let me choose. Please. I know you don't have to take me with you, but give me a chance." William pled.

"Billy, we can't be responsible for you. It's going

to get rough out there." Jay said, acting as a voice of reason. William was unfazed.

"You don't have to worry about that. I'll sign a waiver, whatever." William responded.

"Waiver?!" Mo laughed, "This ain't waiver territory, Billy! We ain't the fucking circus! This is Mexico! Your body wouldn't even be found! It isn't like here, William. Have you ever even been down to Mexico? I'm not talking about Cancun or these resort towns where we're going. It's an old-school die in the desert territory. Banditos, corrupt cops, no running water. Not to mention the terrain itself can kill you, and NOBODY is coming if something goes wrong. No. Sorry Billy, just go back. You had your fun, your adventure. You're done. Go home." Mo said.

William looked Mo directly in the eye. A long pause went by before William spoke.

"You might be right, but God will be the judge of what happens next. Just let me go with you. If I die, I die. Just let me go on my terms. Let God decide." William finished looking at Mo. Mo and Jay looked at each other.

"God has nothing to do with this, Billy." Jay said, rolling his eyes.

"The hell he doesn't! Do you think things happen by chance? Do you think I'd have had the guts to jump on that bike without God? Do you think I'd have faith that I'd be ok out in that desert before I found you guys? I prayed all the time on that road. I haven't prayed since I was a kid. Every time I've prayed, something happened. I prayed for a little more time when my hands were frozen in the desert, and I wasn't sure if I'd make it, and I found you guys. I prayed for you and Jay on the road that you'd be happy, and we wound up at Bud's place. I prayed to see my wife again, and she's here. Maybe not as I thought or imagined, but God is part of it. He's ALL of it. I prayed Rhonda would forgive me and understand why I've done this, and she has, and I prayed to follow you guy until I just couldn't hold that throttle anymore. Now here we are."

"So you got here, Billy. Awesome. Prayers worked. How about praying to live longer? Ever try that?" Mo said, rolling his eyes.

"Don't be a dick, Mo." Jay scolded.

"Oh...I'm the dick? Me? I'm the dick. Billy here didn't even appreciate his fucking life until he was half dead, actually more like three-quarters dead now, but that's beside the point." Mo reached over and tapped William on the right shoulder.

"All of a sudden, he found God and started praying, then POOF! All his little dreams are coming true....So before that, fuck everyone. I'm off to my next meeting." Mo looked at William.

"Before you were sick, you wouldn't have given two shits about him or me! Admit it!" Mo said, staring at William.

William looked over at Jay and then at Rhonda. He did it again.

"Well? You gonna fucking answer?" Mo pressed.

"No, okay? You're right. I wouldn't have, but I

169

didn't know any better. I didn't know you guys then."
William said.

"Oh, but now that you're dying and you found
God, all of a sudden, we're supposed to turn into a
fucking "Make a Wish Motorcycle Foundation" and
drag you along with us! No!" Mo yelled.

"That change in him means something, Mo.
You know that, and he doesn't have much time." Jay
butted in.

"I KNOW that FUCK-O! That's my point!
Everyone out there suddenly finds God in jail or
fucking dying and waste their lives being selfish pricks
no matter WHO tries to tell them otherwise. Even
now. Notice that he's not doing something for someone
else. He's not riding to Mexico to give orphans some
presents on his last Hoo-Rah. He's not taking his wife
to Italy. No, it's all about 'look at poor little me, I'm
dying, and I want to follow these guys to Mexico! Yay!'
and suddenly we're supposed just to jump and feel sorry
for him." Mo said, staring at William.

"Come on, man. It's not his fault, and what's it
going to hurt to bring him?" Jay interjected.

"That's my point, Jay, right there! It's never anybody's
fault. How old are you, Billy? What, forty-something?
That's forty-something years you could have given back
to people. Given to god. You could have helped other
people, helped animals, shit did ANYTHING, and
even now you are in it for you." Mo finished. William's
demeanor shifted to defeat. Mo was right. Everything

he said was true. He looked over at Rhonda and then at Jay.

"You're right." William said. Mo looked over at him, confused.

"What?" Mo asked.

"I am in it for me. I always have been. You're right. I just never saw it until now. If I could do it over again, I would. I would help people. I would tell them there's more to this world than making money or impressing people. I'd tell them there's a God and something out there to strive for. I get it. This feeling here, this adventure, as you called it…..It's been a gift. Probably one I don't deserve." William said.

"Well, wait a minute William. You worked your whole life, and you did help people. You helped them run their business, make money, and, in turn, helped their families. Yes, you made money, but you did help people. Not everyone can be Mother Theresa. You employed people and provided for their families." Rhonda interjected.

"Yeah. I worked. A job I didn't really like, but it paid a lot of money. I guess you're right, too. I did help people, but it was always about me and what I could get out of it. I never taught anyone what I knew, never shared things I didn't have to, and I sure as hell would never give anyone anything for free. So I guess you're both right. The question is now, what am I supposed to do? Baby, maybe Mo is right. Maybe we'll just head home. Thank you, guys." William said, turning towards Rhonda.

171

He reached out for Rhonda's hand, and she took it. They started to walk towards the car. Mo's words rattled him, and he felt a sense of guilt. It wasn't so bad, he thought. Mo was right, he'd probably die on the road, and he didn't want to burden anyone with that. Mo was right again when he said he had led a selfish life even if he didn't mean to, but now he was thinking of others first. He would slow them down.

Mo looked over to Jay who was staring at him intently. He continued to stare, and Mo shrugged his shoulder and threw up his hand in a "what?" gesture. Jay didn't move. His eyes locked on Mo in disapproval, and Mo rolled his eyes.

"FINE! Billy, we'll take you! Yet ANOTHER fucking charity case! I'm so tired of this shit, Jay! Can't we have just ONE vacation where we just go and don't pick up a stray?!" Mo finished and mounted his bike. He fired up his bike and yelled out to William, "YOU BETTER BUY SOME GAS BOTTLES CAUSE WE AIN'T STOPPIN'!!".

William looked over at Rhonda. She nodded for him to go, and he kissed her. He walked over to his bike and mounted it. He heard Jay's bike fire up right next to him. William put his helmet on as quick as he could, and the gloves. He fired up his bike in time to see Jay and Mo pulling out of the parking lot. He dropped into gear as quickly as possible, released the clutch too fast, and stalled out. He quickly pulled in the clutch, started the bike again, and got the bike going. He looked back to see Rhonda backing her rental vehicle out and then pulling forward to follow. He went as quick as he could to catch up, but they were gone.

William began to panic and saw the sign for the highway southbound. Mexico was south. He got on and went as fast as he could, but he couldn't find them. He looked back to see Rhonda following him. About five miles down the road, he realized they had left him. All that talk just to make him look even more like an idiot.

He slowed down and moved to the right lane feeling defeated. He started to travel at the speed limit and looked down. They ditched him. One last joke they just HAD to pull on him. It was a good one. He had to admit that they got him good. He laughed and shook his head. They got him. William prepared to stop and figure out what to do next. How was he going to get the bike back? Where was he going to go now? Sell the bike there and go home?

Jay and Mo passed him on the left, making him jump. They looked over and began pointing and laughing at him on his left side. They were riding side by side and he could see both of them with their hair flowing in the wind behind their helmets. They kept pointing and laughing even harder. A sense of relief came over William as he sped up to catch up with them, and he didn't get ditched after all. He joined the formation, and they continued into the endless highway with Rhonda in the car behind them.

William felt complete. He had everything in "THIS MOMENT." as Bud called it. Even if it was almost nothing compared to what he was used to. He had his friends, this bike, and his wife behind him. No fancy cars, money, computers, houses, or anything. He didn't even have his precious laptop that held millions of dollars worth of clients he never let out of his sight. Yet, somehow, right now, he felt complete.

CHAPTER 9

⸺◈⸺

WEST COAST THROTTLE

hree gas stops. The group was getting close to the border. The landscape changed, but not drastically. It was still desert but seemed a little drier and maybe a little hotter, but then again, he was on a motorcycle. A sign said "Nogales," 20 miles ahead. They must be close, William thought to himself. He started to think about something else when he saw the high beam flashing in his rearview mirror. He looked back to see Rhonda flashing her lights and honking with steam coming up from the hood. Jay and Mo saw it too. The group pulled over to the side. The car stopped, and more steam came from the hood. It was getting dark fast.

"I don't know what happened. It just started doing that." Rhonda said, pointing at the hood and getting out of the car. Jay looked around and saw a building to the highway's right, and Mo walked over and looked.

"Mo, check it out." Jay said, looking at the building. Mo looked into the distance.

"Oh shit! That's West Coast Throttle. We that close already?" Mo said, looking at Jay.

"Did you get the insurance with the rental?" William asked Rhonda.

"Well, yeah, but we need to call them. I don't think the insurance people will have anyone way out here. I was supposed to take it right back to the airport." Rhonda said.

"Let's see if it will make it over there. We can figure out what to do when we're off the road, but we're running out of daylight here, and we're about twenty miles out from where we were planning on staying the night." Jay said.

Rhonda got back into the car and started it. It ran but still steamed. The three got on their bikes and pulled off the freeway, with Rhonda slowly following. The sunset lit up the mountain behind a bar called *West Coast Throttle*. As they pulled into the lot, they could see it was filled with motorcycles. There must have been forty or fifty bikes lined up and parked in a row. Mo led the group around to the back, where a large RV was parked. The RV had flames down the side painted with white highlights. It made it look like the RV was on fire.

"Uh…." Rhonda said, getting out of the car. "Is this place safe?" she asked.

"Depends on what you call safe girly." Mo laughed, dismounting.

"We'll be fine, honey. We'll just get inside, call the rental company and see what they want us to do. Or wait, let me try to call." William said.

"Don't bother….no cell reception out here, Billy." Jay said, taking off his helmet.

"There's a phone inside, though." Jay said, placing his helmet on his rearview mirror.

"Man, we haven't been here for what….how long now?" Mo asked Jay.

"A long time." Jay said.

"Hey…you remember last time we were here what happened?" Mo asked, smiling at Jay.

"Unfortunately." Jay replied. They walked around the building toward the front, and the heat from the wall radiated toward them.

"Man…I've never seen you so pissed, man!! That was a night for sure!!" Mo said, pushing Jay with his right hand. Jay stumbled right and shook his head.

"What? What happened?" William asked, walking with Rhonda behind them.

"A long story." Jay said, continuing to walk.

As they approached the front of the bar, two bikers were guarding the door. Both of them were wearing black leather vests, and one had a big knife on his right side. William picked up on the knife and tension pretty quickly. William thought they were security and tried to show his identification.

"What the fuck are you doing?" Mo scoffed. "Put that shit away, man. You're fucking embarrassing!" he said, pushing William's wallet down.

"Gentlemen." Jay said, opening the door.

"Fuck off." The one on the right said as the three walked through the door.

The climate inside the bar was extremely tense. At least forty bikers were in the center, with a few ordinary people on the sides playing pool. It would look like a regular biker bar any other day, but not tonight. There was tension. One group on one side had a back patch with a snake. William couldn't exactly see what the name was on the vest, and the other group had what looked like a man wearing a Sombrero on the back, but he couldn't see the names on those either because it was too dark. The neon signs throughout the bar were in the right places, and the decor looked like a standard bar with a long wooden bar and two bartenders tending, but there was an eerie calm amongst the loud music and background noises. An unheard silence, but a silence nonetheless. Mo and Jay stepped to the right of the door and stopped. They looked around the room, and for the first time, William saw their expressions change. Their usual look of cool and calm went to a more alert tone. Both stood more upright, and Jay's usual smile turned into a flat line as he scanned the room.

"I need a drink." William said and started to walk towards the bar. Mo grabbed his arm.

"Not that way. This way. Don't walk down the middle." Mo said, walking over to the side, watching the group in the middle.

The bikers took up the entire center, with the snake patches on one side and the Sombreros on the other. William didn't know much about what the patches meant, but Jay and Mo were concerned. The men sat silently. Every once in a while, they stared over at the other group sharply. Mainly keeping their conversations to their groups. It almost looked like friends who got caught fighting and sitting in the principles office together. The leaders of the groups were pretty noticeable. One biker with the snake patch was bald with a long beard that went all the way to his chest and bigger than most of the men. He was a white man but looked weathered and old. William guessed him to be in his sixties but maybe late fifties.

The Sombrero group had almost the opposite. He was a Mexican man with a Mexican flag tattooed on his left arm and the American flag above the Mexican flag. He was clean-shaven, younger, maybe early forties, and had long hair in a braid that went down to the center of his back. Both groups would constantly look at the two men for approval silently as they talked amongst themselves and then scanned the other group.

"What the hell is going on here, Mo? What's up with these guys?" William asked. Mo took a spot at the end of the bar filled with regular people who looked like locals.

"I don't know, but it's not good whatever it is. Those are 1% ers. Did you ever hear of the Hells Angels or the Mongols on TV? Well, they're kind of like them but with different patches. Same breed." Mo said, flagging down the bartender.

"Are we safe?" William asked. Mo shrugged.

"Usually, they just do their own thing and don't bother anybody, but those guys at the door are there to tell them when their leaders get there. There are no presidents here right now." Mo said as the bartender walked up and he ordered four beers.

"Presidents? What do you mean?" William asked, looking over at the group.

"Their leaders. They're not here. Do you see those two with the strip above the left pocket? Both say 'Vice President,' just like the oval office. They're organized just like the military. It's almost unheard of that the president is not the first one in the bar, and everyone follows. Them not being here's weird, and somethings brewing." Mo said.

"Don't worry, Billy." Jay chimed in. "They're not concerned with us." Jay said, trying to ease the tension.

"Not yet anyway." Mo said, still looking at the group.

"Well, if you boys need anything else. You know, beer, food, handjob, a new gasket for that piece of shit rental car..." the female bartender said with a slight southern accent from behind the bar. It took a second, but Mo finally looked over.

"LUCY!! What the fuck?! I should knock your fucking teeth out for riggin' Billy's bike, you crazy bitch!" Mo yelled. William looked over to see a petite blonde girl with short hair. Pretty with hoop earrings and a skin-tight blue dress.

"Awww. Did Mo Mo miss me? Go ahead. Right here, slugger. Knock the front ones out. They're my favorite." Lucy said, pointing to the front of her mouth. Mo was visibly angry, and his face turned bright red.

"No? Didn't think so, you big dumb animal. You've always been all talk. What about you, pretty boy? Do you want to knock my teeth out too? Here's, you're hardcore non-alcoholic beer boys." She said, looking at Jay.

"Fuck off, Lucy!" Jay said, drinking his beer.

"What? Not like you boys should be surprised. You know what I am. I did you a favor. You boys were going to ride right by Bud's place and not even say hi. Pretty rude after all these years if you ask me. Besides, I've done way worse, and you know it. Plus, nobody got hurt, and I needed time to catch up with you guys. You guys were going down to Mexico without me….. Shame on you." Lucy said right before taking a shot glass filled with clear liquid and making a "cheers" gesture after drinking in.

"Um. Excuse me. Who is this? How did she know about my car?" Rhonda asked.

"Oh, how rude of me. I'm Lucy, dear, and I know about your car because I'm the one who pulled your radiator cap half off so you'd start steaming and then pinched the gasket so it would make all that pretty steam. You two were in the station, so I took the opportunity to, well, you know, make some magic happen. Otherwise, you would have passed right by me, and my boys here wouldn't have stopped to pick me up on the way down to Mex….ICO!" Lucy said, smiling.

"Hey! I know you! You're the girl from the bar! The night I met Jay and Mo." William shouted.

"Oh, the chemical meatbag speaks! Oh, that's cute. You boys have a pet now." Lucy said, condescending.

"Watch it bitch!" Rhonda said, approaching the counter. Jay held out his arm to stop her.

"Don't let her get under your skin. Once she gets there, you'll never get her out. She's like herpes." Jay said, staring at Lucy. Lucy heard him and smiled a big smile, then giggled.

"He's kind of right, you know, Sweety. Aren't you just the doll now, aren't you? Hmmm, meatbag must have money." Lucy said, looking over at William.

"THAT'S IT!" Rhonda yelled and lunged at Lucy over the bar. William and Jay were able to stop her before she could grab Lucy and pulled her back. Rhonda kept lunging, but they moved her around the corner of the bar outside of Lucy's view. In the background, they could be heard calming her down while Lucy sipped her drink nonchalantly.

Even with Rhonda's outburst, the men in the center of the room didn't budge. It almost seemed like they were background noise to them. Mo looked over at them and then back at Lucy.

"You got something to do with that?" Mo asked.

"Maybe." Lucy said, smiling and rocking side to side holding her elbows.

"That's why you're here? To watch the show of some fucking chaos you made up?" Mo asked.

"Well, that, and I didn't want to go on vacation alone. You know a girl gets lonely, and it's dddaaaannnnggggeeeerrrrooooouuuussss down in Mexico for a girl all by herself, you know. So, I figured I'd jump in with you guys. Ok, fine….maybe I missed you two a little." Lucy said.

"No way, Lucy! Every time we go anywhere with

you, it gets fucking weird and crazy really quick! There's a reason we didn't invite you!" Mo said, staring at Lucy.

"Oh, come on, Mo! Don't be so dramatic. It's not ALL the time." Lucy said, taking another shot. Mo stared at her.

"Ok...so maybe it is ALL the time, but at least it's entertaining." Lucy said, smiling at him.

"Yeah, for YOU. We always get the brunt of the mess or the clean-up. No way, you go solo this time." Mo said, looking back at the group.

"Ok, what the fuck did you do, Lucy? Last I heard, these guys were friends." Mo said, looking at Lucy. Lucy looked over at the group and giggled.

"Well, Chewbacca, I'm glad you asked. It took me weeks to make this happen." Lucy said, taking another shot. "See, here's what happened. Those guys over there are the -"

"I know the names, Lucy! What the fuck did you do?" Mo interrupted.

"Well. Before I was so rudely interrupted by the ill-mannered peasant beast, I was going to tell the story. See, those guys on the left, their president, really likes young petite blondes. Ironically so does theirs!" Lucy said, pointing at the right side. "So, it wasn't too hard to make 'friends' with them. Those guys have a president who likes to, shall we say, import assault weapons into the U.S. through Mexico. Those guys have a president who likes to run heroin into the U.S. through Mexico. He also happens to, shall we say, facilitate border crossings by holding the customers' children at gunpoint until he gets paid.

Well, needless to say, when men fall asleep, they leave things lying around. It's what I do, Mo. I happen to collect things. An anonymous call to the cops and U.S. Customs, and let's just say if you leave a little something behind here, a little there, well, it's pretty clear they told on each other based on the evidence the cops found. Hey, cops are saying it, not me." Lucy said, now sipping another shot.

"Lucy! They're going to kill each other! Why did you do that?" Mo said, looking at the two groups. Things were getting even more intense as time went by.

"What? I'm doing the world a favor. Like God made them smuggle guns and dope, then rip kids away from their parents. They have it coming. They made their choices. Anyway, I also arranged for both presidents to arrive right about....now." Lucy said, looking at the door.

The two men stationed outside came in the door and signaled to their groups. It didn't take long before both groups were on their feet and started walking outside. They didn't get the chance. The door crashed open as the president of the Sombreros came flying through. The other president came in front of him, running at him from behind. Like a pack of wolves, both groups attacked each other almost instantly.

"SHIT! This way, Billy!!" Jay said, pushing Rhonda and William to the side of the bar. The locals seemed to be caught in the middle. Some ran for the door, and others jumped into the chaos and started fighting. A bar stool was smashed over one man and returned with a beer bottle smashed on the other man's head.

"GET DOWN!" Jay yelled and pushed Rhonda and William down. Lucy could be heard laughing at the top of her lungs as Mo ducked from incoming bottles. The fight raged on as Jay and Mo grabbed the other two and headed to the back door. They made it out the back door just in time to hear sirens approaching from the distance.

All four looked back to make sure they were out of danger. The smashing and breaking of glass and wood could be heard as the door closed. Then the sounds were muted as the sirens got closer. The door opened back up, and Lucy walked out casually and lit a cigarette.

"Well. That was fun." Lucy said, taking a drag from her cigarette.

"Lucy....why are you such an asshole?" Jay asked, catching his breath. Lucy shrugged.

"I don't know. Why is a cat a cat? Why is a dog a dog? They just are. I just am. What can I say? So...." Lucy said, walking over to William.

"What is it? Cancer? That's the popular one nowadays. Or some kind of mutant thing like you see on TV?" Lucy asked bluntly, examining William.

"I swear THIS BITCH...." Rhonda said, walking over to Lucy, and Jay stopped her.

"Don't waste your energy, Rhonda. Lucy's different. You can beat on her all you want to, and it won't change anything. She never learns her lesson no matter what, do you, Lucy?" Jay asked. Lucy shrugged.

"It is what it is." Lucy said.

"What was the point of that?" Mo asked.

"What? You did that? That......in there, is YOUR fault? Why am I not surprised?" Jay rolled his eyes and let out a sigh before stroking his hair.

"What? You boys act as if I'm SOOOO evil. Think about it. Those guys were running guns, drugs, and human trafficking up the border. Most of them are already criminals on parole who like to beat and intimidate anything they come across. Some of them are okay, yeah, I'll give you that, but they know better. They know what they're getting into, so that's on them. Think about it. Cops will break it up, half will be put back in jail where they belong, and the other half will be sent home to whimper at their little clubhouses away from everyone else trying to live like good little sheep. Just like God wants, right? Perfectly lined little hedges and white picket fences with 2.5 kids? Hell, I should be getting an award instead of hanging out with Scooby and Shaggy here." Lucy said, taking another puff.

"You realize you are seriously fucked, right? You know they make medicine for this, Lucy." Mo said, putting on his helmet.

"Yeah, I don't think they make enough medicine to fix that." Jay chimed in, taking his helmet from his mirror.

"Wait. Where are you guys going? We didn't get

to call the rental car company to get another car for Rhonda." William said.

"Oh, don't worry, Sweety. I got you covered. You can ride with me, uh, I kind of threw the radiator cap away to your car, so.....hop in!" Lucy said, smiling at Rhonda. She pushed a key fob, and the alarm from the RV with flames honked twice and flashed the hazards.

"Oh hell no! I am NOT riding with this crazy bitch! No way in hell!!" Rhonda protested.

"I'll wait here, thank you." Rhonda finished looking at William. Lucy dropped her cigarette and smashed it with her right foot.

"Okay, Sweety, suit yourself. But....just one thing. In about 30 seconds, the cops are going to round that corner and put anyone associated with that bar in handcuffs while they 'investigate.' I'm sure you'll be fine sitting in the back of a police car. Especially with men like inside the bar that have pissed and vomited in for years. I'm sure the cops will sort things out. You'll be just fine...oh, and of course, there's only so many cop cars, so you'll make friends with whoever they put you in the car with. Ta ta, Sweety." Lucy said, walking towards the RV. Rhonda looked over at Jay, and Mo, who already had their bikes fired up and idling.

"Just get in the RV! She's not kidding about the cops!" Jay yelled. William shrugged his shoulders when she looked at him.

"Just get in, baby. We'll handle it when we stop." William said as the sirens stopped in front of the bar. William quickly put his helmet on and started the bike.

Rhonda reluctantly followed Lucy into the RV and sat in the passenger seat. Lucy looked over at Rhonda and was about to speak.

"NOT a fucking word, you psycho. Just get us out of here." Rhonda said.

Lucy smiled and winked at her as she started the RV. Rhonda looked back to see the RV was decorated just like she thought it would be. Crazy. There was random everything from all over the country and loud colored clothes in the RV all over the place. Everything from make-up to weapons all through the back. Crazy yet organized. Lucy pulled the RV out onto the street as the approaching police cars began stopping in the parking lot. She looked in the rearview mirror and watched the red and blue flashing lights shrink in the mirror.

"Well. It could be worse, and at least it didn't catch fire this time." Lucy said. Rhonda looked back just in time to see the smoke and flames climbing out of the side of the bar.

"Whoops. Well, I'm sure they have insurance." Lucy laughed as the RV rode off into the Arizona darkness. Rhonda looked at her in disbelief, then out to the three motorcycle taillights.

CHAPTER 10

FRED

The group pulled into the first motel they could find in Nogales. The motel was the typical desert hotel you see in the movies with a giant lit neon sign that said "Vacancy." Single story with doors facing the inside of the parking lot. The RV came to a stop in the rear of the motel, with three bikes stopped in the front.

"Billy. Your turn. We got the last one." Mo said, looking over at William. He was right. They paid for the last room they stayed in. William nodded and dismounted. He put his helmet on his mirror, adjusted his jacket, and walked through the front door. He looked around the small lobby and over the counter. He saw a dark-skinned man writing something at a desk behind the counter. The man looked to be in his fifties and had white hair. He continued writing and didn't appear to acknowledge William. William cleared his throat loudly to get the man's attention. No reaction. He kept writing. He coughed louder. No reaction.

"Uh, excuse me." William said politely. The man kept writing.

"Ok...Pardon Señor?" William tried his best to

remember his 10th-grade Spanish. The man stopped and looked up at William through very thick glasses.

"Oh." the man said in an East Indian accent. "So, because I'm brown, I'm Mexican is that it?"

"Well, no, I said excuse me first." William said in defense.

"Oh, so a man can't finish writing in his ledger before serving you. Sorry, your highness!" The man said, staring at William, and his eyes were amplified through the glasses.

"No, I didn't mean...ok, look, can we get three rooms, please? I have cash." William said, frustrated. William took out a wad of cash from his pocket and showed it to the man. He looked at the money, then looked behind William.

"What kind of place do you think I'm running here? You're not setting up your brothel here!" the man slammed his hand down on the desk. William looked over at the man, confused, and then looked behind him to see Lucy dressed in a very high cut dress, wearing hoop earrings and smoking a cigarette, talking to Jay and Mo.

"Oh...oh no, that's not what it looks like. She's not....no, we're not.... together. Well, we're together, but it's not...." William realized what it looked like with Jay and Mo on motorcycles, and Lucy wasn't shy with her body in those clothes.

"Look, I'm married. It's not like that! Can we just get three rooms, please?" William asked.

"Oh. I get it. So you pay me cash so your wife

doesn't find out about it? Just because I'm Indian doesn't mean you can Kama Sutra all over my motel! This is a reputable place, my friend. I even got that award." the man said, pointing to the newspaper article framed on the wall. William hadn't even noticed it.

"No, look, my wife's with me. She's not a prostitute, and I'm not a pimp. Those are my friends. I just want three rooms, please." William tried again.

"No, no, no! You get out of here, sir. You take all this circus nonsense down to the Mexicali Casa down the road. I'm not having this Tom Foolery here! No sir!" The man said, getting up from the counter and pointing towards the door. His accent was getting even heavier.

"Look…" William started.

"OUT! Before I open up a can of ass soup!" The man growled. William tried to figure out what he meant by ass soup.

"You mean whoop-ass?" William asked.

"GET OUT!!" The man yelled. William put his hands up with his palms facing the man as a sign of acknowledgment and then backed towards the door. He opened the door and walked up to Jay, Mo, and Lucy.

"Where's my wife?" William asked.

"Right there." Lucy said, pointing to Rhonda, sitting on the planter box smoking one of Lucy's cigarettes.

"He won't rent us any rooms. He thinks Lucy's a hooker." William said.

"Well….I do fuck people for money, Sugar, but not

in the biblical sense. So, he's kind of right." Lucy said, smiling.

"I think you are truly the genesis of all mental illness Lucy. I think they should just stick you in a room with all the shrinks of the world and name all the fucked up things that come out of your mouth in that DSM book thingy. You know, the one they have for psychologists." Jay said. Lucy continued to smile as she raised her left hand to Jay with her middle finger out.

"Well, we can go down a few miles and try another spot." Mo said. Lucy rolled her eyes.

"Do women have to do EVERYTHING around here?" Lucy said, walking over to William.

"Give me the money." Lucy said, holding out her palm.

"What? No. I'm not giving you my money; I don't even know you!" William said.

"Give me the money, or I'll rip it out of that silly little bad-boy biker vest you got!" Lucy said with a changed tone and a stare that would intimidate almost anyone. There even seemed to be a small red flash in her eyes that shook him, and he didn't know why. William reached into his pocket and gave Lucy his cash. Lucy took the cash and walked away towards the office.

"Boys…." Lucy said condescendingly. Lucy walked into the front office and, after about five minutes, came out holding two keys.

"One for you." Lucy said, handing one key to William. "….and one for you. I'll see you boys in the morning. Rhonda, beautiful, you sure you don't want to stay with me in the RV?" Lucy yelled out to Rhonda, who was emotionally fried, staring at the ground.

"Fuck you, psycho lady..." Rhonda responded without looking up. Lucy smiled again.

"Don't worry. I take a while to grow on people, but eventually, they accept me." Lucy said to William.

"Yeah, like I said, just like herpes. Except the flare-ups never go away." Jay chimed in. Lucy stuck her tongue out at Jay in response.

"Wait...how did you get the rooms? How did you...." William started to ask.

"I have my ways. See you boys in the morning. Good night beautiful." Lucy said in Rhonda's direction. Rhonda responded by sticking up her middle finger at Lucy, still looking at the ground, not looking in her direction.

"Hey, what about my change? I gave you like five hundred bucks!" William asked Lucy while she was walking away.

"Six hundred and twenty actually, and I don't work for free, Billy. Good night." Lucy said, continuing to walk away. She walked until she was out of sight, but her heels could still be heard clicking away.

"Let it go, Billy. She'll give it back. She's just fucking with you. She doesn't need your money. " Mo said.

"Yeah, you'll get used to her. Kind of like having an annoying little sister around that wants attention 24/7, and she's not that bad when you get past all that bullshit." Jay added.

Rhonda smashed out her cigarette and stood up.

She fluffed her hair slightly and then walked over to the three of them.

"Ok. So what's the plan. Please tell me I don't have to get back in and ride with queen crazy. I'd rather ride on the back of that thing." Rhonda said pointing at William's single-seat Sportster. "Than ride with queen crazy again. Did we call the rental car company yet?" Rhonda asked in business mode.

"No. Let's just call it a night, shall we? We got rooms here, and we can call in the morning." William said.

"Oh, thank God. I need a shower….and a drink. A big drink, no actually, like a bottle, and a therapist after riding with that one." Rhonda said, pointing towards the RV.

"Well. Thank you for another interesting evening, Billy. I don't think we've had a vacation like this for a LONG time, man!!" Jay said, laughing loudly. Mo rolled his eyes and started walking towards the room.

The following day William was awakened by a loud knock at the door. Rhonda and William sat up, startled.

"YO! BILLY! BREAKFAST IN TEN!" Mo yelled out from the other side. William looked around, trying to wake up. He felt sick again, but different this time. Not a chemical sickness, but sick like he was exhausted. It took him a few minutes to realize Rhonda looked about the same. Both of them looked like they had been up for two days straight.

William got out of bed and went into the bathroom for his morning urination. Something was different this time when he urinated. He was standing up straight. Since he had been sick and started treatment, he had always slumped when he urinated and when he walked. Kind of like an old dog with his neck down. He was standing straight. It was a small thing, but something he noticed. It was almost as if he somehow had more vitality and more vigor. He finished and walked over to the sink. He washed his hands and splashed water on his face. He used the towel to dry his face and looked in the mirror. He started laughing. He saw his face and how ragged he looked. He looked like he had aged about ten years. His face looked weathered. He laughed even harder.

"What's so funny?" Rhonda asked, sitting on the toilet to urinate. William's laugh came to a close, and he looked over at her.

"Well, I don't think we will be doing our routine today." William said, looking over at her. He was referring to their daily routine before he got sick. They would spend about 20-30 minutes putting on face creams and serums to look younger and more vibrant. William spent just as much time as Rhonda getting ready to make sure he looked his best for his clients. Rhonda used to joke and call him a "metrosexual." but he sure was handsome.

Rhonda looked up at him and laughed, "No. No, I don't think we are."

She liked seeing him like this. They were closer than before, and the love was always there, but now this was real. No distractions, nothing superficial, raw.

A toilet and a sink in a cheap motel a few miles from the border. That motel now trumped their daily ritual in a million dollar house with all the bells and whistles.

The two of them put on their clothes and got ready. There was not much to do to get ready since neither had any toiletries or new clothes to put on. The two walked out to see Jay and Mo sitting on the bikes. William walked out with Rhonda, following on the phone with the rental car company.

"Yes. This is Rhonda. Yes, the rental car broke down near…." She looked at her phone map. "Nogales. Can we get another one?" Rhonda continued and slowly fell behind William.

William looked out at the desert behind the motel and noticed how populated the small town was. At night, it looked deserted, but it was a bustling little town in the daytime.

"We're going to eat there." Jay said, pointing across the street to an IHOP.

"Okay." William replied. Rhonda was in the background on hold, getting annoyed.

"We need to check out first, or they call the cops in towns like this. You got your key?" Mo asked.

"Yeah. It's right here." William replied.

"Where's Lucy?" William asked.

"She'll make an appearance at some point. Probably went to blow up a shopping mall or something she thinks is funny." Jay said. Mo started walking towards the office, and Jay and William followed. They were greeted by the man from the night before with the giant coke bottle glasses. This time he was very inviting and smiled.

"Oh, I hope you officers had a good night. I'll take those." The man said, holding out his hand.

"Officers?" William asked. The man winced.

"Oh, I'm SO sorry." the man shrugged.

"I forgot, you're undercover!" the man whispered. Jay and Mo looked at each other.

"Lucy." Jay said. Mo nodded.

"I am law and order all the way! In my country, the police are corrupt! They beat you up. Take your money! Not here. Not like you. Where's your Captain? She was so nice. I respect you." the man asked, looking behind them for Lucy.

"She's.. on assignment. You know, she has to get there first because she's the Captain." Mo said, looking at Jay.

"Yeah, you know, she has to make sure to plan everything so she can, uh, plan it out." Mo added.

"Oh. I see. You guys sure had me fooled. I thought you were a degenerate, low-life scum! You'll catch those guys!" the man said, putting the keys behind the counter.

"Indeed they will." A man said from the side room in perfect English but with a British accent. A younger East Indian man stepped out wearing a suit. Not just any suit, clearly a tailor-made custom suit. He was about 5'9", slightly muscular build but with a very well-groomed face. William couldn't stop staring. The man looked like a model.

"KRIS!!!" Jay and Mo both shouted. William looked startled. The man smiled and came around the counter. The men hugged and embraced like old friends.

"Is there anyone you guys DON'T know?" William asked.

"Oh, sorry, Kris, this is Billy. We picked him up along the way, and he's going with us down to Mexico. Man, what are you doing here?" Jay asked.

"Well, it just so happens this is MY holiday now too. I happen to own this place with my friend Joe here." Kris replied.

"Joe?" William asked.

"That's right. My name is Joe Johnson. I'm an American!" Joe replied from behind the counter. William looked at him.

"What? I can be whatever I want in this country. I can go wherever I want. America is the greatest country in the world! I am an American citizen! Not like these wretches....rats out there." Joe said, motioning in a shooing gesture with his right hand.

"Joe and I go way back. He used to be part of the untouchables back in India. He was responsible for cleaning the brothels. We met one day when I was back on business because he was tasked with delivering a note. We started talking, and he told me how he loved America. He had American television. Couldn't read or write but memorized every line of the movie Top Gun. I told him if he prayed hard to his deity, they would bring him here. Little did I know he'd bring me that ONE little piece of information I needed to close out a very large real estate deal. Naturally, I had to sponsor him after that, so the prayers worked." Kris said.

"What's an untouchable?" William asked.

"They're called the Dalit. Considered lower class in India. They're treated very poorly. If I weren't speaking English, he would not dare have even spoken with me. It's a very harsh country. Anyway, nonetheless, I brought Joe here because I saw potential. Look what he's done. He went from being illiterate and afraid of his own shadow to owning his own business and reads, what, two books a day?" Kris asked.

"Pfft. Two is the minimum, sir!" Joe scoffed.

"Amazing what the universe can do if people believe, isn't it, Jay?" Kris asked. Jay looked over at him and shook his head as if it was an inside joke.

"So. Gentlemen. I'm sorry to have to run, but I do need to get going. The only thing I do here is to double-check Joe's books when I'm in the area. Say, Joe said Lucy was with you. Well, I assume it's her by the way he described her. Where is she?" Kris asked.

"Probably setting off World War 3 somewhere." Mo replied.

"Ah yes. She does do that, doesn't she?" Kris said in his proper accent.

"We are going to eat. You want to go?" Jay asked.

"Well, tempting, but I'll pass. Special diet." Kris replied. William looked at his clothes and still couldn't believe this man was in the desert. He looked like he should be on Wall Street in New York or somewhere in London. William knew the style, and he knew suits.

His suit was a tailored suit with custom-made shoes. William's instinct was to network with Kris to pitch his services or somehow get in the group this man was in, but he resisted the urge.

"It was nice to meet you, sir." William said.

"Likewise." Kris responded. Jay hugged Kris in a friendly embrace, and he worked his way over to Mo to do the same. When it came to William, Kris held his hand out and shook William's hand politely. Firm grip, but not too firm. A businessman, William thought to himself. Kris went out the front door, and William could see Rhonda getting irritated on the phone. He went outside and looked at her. She turned away, saying, "What do you mean you have no cars? You are a rental car company, aren't you?".

"Well, at least he didn't make some dramatic exit this time." Mo said, putting on his sunglass. No sooner did he finish when a yellow Ferrari rounded the corner with its loud exhaust revving. A quick look inside, Kris could be seen throwing up a peace sign as he passed by. The Ferrari squealed and revved as it sped off down the highway.

Mo looked over at Jay. Jay brushed back his hair with his hand and said, "You were saying?" Mo just shook his head. The three walked over to the IHOP with Rhonda still on the phone. They entered and were greeted by a teenage hostess who sat them at a center booth. Rhonda remained outside, still on the phone. The three sat down, and William looked around. It was a nice diner that looked like it was out of the 1950s.

It was different than the other IHOPs he had seen. This one had decorations that were signed by various celebrities. A guitar signed by Elvis Presley was above them on the wall, and the local heroes signed different local pictures. Rhonda came in and sat down.

"They don't have ANY rental cars from here to Scottsdale. They said they're expecting a few returns but not until about one in Scottsdale." Rhonda said.

"Shit." William said. Mo and Jay looked at them.

"Sorry guys, at this point, we're on a timeline. If you got to bow out, Billy, maybe that's what was meant to happen. You know that whole God thingy you were talking about." Mo said, making a swirling motion with his right pointer finger.

"Oh, that's not necessary, Sugar. You can ride with me!" Lucy's voice let out as she walked up to the table. Rhonda winced.

"Oh no. No, no, no, no, no!" Rhonda let out almost instinctively. Lucy pulled up a chair from another table, ignoring the family sitting at it. They looked at her, confused. Lucy adjusted her hair and sat down.

"William, you can't be serious. You can't expect me to ride with this sociopath." Rhonda said, looking over at William. Lucy smiled and let out a sigh.

Lucy looked over at Rhonda and adjusted her tone from light and bubbly to cordial. "I'm sorry we got off on the wrong foot. We girls have to stick together, you know. I promise, from this point, I'll behave. We're all going to the same place, I let loose a little here and there, but that's just me. Once we cross the border,

I always mellow out. Have to. It's different there. I apologize for our initial meeting. I'm not normally like that, but those guys had that coming. Besides, I got you guys your rooms, didn't I?" Lucy finished. She did have a point.

"Yes, Captain, you did." Jay said, laughing.

"Well....I might have told just a LITTLE fib, but it worked, right?" Lucy said. Mo shook his head and smiled.

"Yeah, Billy. As annoying as Lucy is, she always manages to pull through for us at the last second. Hey, where'd you go anyway?" Mo asked. Lucy reached into her purse, pulled out three passports, and held them up.

"Betcha boys didn't think of that now, did ya?" Lucy said, handing William and Rhonda each a passport. William opened his passport.

"Kobi Bryant?" William asked.

"Madeline Monroe?" Rhonda asked. Lucy pulled out a tube of lipstick and used the reflection of the sugar container to put it on.

"Don't worry, Sweety. Mexican border guards don't even look at the names." Lucy said, puckering her lips focused on the reflection.

"Well, how are we supposed to get back?" William asked.

"Well, that's YOU'RE problem there. I'm sure you'll figure something out." Lucy said.

"William! We can't do this! It's illegal! And how did you get our pictures?" Rhonda whispered, looking at the picture. Lucy held her lipstick in her right hand

and reached her left hand into her small purple purse on her left side. She handed both of their driver's licenses to them with their fake names.

"Let's just say the boys at the DMV like me a little." Lucy said, capping her lipstick. Then she pulled out their original driver's licenses and handed them to Rhonda. Rhonda looked at them, then up at Lucy with a shocked and confused look.

"How did you...when?" Rhonda started, and Jay held up his hand.

"Don't bother asking. Trust me. Lucy's right. You need a passport. I forgot about that." Jay said.

The middle-aged waitress came up to the table and placed the waters down.

"I'm so sorry! It's hectic. I know that's not an excuse. Are you guys ready to order?" She asked.

"Mary. That was my mom's name." Jay said and smiled at her.

"Must be a sign." Mo said, interrupting, "I'll take the chicken and waffles with a coffee, please."

"Same." Jay said.

"I'll have the All-American Slam, please." Lucy said, not looking at the waitress. A long pause went by.

"I'm sorry, miss, but we don't have that here." Mary started.

"I'm just kidding, dear. I'll have the same." Lucy said, smiling and looking at Mary. She laughed and looked over at William.

"I guess the same. I didn't get to see the menu yet." William said.

"Oh, I can come back." Mary said.

"No, that's fine, all the same." Rhonda finished for William. "Don't be rude, honey. You can see she's busy."

"Ok. That was easy, all chicken and waffles and coffee." Mary said.

"I'll have water." William said.

"Just HAVE to be different, don't you, Billy?" Mo laughed. Mary smiled and walked off.

"So...where are we going anyway?" William asked.

"Hey, man. YOU asked to come with US. You can go anytime." Mo said.

"Damn, Mo, a little harsh." Lucy said, looking at Mo in disapproval. Jay interjected.

"Mexico Billy. We already told you." Jay said.

"Yeah, but Mexico is huge." William said.

"That's what she said!" Mo laughed, and it spread to Jay, who started laughing with him. Lucy rolled her eyes.

"Is it dangerous?" Rhonda asked.

"Very." Mo replied. Lucy rolled her eyes again.

"Sweety, it's not that bad. It's just remote, like going camping. Except these two clowns like to act like tough guys on their little bikes, but you watch. They always wind up with me because they're 'too hot' or 'too tired' or 'whaaa, I broke my leg.' Lucy, can I stay in the RV?" Lucy said, pointing at Mo.

"Hey! I did!" Mo scoffed.

"Who's fault was that? Nobody told you to ride those little....things. They're loud, and you just like them because you get to dress like a pirate. You watch Sweety. Mo here's always the tough guy. He's always the first one in the RV running back to mamma.

Then Jay always gets lonely because Mo's in with me in the RV, nice and comfy, and then we all end up like the Brady bunch. Every year it's the same. Oh, they'll try to say it's not true or tough it out to prove me wrong, but that's how legs get broken, isn't it, big guy? Get all loopy and dehydrated, and then, awww poor baby….you fell." Lucy said, looking at Mo.

"Hey, that's not funny! I scrap piled a 72 Shovelhead behind that. That year sucked." Mo said.

Mary returned with the food, and they started eating. A good two minutes went by as they ate their food when Mo began to focus on the television. Nobody had noticed it before when they were talking. The news was on, and the reporter talked about the weather and traffic conditions.

"Now taking us to world news is Samir Hadin in Cairo, Egypt…" the reporter said as Mo intently focused. A reporter could be seen in front of what appeared to be a car bombing.

"Islamic extremist group Islamic State Affiliate, Sinai Province has claimed responsibility for killing a hundred at this mosque. Behind me is one of several car bombs that blew up…." The television smashed into pieces as Mo's helmet hit it. William didn't even realize that he had brought it in with him.

The entire restaurant was silent as Mo stood with his hands balled into fists and breathing heavily. Jay jumped up and grabbed him by the arms hugging him from the side and ushering him outside. Jay looked around.

"Sorry, folks. He had family there." Jay said, pushing Mo through the restaurant. The crowd settled back in, and a few "sorry" comments could be heard from random tables as Jay kept ushering Mo outside as quickly as possible.

Lucy sat unfazed by the incident while finishing her meal. She patted her face with her napkin and stood up. She let out a small burp and then walked over to Mary. She reached in her bra and pulled out five one-hundred-dollar bills. She counted them silently and then put them in Mary's apron pocket. She looked over Mary up and down, then straightened out Mary's nametag and gave her a second once-over. Satisfied, Lucy gave a nod before turning and walking out. She paused before leaving and looked back at Mary.

"That should cover everything, Doll. Oh, and do yourself a favor, lose that eyeshadow. Makes you look…. well….you." Lucy finished and walked out. She walked right past Mo and Jay and kept walking. She looked over at them as if it were any other day and put on her sunglasses, and continued to walk.

William looked outside to see Jay and Mo in the parking lot. Mo sat down, and Jay sat with him. William looked over and saw Mo's helmet was still on the ground. The tension from the television breaking seemed to be easing. William got up and picked up the helmet from the floor. He inspected it for damage and saw several scuffs, but for the most part, in good shape. The front was scratched, but other than that, it looked normal.

"William, are you sure about this? I mean, he doesn't seem stable." Rhonda asked, concerned.

"He's not usually like this. He just lost family members to a car bomb. You heard what Jay said. Give him a break." William replied.

"Honey, we can just go right now. Maybe this isn't a good time to be tagging along with him. You just met." Rhonda said, and William shook his head.

"You don't understand. He's my friend." William said and began walking towards the door. Rhonda gathered her purse and followed behind him.

"Friend? You just met." Rhonda said, walking.

Walking outside, William could overhear Jay telling Mo it would be alright and that things would pass. All the things you say to a person who is upset, and it wasn't working.

"What the fuck do you mean 'It's ok?' When the fuck is enough, enough, Jay? Seriously man! Come on! Hundreds! You heard it. Hundreds died, and for what? How much more do we have to take?! I mean, for what?! A fucking book?! These fucking terrorist fucks just killed hundreds over a fucking book!" Mo yelled out. Jay held his hands up with his palms out to calm Mo.

"NO! No, I'm not going to calm down. You shouldn't either! That turn the other cheek shit doesn't work out so well, does it? Oh no, THAT fucking book is just as bad killing just as many people, and you're like a fucking peaceful bunny rabbit! I mean, have you ever even killed a bug? Yet that fucking book has killed thousands!" Mo yelled out. Jay looked at him, then looked down. Mo hit a nerve because Jay didn't look up. Mo ran his fingers through his hair and took a deep breath. He stared at Jay for a good twenty seconds, but it felt like forever to William. Finally, Mo spoke again and leaned his face down to Jay.

"Alright, look. I'm sorry okay?" Mo said, still angry.

"Look...let's just get back on the road again. That's the only fucking place that still makes sense. Just fire the bikes and go. Come on, Jay." Mo said and started walking toward the motel. He got about ten feet away and threw his hands up, frustrated.

"My fucking helmet!" Mo yelled out and turned to walk towards the restaurant. He started to get closer, and William held his helmet up. Rhonda stood behind William, still suspicious of Mo. Mo looked at the helmet and then at William, then to Rhonda. He took the helmet from William.

"Thanks, man. I'm sorry, guys. I kind of lost my shit in there. Won't happen again." Mo said.

"It's okay, man. You just lost your family, and I'm sorry." William said, and Mo shook his head.

"No, man. WE just lost family in Egypt, and that's what people don't get. It's not just about YOUR last names and where YOU come from. We're all family, all of us." Mo said, looking over at William and then at Rhonda. He could see they didn't get what he was saying.

"Never mind, man. Look, let's just get on the road. We're on a schedule now, and we got to be into Mexico by sunset." Mo said.

"But, we're right here. I can see the border, and it's like five minutes away, tops." William said.

"Naw, man....I said Mexico. The border ain't Mexico. You'll see what I mean." Mo said and started walking back toward the motel, carrying the helmet in his right hand. He was walking fast, still upset.

"BEEP BEEP BEEP" blared a loud horn from behind Rhonda and William. They looked back to see Lucy's RV parked and Lucy waving. Rhonda looked over at William, almost pleading, and William shrugged his shoulders. Rhonda stared at him for a few seconds and then walked towards the RV. She got into the RV and climbed into the passenger seat, watching William cross the street to join Jay and Mo. The three of them got their helmets on and fired up their bikes. Lucy looked over at Rhonda, and Rhonda looked back at her reluctantly.

"Well. That was a good twat waffle. Off we go!" Lucy said, moving the RV forward. An orange cat jumped onto Rhonda's lap, which scared her until she almost screamed but realized it was a cat. The cat quickly made itself at home on her lap and twirled around a few times. Rhonda started petting the cat and smiled.

"Oh, that's Beelzebub. You're in his seat, but don't

worry, he's friendly." Lucy said, pulling up and turning. She pulled onto the highway as the bikes pulled away.

"Beelzebub? Like the demon?" Rhonda asked.

"Um-hum." Lucy said, looking in the rearview mirror and fixing her hair.

"Why am I not surprised?" Rhonda said, looking at the cat.

"I would've named you....Morris. Like the nine lives cat." Rhonda said, and a loud thump came from the back of the RV.

"What was that?" Rhonda asked.

"What was what?" Lucy asked back.

"That loud thump." Rhonda said.

"Oh, that's Bill. Don't worry. He's friendly too. Rhonda looked back to see a full-sized Billy Goat standing in the middle of the RV. Rhonda looked again because she couldn't believe it.

"You have a goat....in your RV..." Rhonda asked, still staring at Bill, who stared back at her.

"Yup....and a Raven, his name is Edgar, but he's shy. Oh, and there's a Ferret. His name is Ferris, somewhere in here, and an Iguana named Iggy. He's mean, though. You don't want your fingers anywhere near Iggy." Lucy said, staring at the road.

Rhonda rolled her eyes. She thought back to last week when she went to her support group and hid her smoking from William. Now she was in an RV full of animals with a lady who just helped set fire to a bar, impersonated an officer, and forged all the passports and DMV documents somehow while watching her sick husband on a motorcycle with two strangers going into Mexico. Yet, as crazy as it sounded, this was the best she had felt in years. She began laughing out loud.

"So we're a zoo on wheels!" Rhonda laughed. At this point, she decided it was just going to happen how it happened. She looked out to see William on his bike, looking back at her and waving. She waved back at him, still laughing. Another loud thud came from the back of the RV. Rhonda's laugh slowly died down as she looked back to see Billy still staring at her.

"Did you hear that?" Rhonda asked.

"Oh, that? Oh, that's just Fred." Lucy said, still staring ahead.

"Ok. Who is Fred?" Rhonda asked. She imagined that it must be a dog, or maybe something else exotic like a snake.

"Let me guess, Fred's a...bird....no a snake! Fred's a snake, isn't he?" Rhonda asked. Lucy looked in the rearview.

"Oh no. Fred's the guy I took home from the bar last night. I forgot he was back there. Don't worry, though, Sugar. We'll let him out when we get to the border." Lucy said. Rhonda looked over at her waiting for her to say she was joking. Lucy kept driving.

"Wait, there's a man....back there....in your RV?" Rhonda asked.

"Um-hum." Lucy replied. Rhonda got nervous.

"Oh, don't worry. He's not going to hurt anyone. Likes to be tied up, those accountant type like that." Lucy said, still driving. She reached down and pulled a stick of gum out and popped it in her mouth, and she began chewing. Rhonda waited a few seconds.

"Wait...what?" Rhonda asked. She couldn't believe it. After about ten seconds, she got up out of the passenger seat and walked to the back of the RV. She slid the privacy divider back and then jumped back, gasping and covering her mouth.

Fred was on the bed, covered from the waist down by a sheet with his hands tied above his head, still wearing his black business shoes. He was blindfolded and gagged. Rhonda could see he was a white man, maybe in his mid-forties.

"LUCY!" Rhonda yelled out.

"What?" Lucy yelled back.

"You can't keep this man like this!" Rhonda said, looking back at her.

"Hey, we're on a schedule, Sugar. Don't worry. He'll be fine. Come sit down. We're almost at the border." Lucy said. Fred continued moaning through the gag. The RV stopped, and Lucy popped up from the driver's seat and walked back, moving sideways past Rhonda.

"Oh, shut up! You asked me to do this, and now all of a sudden, you're the victim." Lucy said, reaching over and untying Fred's right hand. Rhonda looked over and then back again and slowly walked back to her seat. Just in time to feel a bite on her left index finger. She yanked it back and yelled, "OW!".

Lucy looked up while ushering Fred to the hurry up.

"Iggy! You be nice! I warned you. He likes fingers." Lucy said.

Fred pulled out his gag and yelled, "You're crazy!" to Lucy while finding his clothes and putting them on frantically.

"That's not what you said last night, big boy." Lucy said, walking towards the middle of the RV. Fred got dressed as fast as he could and dashed for the door.

"You're fucking crazy, lady!" Fred yelled again, opening the door to the RV. Lucy slapped him on his left butt cheek as he left and yelled, "Suck it up, buttercup!!" and laughed, which was in between a genuine laugh and the HA-HAH laugh from the Simpsons show. She watched Fred run to the right, then to the left out of sight, before closing the door.

She walked back up to the driver's seat and sat down. Iggy the Iguana was still on the center console, and Lucy picked him up and put Iggy in her lap.

"Well. Now mamma's back. You be nice." Lucy said to Iggy. Iggy seemed content. Rhonda looked over, still holding her hand.

"What? Oh, don't worry. He's just marking his territory. Now you're his bitch!" Lucy laughed and moved the RV forward a few car lengths. She pulled up behind the bikes and put the RV back into park. Rhonda looked around and then looked at Iggy.

"Where's the Raven?" Rhonda asked cautiously. Lucy pointed outside and up. Rhonda looked over to see a specially made perch on the right side of the roof with a big Raven sitting on it.

"Of course." Rhonda said, not surprised.

"Oh, don't worry. You'll be family before you know it, Sugar!" Lucy said, laughing. Rhonda looked around, blinking. For some reason, she felt at home now, even in this chaos. The RV had something special to it, a calm amongst the chaos. They were right. Lucy was growing on her. She even let out a small laugh.

William pulled up in between Jay and Mo. All three had their bikes in one line. They moved up and then shut their bikes off to keep them from overheating. It was hot, a different kind of hot than William was used to. This heat was a dry hot. The sweat seemed to evaporate before he even felt it. He pulled out his water bottle from his right pocket and drank. The three remained quiet in the heat and moved up whenever a car moved.

William's health was diminished, but he felt like he could make it. He was miserable, but at least he had his friends and his wife with him. *It wouldn't be so bad going out here….*William thought just in time for them to pull up to the Mexican customs officer. The big red, white, and green MEXICO sign got closer, and the seemingly endless metal wall came to the front. It was a stupid wall, William thought. All they had to do was go under it.

"Passport, please. Do you have anything to declare, Señor?" The Mexican customs officer said in a heavy accent. All three produced their passports. William handed his passport over nervously. The man wore mirrored sunglasses like the cops in the movies, and he hated those. The officer on the other side waived Jay and Mo through, but the agent checking Williams stared at the passport.

Even though the agent had already flagged them through, Jay and Mo waited for William.

"Why are you so nervous, my friend." the officer asked William.

"He's not nervous. He's sick. Cancer. This trip is probably his last ride, sir. That's his wife back there. He said he wants to die in the best country on earth." Mo shouted out. The officer looked at Mo, then at the passport again, then back at William.

"Señor, Kobe....Bryant?" the officer asked. William nodded, "Bryant sir. Kobe Bryant." he repeated, looking into the officer's glasses. Another long pause. The pause became uncomfortable for William. Jay and Mo looked on helplessly, and Rhonda could be seen fidgeting in the RV behind him when he looked back.

"Go ahead, Señor, Kobe Bryant. Enjoy Mexico, my friend." the officer said, stamping the passport and handing it back. A wave of relief flooded over William, and he put the passport in his pocket. He turned the key to his ignition and started the bike, and Jay and Mo did the same. They rode about a half-mile down the road to wait for the RV.

The RV pulled up to the border, and Lucy rolled down the window.

"Maria! How are you, dear?" Lucy said, handing the customs agent her passport.

"Miss Lucy! Where have you been, Chicka?! Good

to see you!" the female customs officer replied, smiling. She immediately handed back the passport and started to wave the RV through. Nobody bothered even to check Rhonda's passport.

"How's Miguel and Cecelia?" Lucy asked, slowly pulling the RV forward.

"They're big! Miguel just turned eight, and Cesi's ten! You come by later!" the officer said as they pulled off. Lucy gave her a thumbs up in acknowledgment. Rhonda looked over at Lucy in shock. Lucy looked back and shrugged her shoulders.

"What? It's not my fault those boys don't like to make friends." Lucy said. Rhonda raised her eyebrows. The RV began to catch up to the bikes.

Williams Sportster was much lighter than the other two bikes, and he found he could move much quicker. As the road stretched on, signs of border security began to fade away. This road was much different than the roads in the United States. They were paved but not maintained. The desert sands seemed to pile up on parts of the road and swirled as they went past them. Very few cars were on the road, and the ones on the road were very dilapidated.

The desert seemed to stretch forever, and they passed small buildings that looked abandoned, but they weren't. Their residents could be seen in random areas going about their day. William started to feel exhausted, but he kept on the throttle, moving in unison with Jay and Mo. He wasn't even sure if he would make it this far, but he did. He wasn't sure how much further he had in him, but he wasn't going to stop. It was an odd feeling. Almost like a second wind knowing this was most likely the area he would die. It was completely different from what he had imagined his whole life, but as he looked around and twisted the throttle, he was good with it.

William thought about what Mo had said about him being selfish. He was right. This trip was a selfish thing to do. The right thing would have probably been to get his paperwork in order and die at home so Rhonda would have less to worry about. He looked back at the RV and saw Rhonda and Lucy talking and laughing through the glared windshield. Rhonda's hands raised as she talked, and clearly, they were having a good time. It had been years since he had seen that smile. A genuine smile. Not the smile you get when you're trying to make someone feel better. He looked back in front of him at Jay and Mo. The three of them riding as one created a feeling that no amount of money could buy. No words could eloquently explain it, and it was just there. A moment that was worth everything, he thought to himself. He thought about Mo's words again and realized he was glad he was selfish. He was glad he fought for this right here. Even if it was selfish, it was perfect.

The perfect moment didn't last long as William's bike started to sputter. He reached down instinctively and moved the switch to reserve on his gas tank. He had mastered that move after the last debacle. He punched the throttle forward, pulled up alongside the other bikes, and pointed down at his gas tank. Jay nodded, and the three bikes pulled over to the side with the RV following. William reached back for his gas bottle and dumped it into his gas tank.

"Shit, guys, that's not a lot of gas." William said.

"Well, if you had a real bike, you wouldn't have that problem." Mo said, laughing.

"HEY! I'm keeping up with you fuckers just fine! I'd even bet mine would beat yours off the jump. Quarter mile, I'd have you down. You guys are slow off the start." William said, joking.

"Lucky for you, we have a mobile gas station." Jay said, looking back at the RV. Lucy's head popped out from the driver's side and yelled, "You pump your gas! I'm not your slave!" and popped right back in. Jay started his bike, followed by Mo. The two of them pulled to the rear of the RV, and William followed, confused. Jay stopped the bike and pulled out a large gas can from the back. He filled up his tank, then moved over to Mo, then to William.

"Your turn next." Jay said, putting the gas can back.

"Yeah, Lucy's been our chase car forever now. Even when we try to ditch her, she somehow finds us. We kinda knew this was coming." Mo said.

"Yeah, we'd never make it there without a chase car anyway." Jay said, tightening the strap to secure the gas can.

"Wait, so you were just hoping to run into Lucy? You guys didn't like plan to meet up or call?" William asked.

"Nope. Never do." Mo said, starting his bike. Jay mounted his bike and started it. William wanted to ask more questions, but the two were already gone. He started his bike, pushed his left foot down into first gear, and rounded the RV, expecting them to be about a mile ahead, but they weren't. They were stopped in the middle of the road, waiting for him. William pulled up behind them, and Mo signaled for him to come up in between them. The engines were loud, but he could hear Mo yell out, "LET'S SEE WHAT SHE CAN DO!". Mo revved his motor, and Jay followed. Mo followed up a rev with a burnout holding the front brake and making the rear tire spin.

"WHAT?" William asked. Before he could say anything else, the bikes were off. Jay and Mo got a slight jump, but he reacted quickly and let out the clutch giving as much throttle as possible to keep up. The three bikes flew down the road as fast as possible, with Mo slightly leading Jay….until William twisted his throttle as far as he could after shifting up…and up…and up….and he passed them!

He was so excited he twisted that throttle until the engine was screaming and it wouldn't twist anymore. The wind was going so fast he didn't even know how fast he was going, but it was faster than he had ever gone. His heart was pounding, and he was laser-focused on staying in front. That was until the other two bikes passed him like he was standing still. William stayed on the throttle to keep up, but Jay and Mo were at least a mile ahead.

William eventually caught up as the two went back to a cruising speed. William took his position with the other two bikes. Mo looked back and gave him a thumbs up. Jay just remained in cruising mode without looking at him. They slowed slightly, and the RV caught up about ten minutes later. Mo turned onto an unmarked dirt road, and the dust started to kick up and made William cough.

They kept on the dirt road for what felt like forever with a couple of bathroom breaks and water from the RV. They were back on the road for a few more hours, and the sun was starting to set. In the background of the desert stood a small rock pillar that looked like someone stacked up to about eight feet high in the distance. Mo and Jay headed towards the pillar, and it got closer. The bikes pulled up to the pillar, which now stood about fifteen feet high by Williams's estimate, and Mo turned off his bike. Jay followed.

"We're here." Jay said. William looked around, and there was nothing but desert. Aside from the rock pillar, there was nothing out here. There were no buildings, not even a real road, just a dirt path.

William shut off his bike and watched the RV pull up. William looked again, thinking he missed something. This spot couldn't be the "vacation" they talked about. There was NOTHING out here.

"Hey....guys. What do you mean we're here. Like here-here? Right here? There's nothing out here." William said. Mo looked back at him and then walked over and urinated behind the rock pillar. Jay looked over at William, and he didn't say anything.

"Wait. This can't be right. What was all that talk about DANGER and...YOU'RE NOT GONNA MAKE IT BILLY....and OH God, YOU HAVE TO BE BEAR GRYLLS TO MAKE IT OUT HERE talk? We're literally in the middle of the desert. I could have driven here, and I thought you said we're going to have to walk part of the way there." William said, looking back and forth between Mo and Jay.

"I never said that. Change your tampon or do something useful. Stop killing the vibe." Jay said, putting his helmet on his sissy bar. Mo started walking back towards William. Jay shook out his long hair and then walked over to where Mo was and urinated in the same spot.

"You were right, Billy. You had me on the jump. Still. It's a bitch bike." Mo said, walking towards the RV.

"Yo! Lucy! You got any food?" Mo yelled out.

"Not for you!" Lucy yelled back.

"Then I'll eat Beezlebub!" Mo laughed and kept walking. William looked back and forth, completely confused. He didn't know what he was expecting, but it wasn't this. They made it sound like this vacation was a long trip to some mysterious place that nobody knew about. After a few minutes, he put his helmet on his mirror and got off the bike. At least he wasn't in a chemo chair. The sun was starting to set, and it was cooler.

Jay, Mo, and Lucy seemed to be in good spirits

laughing and joking with each other as they put out folding chairs in a circle in front of a rock fire pit that William had somehow missed pulling in. Mo built a fire with wood Lucy had brought in the RV. The fire began crackling. William and Rhonda made small talk with everyone. This place wasn't what William had expected, but he sure was grateful for this time. He looked around to see everyone smiling and laughing, Lucy's smart-witted jokes coming in at the perfect time. Mo's gruff barking, Jay's smile, and Rhonda next to him. It felt like family.

The sun finally set, and there were so many stars in the sky William thought it must be fake. It looked so beautiful it was unreal. He had never seen so many stars, not even at Bud's. They seemed to light up the entire sky. Bugs could be heard being zapped by Lucy's bug-zapper hanging on the other side of the RV, and a slight chill came in the air.

"So, Billy. I don't mean to be rude, but what's it feel like to be dying?" Jay asked, which kind of shocked William for a minute. He had forgotten about being sick. For some reason, though, he realized he didn't feel sick.

"I don't know. I try not to think about it. I can tell you what it's like to feel like complete shit and go crazy jumping on a bike riding out to the middle of nowhere to meet you two fuckers!" William laughed. Rhonda looked over at him, surprised. He was usually so reserved. Also, she wasn't used to him using foul language. This was a very different side to the polished

William she had seen for so long. She kind of liked it. It felt genuine. Mo and Jay laughed.

"On a serious note, guys, I never thought about it. Not until you guys and Bud, Bud made me think a lot about it." William started.

"Yeah, he does that." Mo chimed in.

"Sorry, who's Bud?" Rhonda asked.

"A friend of ours. Billy met him." Jay said. Rhonda nodded and looked back at William.

"I guess it's kind of like...well, how do I put it. I mean, we're all dying every day since we're born, right? We just don't think about it. I guess the best way I can put it to what you guys might get is it's like riding. You're riding on your bike down the road with a full gas tank. You know the ride will end, or you'll run out of gas. You just don't know when. If you plan it, you might get to where you think you're going to go, nobody knows, but ultimately you know the ride will end. In my case, it's like you realize that you don't have a full tank like you thought. You got a quarter tank, then less and less. On top of that, the engine is overheating and burning itself up. You try to make the engine keep going however you can, with whatever you can, but you pretty much know at some point that engines going to go. That's pretty much how it feels. The end, though, that's still coming." William said.

"Beautiful, man. Beautiful. I wish I could die." Jay said, then used his vape pen. The statement didn't seem to phase Mo or Lucy, who stared into the fire. William looked over at Rhonda, who looked back at him just as confused. That was an odd statement. The crickets started to chirp in the background, and William looked over at Jay.

"Well...you will someday. Let's hope not for a long time." William said.

"Nope. I'd go right now if I could." Jay said.

"Yeah, me too." Mo chimed in.

"Me three." Lucy said. The three just continued to look at the flames.

William and Rhonda looked at each other again. They weren't sure whether to be completely creeped out or if they had just heard them wrong. They didn't feel unsafe. It just seemed weird. They sat in silence as William continued to look at them, waiting for someone to say something like they were joking, but they didn't.

"Ok, that's just fucking weird." William finally broke the silence.

"What's weird?" Jay asked.

"That you wish for death. You're going to die, and everyone does." William said. There was a slight pause before all three started laughing. Rhonda and William just looked at them. Mo took a drink from his water bottle and looked over at William. Then he looked over at Jay.

"Should I tell him, or do you want to?" Mo asked. Jay sighed.

"I'll do it. You're just too....well...you. No way she's allowed to tell anyone." Jay said, looking at Lucy.

"I'll just have you know I'd be great at it if I were

allowed to. Woman's touch, you know. Corndog? Anyone?" Lucy said, pulling up a corndog on a stick she had been heating with the fire. Jay looked over at William, then put his chair down and sat on William's left side. Rhonda was on his right.

"You haven't figured it out yet, have you, Billy?" Jay said.

"Figured what out?" William asked. Jay sighed.

"We're not exactly the 'normal' people you run into." Jay said, holding up his fingers in air quotes saying normal.

"Yeah, you're a little different, but so what?" William asked.

"No, Billy, we're a lot different. See, there's a reason you found us in the desert out there. Did you bother looking to see how long it would take for you to get from your place to where you met us? Probably not." Jay started.

"13 hours. Actually, like 15, and I mapped it." Rhonda said.

"Exactly. Billy, how long do you think you were gone from your house? When you started riding." Jay asked.

"He was gone four hours before I got home. I can tell you that! Asshole!" Rhonda said, smacking his left arm, and Jay nodded. William looked at the two of them.

"Rhonda, how long was it before you found us?" Jay asked.

"Well, I was on a plane by eleven, so probably ten hours?" Rhonda estimated. Jay nodded again.

"So….Billy. Tell me. How long were we on the road together?" Jay asked. William thought back.

"I don't know, two, three days? No, four. I think it was four." William replied, perplexed.

"Right. So how did you spend four days with us, and Rhonda found you and caught up with you within a day?" Jay asked. William looked at him, confused. Jay raised his eyebrows and looked at him patiently.

"Oh yeah, it was all real. You did spend four days with us. Bud's place, all that happened. How do you explain that?" Jay asked. Rhonda looked just as confused as William.

"You think it was an accident you happened to find us? I mean, of all people, you run into us. You could have gone to a police officer for help, and they would have gotten you home. You could have gone to a hospital, hell, any business, and asked for help. You could have asked for the bartender at any of those places to call information for you, or even used someone's cell phone to email or somehow contact Rhonda, but you didn't. It wasn't that you didn't want to. It just didn't happen that way, did it?" Jay asked. Mo snatched the corndog away from Lucy.

"HEY! I didn't think anyone would ACTUALLY take it. PIG!" Lucy said, getting another corndog out and putting it to the fire inches away to warm it.

"You know that those are made out of pig, right?" Lucy said sneering at Mo. Mo looked at her and kept eating. They locked eyes in a staring contest until Lucy finally rolled her eyes.

"Think I don't know the difference between your tofu foo-foo dogs and a real one? There's a reason nobody eats these nasty ass things. They taste like styrofoam." Mo barked. Then he took another bite.

"Well, a girls got to keep her figure. Besides, they're three dollars cheaper." Lucy sneered.

"Excuse me. I know the tofu dog is riveting, but Jay, I don't understand what you mean." William said. What Jay said made sense on the one hand. He could have done any of those things, yet, he didn't.

"Every year, we take this trip, Billy. Every year, except two, we always wind up with a straggler. The two years we didn't was the plague, and World War II, don't ask why. We don't know. Anyway, every year we get a straggler or two. It's just meant to happen." Jay said.

"Did you say the plague and World War I?" William laughed.

"No, Billy, I said World War II." Jay said, looking at him. William's laugh stopped when he realized Jay was serious.

"Oh, come on, man! You expect me to believe you're that old! Come on, stop fucking around!' William laughed. Jay's soft demeanor remained, but he didn't laugh, and neither did Mo or Lucy. William tried again.

"Come on! Do you expect me to believe you were around in World War II? Jokes over, guys. HAHA, you got me. Can we stop now, please?" William said, looking around at the other two. Neither of their expressions changed. Rhonda looked over, concerned but interested.

"No, Billy. If you were paying attention, I said the plague. We're much older than that." Jay said softly. William looked into Jay's brown eyes and saw the glimmer of the fire. It was almost as if Jay was looking right at his soul. He couldn't help but keep staring. Kind eyes, but keen and astute.

"It's usually someone like you, someone who is towards the end. Sometimes it's not someone like you, we've had thousands that have come with us in one way or another, but in modern times, well, what you call modern, we just have one or two at a time now. There is a power in the universe that everyone ignores until the end. That power, I call it God." Jay started.

"Allah, thank you very much." Mo said.

"I just call it Dad." Lucy said before biting her corndog.

"Anyway! Like I was saying before being rudely interrupted." Jay started.

"I'm interrupted by your boring ass dramatic monologue!" Lucy yelled out, taking another bite. Jay shook his head at her.

"Anyway, Billy. You're not here by accident, and we've been around a long time, is all I'm saying." Jay said, looking over at Mo for a que of what to say next. Mo shrugged his shoulder, chewing the last bite of his corndog. Jay looked at Lucy.

"A little help here." Jay said.

"Oh, no, Sugar, you're doing just fine like you always do!" Lucy said, taking a sip from her flask. She shook all over after she swallowed and let out a breath blinking rapidly.

"Oh, Jesus Christ, guys! Come on!" William balked. He was trying to laugh it off, but everything Jay said was rattling in his brain. There was no way he could have traveled as far as he did in that short amount of time. Thinking of how things unfolded and the places they had been all seemed different somehow. Not different as if it didn't exist, but just different.

"That's funny. You should mention that…." Mo looked up. "What do you think Jesus has to do with anything?" Mo asked, looking at William.

"I don't know, and it's just a figure of speech. Come on, Mo!" William balked again.

"Yeah, I've never understood why they always say that about you, Jay. Why do you always get yelled at when shit goes wrong. You don't hear Muslims saying MOHAMMED ALLAH DAMN IT!" Mo said, slapping his hands together and dusting off the corndog crumbs. Jay shrugged his shoulders.

"Jay, come on. Stop messing me. It's getting weird." William plead.

"His name is not Jay. His name is Jesus, but down here, they call him HEY ZUESSSSS, right Jay? I'm not Mo, my name is Mohammed, and that's not Lucy. His name is Lucifer. There. Stop beating around the bush, Jay. HA! Get it beat around the bush! Moses! Get it?" Mo let out a big laugh, followed by Lucy laughing with him and Rhonda, though she had no idea why she thought it was funny or why she was laughing.

William looked at Jesus, who shrugged his shoulders. The three stopped laughing, and William let out a sigh of relief.

"Man, you guys had me going there for a minute." William said. Mohammed took a sip of water and looked over at William.

"What do you mean?" Mohammed asked.

"I thought he was Jesus for a second." William said. Rhonda looked confused and wanted to say something but stayed quiet. She looked over as the four talked.

"He is." Mohammed said. William looked over at him.

"Okay, jokes over, Mo. Can we just be normal now?" William asked.

"Who said I was joking? You're the one being weird. He's Jesus." Mohammed said.

"I am. Guilty." Jesus said, holding up his right hand. He reached past William and grabbed a corndog from Lucifer's purse.

"HEY! You're supposed to ASK first! Rude." Lucifer said. William looked around, confused.

"What? Why? They're disgusting. I'm doing you a favor." Jesus replied.

"Wait. You mean like Jesus. Like in the Bible?" William asked.

"Oh, come on, man! Don't even get me started on that thing! That was written like years after I ghosted out of that whole era, man! Don't remind me! Though, it has some really good stuff if people would actually take the time to read it instead of making it about them instead of God." Jesus said, putting the corndog to the flames.

Nothing had changed, this was still the same Jay he had been riding with, but William's eyes got wide. He looked over at Jay and realized he wasn't kidding. There was no WAY this could be Jesus. He was always depicted as wearing a white robe, and….well, he did have long hair.

"That's impossible!" William balked.

"Yeah yeah. We've heard it all, Billy. That's impossible… You're lying…. There's no way….You can't be serious… But Jesus looks like this….Mohammed looked like that….or I'm too big to be Mohammed, or I'm not pure enough to be Mohammed.

One thing is for sure. When Lucifer tries, they always think he's lying. They also try to fight him. That's why he's not allowed to tell anyone. Eventually, everyone freaks the fuck out, and then they realize we're not lying, and before you know it, they croak, and we start all over again. Did I miss anything, guys, or does that pretty much cover every year?" Mohammed asked, reaching for another corndog out of Lucifer's purse, which was met by a slap on his hand.

"ASK first big dumb animal!" Lucifer said.

"Hey! You didn't hit Jay! Why am I always the one getting hit?" Mohammed protested.

"Because I like you more. Now you can have one

more, but the other two are for our guests." Lucifer finished. William stood up.

"Oh, here comes the freakout." Mohammed said, putting the corndog to the fire. William's breathing was heavy, and Rhonda tried to calm him down by talking to him, but he realized they weren't joking. They were who they said they were. William paced around for about ten seconds and then looked over at Lucifer.

"Okay. Okay…." William said.

"Now, here comes twenty questions. Every time I tell ya." Jesus said.

"I thought Lucifer was a man." William said.

"I am. SURPRISE, Sugar!" Lucifer said. Lucy was still Lucy, and she still looked the same. William looked her up and down, still confused.

"What?" Lucifer asked. Jay and Mo just looked at him.

"Come on, at least tell him why you dress like a woman!" Jesus said.

"Well….let's just say men think they run the show…. but at the end of the day…." Lucifer made a sweeping motion with his hands from top to bottom. "THIS gets it done. Oh, I know, Sugar, I'm supposed to have horns and pitchforks, and I'm SO evil! I made them do it! I made them go on a rampage and kill everyone. I made them spend all their money at the casino, and I made them have sex with whoever or whatever. Of COURSE, I did it." Lucifer said, irritated. "Even though I was on another continent at the time….or never even met the person, but it's MY fault." Lucifer lit his cigarette.

"Well, you do have to admit, you do some crazy shit, Lucy." Jay said, taking a drag from his vape pen.

"What? Do you mean the bikers? Oh, come on, Jay! THEY chose to sell guns that will kill people, not me. THEY chose to smuggle drugs in that destroy entire villages, NOT me. Now, I'll admit....I might have lined things up, but THEY are the ones who CHOSE their path. There has to be a balance, Jay, you know that." Lucifer finished. Jesus tilted his head and looked at her, slightly more intense than usual.

"Lucy! You BLEW UP A BUILDING! You also caused ROME to fall!" Jesus said with his eyes widening at her. Lucifer took a drag from his cigarette.

"Ok. I might've gone a little overboard on that one." Lucifer said, nonchalantly blowing out smoke into the air.

William looked at the three of them and back at Rhonda. He did the same a few more times, hoping for them to say they were joking.

"You guys are fucking nuts! You expect me to believe that YOU are Jesus Christ, YOU are Mohammed, and YOU are Lucifer?! This is fucking crazy.... C-R-A-Z-Y! We're out of here! Let's go, Rho..." a set of headlights pulling up cut off William. William looked behind him to see what looked like a caravan of cars. Hundreds of headlights could be seen as far as the road was stretched.

"They're here." Mohammed said, standing up.

"Finally." Lucifer said, standing up and dusting off his thighs.

"They sure know how to keep a girl waiting."

William looked back to see a man walking up, and Jesus started walking toward him. It was Kris from the motel.

"Good to see you! It's been so long! Like what, almost 24 hours now? Seriously, you should write more." Kris laughed, hugging Jesus. He did the same with Lucifer and Mohammed, then looked over at Rhonda and William.

"Well, who is this beautiful young lady?" Kris asked, looking at Rhonda.

"Rhonda, MY wife. We were just getting ready to leave your circus here." William said, looking back at the cars.

"Krishna. Nice to meet you, Rhonda. I saw you back at the motel, but you were on the phone." Krishna said, extending his hand to shake hers. Rhonda was still confused but shook his hand. William looked over at Krishna.

"I thought your name was Kris." William said.

"Well, yeah, it's short for Krishna. Americans get just a little weirded out when they have to say, Krishna." Krishna said and then held his hands out.

"Well, here they come. You ready for vacation or what?" Krishna asked the group.

"Wait….you mean like Krishna. Like Hare Krishna? Like the guys at the airport handing out flowers?

THAT Krishna?" Rhonda asked, looking at him with a bewildered look.

"Well, yeah, but I never told them to do that, and I never told them to wear that RIDICULOUS hair either. Atrocious. Oh, and did you see those clothes? No style. My goodness, they strayed when I left, but yeah, the same person." Krishna said, turning and talking with Jesus and Mohammed.

William looked around at the crowd beginning to gather and greet each other. This wasn't a joke. For some reason, he wanted to stay even though his head was screaming to leave. An internal struggle started in him, and he looked over at Rhonda; just when he decided to leave, he felt a hand on his shoulder. Startled, he turned around to see Bud standing behind him.

"How's she runnin'?" Bud asked, pointing over at William's Sportster. William looked at Bud, shocked, and then gave him a big hug.

"BUD!!" William shouted out as if he had just found his best friend and was saved from something. He wanted to tell him the crazy story about what Jay and Mo had just said; then he realized Bud had just traveled down to this very spot with them, which meant he already knew. Bud gave William a quick couple of pats on his back, and William let go.

"Good to see you too, my friend. Who is this?" Bud asked.

"Oh. Rhonda. She's my wife. Bud fixed my bike. He's the one Lucy was talking about." William said as Bud held out his hand as a handshake gesture and smiled. Rhonda shook his hand. Bud's smile made her smile even though she was still confused. Even a little disturbed. Not scared, but disturbed.

"William, what's going on?" Rhonda asked.

"I don't know." he said, looking around at all the people walking up. After a few more greetings here and there, Jesus walked back over to William and Rhonda, and Bud was still standing next to them.

"I see you met Bud, or Buddha, as the world likes to call him. Anyway, Billy, you're free to go. I know you said you wanted to go before everyone started showing up, and you're not a prisoner here or anything. I know it's a bit overwhelming." Jesus said, looking at the crowd.

"Wait...what...did you say, Buddha?" William asked. It all made sense now, the whole trip.

"Yup, sure did. He's Buddha, and I even told you he was a prince, and you didn't believe me. Anyway, we're staying. We're just waiting on one more, and then we're going. If you want to go, though, that road will lead you straight back to the border." Jesus said, pointing at the road.

"Here." Lucifer said, throwing her keys to Rhonda. Rhonda caught them and looked up.

"I don't need it anyway. I'll get another ride. I am Lucifer, you know, and kind of have a grip on things here and there. Oh, here's your money too from the motel." Lucifer winked at Rhonda and then threw a wad of cash at her.

"Told you she wouldn't keep it." Mohammed said. William looked around.

"Yeah, with our awesome passports, you think the American border patrol will let us in?" William asked. Jesus smiled.

"Look again, Billy." Jesus said. William pulled out his passport from his back pocket. He looked at it closely, and it had all of his correct information, and Rhonda did the same. Hers also had her correct information. William looked over at the road and then back to Jesus, astonished.

"How?" Rhonda asked. Mohammed stepped up to the group.

"Who cares? Are you in or not? I need a headcount for our party?" Mohammed barked.

William looked at Rhonda, and both had the same look. It was almost like they were watching a movie, and it JUST started to reveal itself. William should have been scared, and Rhonda should have felt terrified, but they didn't. They both turned in unison and said, "We're in."

CHAPTER 11

THE GATHERING

By Williams's estimate, the crowd continued to grow to what appeared to be at least 200 people. All different races and ages, and dressed in everything from suits to shorts and a t-shirt.

"AH! Hey, listen up, everyone!" Jesus yelled out. He stood up on one of the stones and looked over the crowd.

"HEY! Look! He's here, everyone!" Jesus said, pointing out into the crowd. Several cheers could be heard as a man emerged from the crowd, slowly waving at people and greeting them as he moved. He appeared to be a celebrity amongst this crowd.

He looked average to William. He couldn't quite pinpoint the man's race, but he was neither White nor Black, maybe a little Asian, William couldn't tell. The man had olive skin and slicked-back jet-black hair and appeared in his mid to late '40s. He was dressed in what looked like a suit, but it was a Mandarin-style shirt with no collar and a black vest with no jacket. He slowly worked his way up to Jesus, who opened his arms. The man opened his arms back, smiling, and the two gave each other a big hug. After the hug, the crowd slowly quieted.

"Welcome back, everyone! Another year down, and we get a break. I'm glad to see all of you again….and this year, we have a couple of guests." the man said, waving his hand in William and Rhonda's direction. The two immediately began to look around them. Out of all the people here, they were the ONLY guests?

"I know you don't know me. Not a lot of people do. Well, except them, of course." he said, motioning out to the crowd. "My name is Thoth. It's pronounced THO like Toe and OTH like Moth. Last year someone called me tooth." Thoth laughed. It was a genuine laugh that made even William laugh. He couldn't figure it out. He should be scared of all these strangers, yet he felt like he was at a family reunion. He was confused, but somehow, like he was supposed….

"Supposed to be here? Is that what you were going to say, William?" Thoth asked while looking at the crowd still. He slowly turned his head over to William.

"Uh….yeah. Actually. How did you know that?" William asked. The crowd burst into laughter. After a few moments, it died down. Thoth had a slight accent, but he didn't know what type. It was an accent he had never heard.

"You're not the first person to have those same thoughts, William, and your beautiful wife, Rhonda. Welcome. I apologize. Where are my manners? Welcome both William and Rhonda.

Well, folks, another year, and here we are. Another

year, we all hoped, wouldn't happen, but here we are. At least we're in good company, right?" Thoth asked the crowd, who nodded in agreement. Thoth had a relationship with each of them. That was clear.

"Hey, Jesus, what's going on? What's he mean?" William asked Jesus, and Jesus shushed him, listening to Thoth.

"Don't worry, sir, I'll explain later." Thoth said to William before turning back to the crowd. How did he hear him? Impossible. He was whispering.

"Well.....how about we get this party started? What do you think, folks?" Thoth asked, and the crowd began to cheer.

Thoth waited a moment and then walked over to the stone in the center that William had noticed when they stopped. From the rear of the stone, Thoth reached down and pulled out two slabs of flat stone. The firelight gleamed over them, and William could see they were green and about the side of a laptop. Thoth looked back at the crowd, who gave another cheer and placed the tablets on the stone. Thoth took a few steps back, smiling, and held his hands to his chest with his fingers touching and steepled together. He moved his upper torso elegantly as he stepped back again, almost as if he were floating.

Within a few seconds, the crowd fell silent. A small light emerged from the top of the stone and pulsated white. It did this for a few seconds before shooting a beam of light directly into the night sky, and as quick as it went up, it was gone.

William looked around to see he was in a city, a big city, and daylight. It was a vast city because he could see skyscrapers, but it was different from anything he had ever seen. A second ago, he was in the desert.

He looked back at the crowd. Everyone seemed like they were waiting on a bus. The air was different. Clean, like when William went camping in the woods, but he was in the middle of a big city. Buildings towered in the background, but they somehow looked like they belonged in their places.

William looked around dazed as the crowd started to shuffle away, wave goodbye to one another, and start walking in different directions. William looked closely at the nearest building. It wasn't a building at all. It was a tree.... A tree was a building....with windows, but the tree was somehow grown and shaped AROUND the window with its leaves neatly trimmed on top, so the building sat flat.

William kept looking and then looked down to see he was in a large parking lot, but he wasn't standing on concrete. It was black and looked like concrete, but it was different, and it wasn't hot like asphalt. Rhonda also noticed that several animals were milling about, unafraid of humans. Rhonda tapped William on the shoulder and pointed to a deer standing next to the building. People walked by the deer, and it didn't' move.

"They're only afraid of mountain lions and predators." Mohammed said, pointing at the deer. "Don't try to pet them, though. They bite." Mohammed walked past them, waving them to follow him with his right hand. Jesus appeared on Mohammed's left, and they walked over to Thoth, who was greeting people and saying things like "Have a nice time. Have fun! See you next year!" to the passersby.

"OH good good good." Thoth said, clapping his hands together.

"Where are we?" Rhonda asked.

"Well...that's a loaded question, my dear. There's the long answer which requires a VERY long lecture on how prisms work as well as dimensions, but the short answer is your right here." Thoth replied.

"Yeah...but where is here?" Rhonda asked. William remembered his talk with Bud or Buddha as he learned about the moment. He held up his hand and shook his head to stop Rhonda from asking more questions.

"It's alright, William. Rhonda, here is a concept, a human concept. Location is a human concept. Time is a human concept. So, all you have to know is you are here. Now, a better question may be WHY you are here. Would you not agree?" Thoth said as he began to walk. They walked toward the buildings. More and more buildings became visible. They were ALL trees or some type of plant that was somehow molded into a building. William looked at them in amazement and continued walking.

"Well, before I get into the why, I could answer your question a little further, Rhonda. See this here, THIS...." Thoth held his arms out wide, "THIS is what you would call....Heaven." Thoth said. Rhonda looked at him. Her eyes widened, her breath became rapid, and she began to hyperventilate. Jesus and Mohammed looked over at Thoth wide-eyed. They had seen this before.

"OH MY GOD! ARE WE DEAD?" Rhonda blurted out instinctively.

"OH MY GOD! OH MY GOD!....." Rhonda said, starting to hyperventilate further.

Mohammed whispered something in Thoth's ear, and he raised his eyebrows and said, "Oh..".

"I'm sorry, Rhonda. I used the wrong word. Forgive me. English is not my first language. This place is what you would call.....Shangri La? Eden? Utopia? Forgive me, I don't know the exact English word, but it's the perfect place. How the world should be." Thoth said. He watched, and Rhonda calmed down slightly but looked at him curiously.

"So....we're not dead?" Rhonda asked. Thoth smiled, and grandfather-like energy came from him, which sent her immediately into a state of calm.

"Dead? No child....another human concept. Death. No, you are not dead." Thoth said, continuing to walk again. Rhonda let out a sigh of relief.

William was distracted by a small child running to his right. The child ran up to his mother and took her hand. They were dressed in what looked like modern clothes, but also simple. It was both a beautiful and a simple outfit all at once. The woman had long hair in a ponytail and appeared to be wearing makeup, but maybe she wasn't. Her light skin radiated, and she and the child looked healthy. A different kind of healthy than he had seen before, almost radiant. Vibrant.

"They can't see you, Billy." Mohammed said, noticing William watching the lady and her child.

"What do you mean they can't see me? How can she not see me? I'm right here." William said, waving at the woman, and she didn't wave back.

"Billy, shut up and pay attention." Jesus barked. They continued to walk, and William was thoroughly confused as he saw the people from this place walking all over....that was another thing he noticed. No vehicles. This place was a modern city, but there were no vehicles, at least none that he could see.

Thoth stopped and looked around. William tried to comprehend what was happening. He heard what Thoth had said, but it didn't make any sense. They were in the desert less than five minutes ago. William looked around and then at Jesus.

"PEYOTE!! That's what this is!" William shouted out. William looked around wide-eyed and pointed around him in a circle. The group stopped and looked at him. Thoth raised his right eyebrow, and Rhonda looked at him, embarrassed.

"Seriously? So we ALL are having the same trip? Come on, William! Do you remember when we dropped acid when we first got together? We wouldn't ALL see the same thing." Rhonda scoffed and rolled her eyes. She looked over at Jesus.

"So...did you walk on water?" Rhonda asked.

"YES! Okay! You're like the millionth person to

ask. The water was 2 inches deep! That's the part they leave out! I did it to be dramatic. Now pay attention!" Jesus interrupted. Rhonda blinked a few times and looked over at Mohammed.

"What? I have questions? What do you expect?" Rhonda shrugged. Mohammed didn't answer.

"Questions. Questions are a good thing, my lady. Questions brought you fire. Fire allowed you to cook. Cooking led to living longer. Living longer led to more questions, and here we are." Thoth said, beginning to walk.

"Questions are a beginning, like a seed, and then the answer grows into something beautiful. Well, usually, but not all seeds grow, and some grow the unexpected….and sometimes the unwanted. Sometimes those questions…..well. You get the point. You can ask all the questions you want while you're here, but you'll find every question leads to a million more. That's the beauty of it all." Thoth pointed at a building in the distance. The building resembled a pyramid, but it was modified to accommodate the surrounding trees. The windows were tinted, or at least they looked tinted.

"You might find some of those answers there." Thoth said.

"Aww, man! Not again!" Jesus said, shaking his head. Thoth looked over at him. Jesus shrugged in defeat, then shook his head and muttered, "Fine….".

"Well, this is where we part ways for now. I have some others to see." Thoth said, nodding.

"Wait. Are you leaving? We just got here. I have

questions too. Like who are you? What's your story? Where do we go?" William burst out. Thoth gazed at him. He had a very wise posture, almost like someone who has the answers but isn't sure you would like the answer. Thoth smiled.

"I'll be back later, I assure you. You're our guest. Of course, I'll be back. You just got here, well, at least your consciousness just got here anyway." Thoth said to William.

"What?" William asked. Thoth smiled and patted William on the right shoulder. He looked over at Jesus, nodded, and walked to the left. A group of people walking waved at Thoth, and he waved back at them. He greeted them and began walking with them as old friends reunited.

"What is he like the leader?" William asked Mohammed.

"He's more like a mentor." Mohammed responded.

Walking as a group, William looked around. This place was earth, definitely a city, but the whole place felt different. Organic was the only word he could muster to describe it. Rhonda appeared to be a little more grounded as they walked and looked around occasionally.

As they walked, a large building appeared in the distance, about forty feet away. It was a glass structure, and William could see trees inside it. It had a dome-like appearance but appeared triangular at the top, at least twenty stories tall. As they got closer, a glass archway led into the building.

"All the answers are in there, Billy." Jesus said, lifting his chin towards the building.

"What do you mean?" William asked.

"Man, Jesus is speaking English isn't he?" Mohammed rolled his eyes.

"He said...ALL....YOUR....answers...are...in... there." Mohammed said with a smart-aleck tone. William looked over at him.

"What answers? I didn't ask anything." William said, looking first at Jesus, then at Mohammed.

"Just...get your ass in there, would ya? We got shit to do." Mohammed shoo'd William forward with both hands in a sweeping motion.

"Easy there, Mo. He'll go eventually." Jesus responded and stood looking at Billy patiently.

"Ah. Yes. Rhonda, is it? I would like to show you something if you would be so kind as to accompany me." Thoth said from behind the group. Rhonda turned around to see Thoth standing with a cordial smile holding out his hand. His demeanor was that of a grandfather offering to show his grandchildren something. Rhonda looked around over at William.

"Uh...I don't know. William?" Rhonda asked. William had reservations at first about letting his wife separate from him, but a feeling inside made it seem alright. Even though he should have been completely freaked out, he wasn't. It felt safe. He nodded over to Rhonda and Thoth.

"Oh, you'll like these. It's a rare flower that only grows in one place on earth, and it's in the ice! Also, you'll like the gaming area we have, and you like to gamble, right? But unlike the ones you're used to, these are different…." Thoth continued as they began to walk away.

Mohammed and Jesus remained behind and waved at the two as they walked away. William watched as Thoth led Rhonda to another building nearby. He knew she was going to be okay, but he felt….

"Afraid, Billy. That's what it's called." Mohammed said, still looking over at Thoth and Rhonda. William looked over at him.

"It's okay, Billy. I was too. She can't go in there, though. Only you can go. This place is interesting, to say the least." Mohammed said, turning towards William. Jesus held his palms up and beckoned for William to enter the building.

"I don't get it. It's just an atrium, right? Like a garden? What's the big deal? Why can't Rhonda go?" William asked.

"Well, let's go find out." Jesus said. William looked over at Jesus, then at Mohammed. He thought back to the fire pit with Bud, who he now learned was Buddha, and their other times together on the road. The motorcycle ride together just happened but felt like a lifetime ago. In either case, he felt trust. A trust he had never felt with anyone else, and he walked through the archway.

CHAPTER 12

---◇---

THE ARCHWAY

Walking through the archway, William expected some miracle transformation or something to happen, but it didn't. They walked through the garden that had plants and trees of all kinds. He could hear water flowing in the background, and the climate became tropical but not too hot.

As they walked through the building, it seemed endless. After what felt like about fifteen minutes, William finally looked over at Jesus and Mohammed, who were patiently walking a few paces behind him.

"Ok. I don't get it. It looks like a fucking atrium- like you see in the tourist towns. You know, a botanical garden, so what's the big deal?" William asked.

"Really? Even that flower over there? Did you ever stop to look at it? I don't think you've even stopped to look at one thing here." Jesus asked, pointing over at what looked like a red poinsettia like the ones they have at the store at Christmas time. William looked at the two and then rolled his eyes.

"Whatever. What the hell is this thing anyway? You'd think they'd put signs up or something like normal. What's the name of this...thing...anyway...."

Williams's thoughts were delayed as he focused on the red flower.

It seemed to hypnotize him as he was drawn closer and closer to it. Before he knew it, the flower seemed to be radiating back to him with an energy that he had never felt. Love, but in a way that seemed to overpower every doubt or fear in his being. He felt a peace that he had never felt, and it seemed like no matter what, everything was alright. A bomb could go off next to him, and he'd be fine. The love seemed to pierce deep inside of him, and the flower became just a symbol as he started to cry as if this flower was what he had been seeking his whole life. A flower. Just a flower.

"Welcome to the Garden of Eden, William." Jesus said, startling William, who was still focused on the flower. William had forgotten all about Jesus and Mohammed. He stopped looking at the flower and looked over at them, still crying. He looked back at the flower. The flower was gone, but the feeling of joy and love emanated from somewhere inside him. William looked around to see darkness around Jesus and Mohammed. The entire atrium was gone, and it was just the three of them surrounded by darkness. The three of them sat in what felt like suspended animation.

"Am I….am I dead?" William asked. Jesus giggled.

"Not yet, buddy. But pretty fucking close! Why does everyone always ask that?" Mohammed laughed. Jesus looked over at William and then opened both of his arms wide open and looked up.

"Just think Billy, your whole life, this was here the

whole time. All you had to do was let go and focus." Jesus took a deep breath.

"Imagine Billy, a whole world where everyone felt this...right here. This is what God is, this. " Jesus closed his eyes for a minute. Mohammed nodded in agreement. William remained silent, absorbing the feeling. He could remain forever in this place. Pure love, in a way that he couldn't put into words. It was like his grandfather, grandmother, and parents were hugging him. A long time passed before William spoke.

"Why can't everyone feel like this? We'd never have a war, and there'd be no fighting. Why don't you guys make this happen out there?" William asked.

"Oh, please, Sugar. Like they didn't try." Lucifer said, walking up from behind Jesus in the darkness. William focused on Lucifer, who was now wearing a skin-tight red dress. Lucifer seemed to move elegantly yet, in a way that seemed unnatural. Etherial.

Usually, that would have startled William under most circumstances, but it felt like it was meant to happen.

"Don't worry, Sugar. You'll get used to it. See, I'm the only one here that can come here any time I want to. You know. Angel and all. Well, we're not called 'angels.' You guys named us that. Well...technically, we're not even here. See, our atoms work differently than yours–" Lucifer started and was quickly interrupted.

"Lucy, shut the fuck up already! Nobody cares. He wouldn't get it anyway. Just....chill and be present, man....we don't get to be here that often, and we don't want to hear that whole thing again." Mohammed interrupted.

Lucifer looked at him with angry eyes and then thought about it. William watched as Lucifer's facial expressions instantly went from annoyed to understanding. The group remained in silence for a while before Jesus spoke.

"So....Billy. Imagine trying to explain this to people. Going back to what you said. Try to explain it...go ahead. Explain God's love, how you feel." Jesus said. William looked around.

"I guess you can't, but you can try, right?" William responded. Almost instantly, all of the other three were laughing hysterically. Mohammed snorted a few times, laughing. When they were done laughing, Jesus looked over at William.

"Yo. Billy. You ever read the Bible? You know, because it's a sin if you don't." Jesus asked.

William, still in this feeling of peace, responded, "Yes. I read it."

"So, you followed every rule, right? Because, you know, God's watching." Jesus laughed, causing Lucifer to giggle behind him and cover his mouth. William looked over at Jesus, confused.

"I don't get it. What's so funny?" William said. Mohammed took a second and then looked over at William.

"Billy. Jay told you that all your answers were in here. You could ask anything, and you ask why can't everyone feel like this and be like this. You're sitting on a water-filled ball spinning through space at thousands of miles an hour, powered by a huge ball of fire that is just far enough away not to boil the planet away. You're only saving grace is a moon that pulls you away from that ball of fire, which also blinds you if you look at it, and if just a FEW degrees go off from that moon, you die, and the planet is done. Yet, your question wasn't how any of that works, no. Your question was about other people. Like only people matter. Doesn't that make you wonder what the hell is wrong with you?" Mohammed said, looking over at William.

He was right. William was unfazed by his words, still in this feeling, but he was right. The only thing he had thought of was other people. Weird, and not about the answers to the universe or even anything to do with anything other than people.

"Don't worry, Billy. We both did the same thing." Jesus said, and he looked over at Mohammed, and then at Lucifer, before speaking again.

"We tried Billy. We still try. Even though Lucifer told us not to, Lucifer said it would only lead to disaster, but we tried and tried. That's the funny thing. We still keep trying. You're the perfect example. You know.... you read the Bible, right? Did you read the Quran too? You know, Mo's book?" Jesus asked. William shook his head no.

"Well." Jesus said. "It's probably a good thing because neither of us wrote those fucking things. The people we taught did, and they had good intentions. Also, it's accurate, but like anything, it can be misinterpreted or abused."

"Well, actually, I did write part of that, but it was more like notes. It was never meant to be a book, I just wrote some things down, and THEY turned it into a book. I was just, you know, writing my thoughts. Didn't know they would be using my notes as 'companion codices' and all that complicated crap. Hell, when I wrote those, most people couldn't even read! I was just writing some stuff down to get people on the same page. That was the plan. Ideas. Ways to influence people and teach them. Guide them towards Allah. Then they took the stuff I wrote and well....you know the rest." Mohammed jumped in.

"True dat, as the young people nowadays say. I did the same thing, but I didn't know how to write like Mo here. You know, we were both on foot, on the ground, trying to convince people that this place right here was RIGHT at our fingertips. God's love is real. Anything can be done with God.

I tried to get them here with metaphors and prayer. Prayer, teaching every day nonstop. Didn't matter who it was. Everyone is the same in the end. Think about it. That same bum asking for money is the same guy living in a mansion. There's no difference in their DNA. No difference. If you're outside looking in, there is no difference. To us, though, very different, right? If you look at it now, people have good intentions, but they focus on the words in the prayers. That's not what it was about for Mo or me. We were trying to use those words to make FEELINGS happen inside them. The same ones that are there all the time. They can have THIS right here, but they don't. God's RIGHT HERE ALL the time. He never once leaves us.

Now, after being here, how would you try to tell those same people who judge daily how to get this here?" Jesus asked William, and William didn't have an answer.

"Shit, Billy. We try. Nobody listens. Well, some do. Very few. The ones that do listen get distracted now by their cell phones and TV. You know, I once had many followers that understood what I was trying to say. Even a few felt this. I was able to walk with them into Mecca, the biggest city in the world back then, and take it over without hurting a single soul. Man! I was on FIRE back then, and I thought FOR SURE that I would get EVERYONE on board. We were ALL going to get here! They were trying to get here worshipping, like, weird goats and all kinds of nonsense. I was SURE that I would get in there and get everyone on the right path. I was RIGHT there too…... Billy, I had ten THOUSAND people with me, and I was going to get every person right where we are right now. I even had Jay and Bud on board. We were rockin'! Well. Anyway, I was almost there. SO close." Mohammed jumped in.

"So. What happened?" William asked.

"I died." Mohammed responded. "Not dead like dead-dead, but I died. When I came back, nobody believed me. They didn't believe I was me. I went from being the land's ruler and leader of ten thousand people to a crazy person impersonating myself. Talk about a shot to the nuts on that one. Hero to Zero real quick, buddy. Anyway, Jay and I took off after that. Now we're here." Mohammed laughed.

"Me too. You know my story or at least part of it. I didn't have ten thousand, but I had a few followers, especially back then. I got a couple of people to this place as well, but then you saw what happened. They decided to make me a pincushion and beat the hell out of me in public just to make a statement. You know the most fucked up part about all that is I didn't even fight back. I kept thinking at some point. They would get this feeling and stop. Something would intervene. They would be in this place we're in here and realize how great things can be, and it would stop. Thorns slammed on my head, whipped, and then, yay, the whole nails to the hands and legs, then vulture food. Man, that sucked.

Do you know what the worst part is? Of ALL the symbols they could have used to try to keep my message alive, they used the image of me dead on a couple of sticks roasting in the sun. Do you know how fucked up that is? They could've used a nice flower or a bird from when I talked about life being beautiful and this place we can get together, or even a basket talking about giving something to each other. Nope. Not my followers. These guys use my bloody corpse on a cross. Man. Different times." Jesus said, shaking his head. "When I woke up, I tried to bail, but a couple of people

258

saw me. Didn't want round 2 of the whole beat the shit out of Jesus thing, so I took off. Romans. Man. That's why I was killed, sedition. People think it was because I was teaching. It wasn't.

Of course, that led to the whole Easter thing. Never understood the whole rabbit crapping out eggs, though….Anyway, yeah, man, that's when I took off east and wound up finding Bud. I had heard about a guy, a prince actually, trying to do the same thing I was doing. Found him. Different method, though. Man, Bud was something else back in that day, though. You think he's chill now? I saw that dude sit and meditate for a week straight. A lot of gurus back then, just like now. Had to sift through them to find Bud. He is the one who showed me how to keep a low profile and keep learning, being present, and all that.

This feeling here….you can do anything. When you are in tune with God, the universe, there's no sadness and no want of anything. I hung out with Bud for a while until I heard about THIS dude in Mecca." Jesus said, pointing over at Mohammed. "Then I decided to go see for myself. We've been friends ever since. Ain't that right, Mo?" Jesus said.

"Yup. The only one who puts up with my bullshit throughout the years." Mohammed laughed. Lucifer rolled his eyes.

"You two little Jackwagons should've listened to me in the first place and left things alone." Lucifer said.

"Agreed, my dear Lucifer, but what's done is done." Mohammed said.

"You know, I told these idiots what would happen if they went out there. The world isn't ready, and still isn't. Oh no, don't listen to the one being created to watch over things and keep the balance...oh no. Not like I was created to look after you, but at the same time, be tied to this place and keep things balanced. Why listen to me?

Anyway, Jay, I didn't even see that coming. I thought he had proven me wrong. Humans were BRUTAL back then, and somehow Jay kept turning them around. Turning the most violent souls into peaceful followers. Billy, let me tell you. You think you got it bad now.... oh man. The world was MUCH worse back then.

Anyway, that whole 'tempting Jesus' thing. I didn't tempt anyone. I just told him to keep his butt here, but NOOOO. Not him. He had to go try to get EVERYONE here. Spread the word, heal the world. Didn't work. TOLD YOU!" Lucifer said, looking at Jesus.

"Yeah.... yeah, you did. Should've offered me an apple!" Jesus laughed, inferring the Adam and Eve story. Lucifer rolled his eyes, and William stopped for a second.

"So...what is that story? Adam and Eve? We're here now in the Garden of Eden, right? So what happened?" William asked. Lucifer rolled his eyes again, annoyed. Mohammed looked over at Lucifer and shrugged his shoulders as if he had heard this story before.

"That's ANOTHER one they get all fucked up. I didn't tempt Eve with a fucking apple. Do you see any apples here? NO! I told BOTH of them to stay here. Let me ask you, Billy, do you have anything you want right now? Feel like getting rich? Want to bang that 20-year-old barista?" Lucifer asked. William thought about it. He was in such a state of peace and love. He didn't want anything other than to be here. He shook his head.

"EXACTLY! Just stay where you're at, I said. They wanted to leave. I even said I'd get them something to eat, and then Eve, EVE NOT ME, picked a fucking apple and started eating it. I had NOTHING to do with it. Then she took some more for the road, and they left. They could have simply come RIGHT back, but NOOOO. They STAYED out there, and instead of coming back for this, they wanted to make things on their own. That's where all the greed and lust come from. Here, you don't have any of that. It's God's love, and it's everything you need or want. I TRIED to keep them here, but they made choices, yet, it's my fault. Go figure. God never punished them or hurt them. THEY did that to themselves. God's love knows no boundaries, and he forgives you guys for some reason. I have no idea why. You fuckers do all this shit to yourselves. God has nothing to do with it.

I even tried to warn them REPEATEDLY, but then they started blaming ME when it went wrong. So, I figured, if people want to be stupid, fine. I can't stop them, but I can sure get some entertainment out of it! Anyway, I only mess with the bad ones. The ones that hurt other people. It can get quite interesting though.

It's been so long though, people are genuinely lost, and I don't know if they can ever get back in tune with things." Lucifer said.

William started to laugh. A little at first, then a full roar. It kept going for about a minute or two when he looked up to see the three looking at him.

"It's real. This is all real." William said, smiling. The statement didn't even seem to change the vibe of the room. The peace and calm that had swarmed over William seemed like it had always been with him, and he didn't want to move, but curiosity got the better of him.

"So, Jay, are you saying you and Mo have been together the whole time?" William asked.

"Yeah. Well, ever since Bud and I found him." Jesus responded.

"So.... were you born in a barn? Was your mom a virgin? What about the three wise men?" William asked back to back. Mohammed laughed.

"Why does everyone always ask me that? How the hell would I know? I was a baby!" Jesus responded. Mohammed laughed again, this time shrugging his shoulders.

"I'll just say it ahead of time before you ask Billy. No, I did not say a 'Jihad' was a green light to wage war with anyone who disagreed with Islam. It wasn't even called that then. We didn't have names for religions, people were looking for something at the time, but it wasn't called 'Islam' or 'Christianity.' When I said that, I meant there's an internal struggle for what you're seeking, and you have to fight what is out there in front of you, to get here to what's inside of you. It's alright to love Allah and express it. Not to actually hurt people in Allah's name!

You're here now, Billy. This....this is God, Allah, right here. This place, and it's in all of us. You don't need or want anything here. It's just love. We've somehow made that word love sound weak, but it's the most potent force in the universe. Soldiers don't fight because they are angry. They fight to protect the country and the ones they love. Love is so strong. It gives mothers the strength to pick up cars off their children to save them. Lovers die for each other, and those people just get a sliver of this here. It's always been here, in all of us, all around us. God is love.

You can't get here worshipping a tree. You'll just focus on the tree. That's why I destroyed all the false idols. They were a distraction. I wasn't trying to condemn anyone. I was trying to show them how to get here. To get here, you have to focus on the inside, where it counts, and.... well, you try to explain how you feel right now, where we are. Then try to explain what I meant hundreds of years ago. Good luck with that.

Allah was the word we used. It was supposed to mean all, and one path, one God. Language had come a long way since Jay's time. We were able to communicate better and write things. I was lucky enough to know how to write, so I did. Well, ever play the telephone game where one person says something on one end of the room, and by the time it gets all the way around, it's different? Well...welcome to now." Mohammed said, moving closer to William.

William looked around to see the darkness that was once around them had turned into a light grey with pink highlights as if they were in a cloud. He looked around him.

"Oh, that....William, that's you doing that. Concentrate on a forest." Jesus said to William. William began to focus, and before he could obtain the thought, they were in a forest. A different kind of forest. Dense, beautiful, and just enough light to keep the serenity around them.

"See? Now you know why both of us wanted to get rid of false idols. What you focus on is what you see. Every single day. If you focus on God, you'll see him or feel him." Jesus said.

"Yeah, that turned into a shit show real quick. Made it seem like we were taking a baby's toy away. Egos never change." Mohammed said.

"You think that's bad, Sweety, I get blamed for everything wrong in the world, and I didn't do anything. Shit, I even tried to guide people in the right direction, but NOOOO.... They need someone to blame. Taking responsibility for your own choices? Nope. It's my fault. Lucifer made me do it. Mo's people call me Iblis, and it goes on and on. Every culture has a name for me. Anyway, continue, boys. I'm going to pop back in downstairs." Lucifer said, lighting a cigarette. He gave a goodbye wave to William.

"If I don't see you again, Sweety, it's been fun." Lucifer said, winking at him. He walked away into the forest and disappeared into the trees. William locked on to Lucifer and waved. He was about to talk when Mo interrupted him.

"So…. yeah. To answer your question, we've been together a long time now. Jay was one of the reasons I was so successful back then. They left him out of the story on purpose. I promised to protect his identity after what happened. Gabriel, well, I'm sure you heard that story, but Jay was there with me the whole time. Told me his story, and then Bud. We haven't even talked about Bud. He's been around the longest beside Thoth. He tried to get everyone to just chill the fuck out and be here. He called it Nirvana, a place of inner peace. You know, right here, man. Man, he was big back in the day, but Jay's story ended up being the one everyone hooked on to. Mine was good too, but something about how Jay went out getting beat down in public, I think, clicked with people. Dark, but it worked. Plus, you know, he had all those different chapters and authors in his book." Mohammed said, looking around at the forest. "Good work Billy…. I like it."

"Man! I didn't even write that thing! Plus, they mixed up half of what I said." Jesus chimed in.

"BUT….they did include some of the good stuff. Imagine what the world would be like without those books, Jay. You remember how bad it can get." Mohammed pointed at the ground.

"True." Jesus said.

"Wait. How are you two still alive? I mean…. I know you're sons of God and all…..but how are you here?" William asked. Both Jesus and Mohammed laughed. They looked at each other.

"Every time, Billy. That's another question we get all the time. Sons of God. We're all sons and daughters of God. We have no idea, Billy. We're no different. Try explaining THAT to others too. You wind up in a loony bin. All I know is I woke up after getting stuck with a spear. Mo woke up after he died. We still have no idea how that happened. It just happens. We don't know why. We live and die, then live again. I think it has something to do with finishing what we started.

I'm still human, nothing special. We get sick. We get hurt. Life happens over and over again. We found out that if we come here, to God's love, we get to be reborn but don't have to have that whole shock factor. No pain involved. We know we'll be starting over and skip the whole death thing when we leave.

Anyway, every year we're allowed to come here. Once in a while, we get a guest, like you, Billy. Actually, every year we get one of you. You see all those people out there in the desert? Yeah, Mo and I aren't the only ones. All those out there, they're like us. You just haven't heard of them. Every one of us has tried to get people to sync up and be like this with God. Think about what the world would be like if everyone had this right here. No killing. No raping. No fighting for power. Happy and content people don't want to harm others. That's why people who get high,

266

like the hippies, just let go of everything, but drugs are like that tree that Mo talked about. False prophets." Jesus looked over at a deer that had come through the forest. A large 12-point buck was staring at them. "Did you do that, Billy? Looks like you're getting this thing down." Jesus said.

"I don't get it. You're still here. You...you guys can get out there; you can make it right. Right? I mean.... you can..." William started.

"What, Billy? We can what?" Mohammed interrupted.

Mohammed looked over at William. "You think we haven't tried? Billy, we've been involved in ANY movement that has come up since. We tried to get in there and nudge, here and there, just to get it on the right track. That's how we wound up here in the United States. Yoga, hippies, all that. We spent so much time in India and the Himalayas. I can't even tell you. I can tell you damn near each rock over there. They got it, by the way. Nepal. 100%. The Tibetans got it. Then China came in. Anyway, we try, but these religions have taken on a life of their own. People in power get a little tiny piece of what we have here, and they destroy everyone and everything to keep it. They miss the whole point. It's for everyone, not just THEIR people. Would you fight for this Billy? Yes, you would. You would die for it, and that's what we're up against. They don't know there's more to the story. God loves indiscriminately. So, we try where we can, but it's like watching a broken record. It skips RIGHT where the song gets good, but then keeps skipping."

Jay looked over and raised his hand. "You know, there is hope, my friend. Those motorcycles, I know they're new, but man, you guys are on the right track. Think about when you are on that bike and on the road. You're sitting on a machine hurling you down the road with nothing around you but the air, and you can get clipped at any time. You can't think. You have to focus. You can't slack off, and you are right at the edge all the time. The same thing as meditation, but you get so close to this place right here. Right there, and there are no books or words to confuse. No person telling you how to do it. It just happens. It doesn't happen in a car or an RV, just on these bikes. People are catching on, though, and fast. I like it. This motorcycle culture seems to get it and doesn't say a word about it. That's a good thing. They just get it and hang out together, then they ride, and more people show up. It's great. " Jesus said, holding his hands up like he was riding a motorcycle.

"Jay's right, man. I tell you what, this dude and I have been together a LONG time. I mean, we go other ways here and there, but we've stuck together because we know what this place is. Actually, more of a state than a place. Not even really a place. This guy's my brother for sure, but it wasn't until those bikes came along that we locked in even closer. Now we go everywhere on them. When they came out in the 1920s, they didn't go fast enough, and it was kind of like riding the bumper cars. They were whatever. Then came the 1940's and that's where the magic happened. You can ride with people on these bikes, and nothing needs to be said. I'm closer to that guy over there now than all these years. Can't explain it. Go figure.

We got those bikes you saw; I think, back in the '80s? We've taken those things all over the world. Those American-made bikes, I don't know what it is. It's just special. We swap motors and modify them, but it's the bikes that are magic. Well, you get it, don't ya, Billy?" Mohammed said, looking over at him.

"I get it." William said. He thought of a sunset, and it happened. The most beautiful sunset peered through the trees. William took a few moments and then thought of a sunrise, and it appeared behind him. Jesus and Mohammed looked at William, nodding in approval of the sunset. William thought of Rhonda and then looked around. The forest started to fade, and William thought harder. Now the forest fell into the neutral darkness. Jesus figured it out.

"She can't come here yet, Billy. Only you." Jesus said, looking at him.

"What do you mean? You just said you're trying to get everyone here, and I can make a sunrise. I want her to see this, and I want her to have this too." William said.

"That's…. entirely up to her, Billy." Mohammed said solemnly.

"Well, she's with Thoth, right? He can bring her here, right?" William asked.

"No, Billy. Thoth is like us. He's just the oldest of us. He doesn't even know where he came from. They call him Thoth the Atlantean, you know, the city that sank, but he doesn't even know. He tried to put his story out there, too, even carved them into emerald tablets. Emerald! Damn, if that ain't a way to bling things out, I don't know what is. Hell, they're still out there, you know, supposably in the pyramids of Egypt, but that's not where they're at. Thoth won't tell anyone. He let some doctor translate them, but you know. It's like any other story, worthless unless people take an interest in it. Anyway, even he can't bring her here. See, this place here is only accessible to those of us like Jay and me, and... you." Mohammed said.

"Wait. I thought you said I wasn't dead." William said.

"You're not. I said damn near." Mohammed responded. William thought long and hard for a moment, and they looked around. It was the clinic.

The beeping of the chemotherapy drips hummed in unison. The television was playing, and William looked over to see himself in the chair. His eyes were open, and he looked at himself. Lifeless eyes, but he was still alive. Normally he would've jumped out of his skin with fright, but he still felt the same peace and calm.

"How…. how is this possible?" William asked.

"This place, the one we're in now, is not accessible to the living. That's why Rhonda can't come here. Thoth can, but she can't. The love is real, but the actual place is not." Jesus said, looking at William's body in the chair.

"You notice you ain't been in pain, Billy? How that pain gone in and out the whole trip? Yeah…. that pain was in your head. The whole time, you made that happen. It's not here at all. At the same time, though, it's real Billy. All this is real. Hard to explain it." Mohammed added. William looked around at the others in the chairs. Some were looking at magazines. Others were playing on their cell phones. All of them were hooked up to the machines.

"Wait, so if I'm not dead, how can this…." William started.

"You're damn near it. Look. You know, your body, but that's not you, is it? You're almost there, buddy! Almost crossed that finish line, baby!!" Jesus made a running motion with his arms.

"Wait, that means if I'm almost dead, that would mean you're both…."

"Dead? Yeah. That's us, buddy. Every year. Except we come back, other people don't." Mohammed said, saluting with his right hand.

"What? I mean…if I'm here, how…. I mean, we were in Arizona, right? I mean, how can that happen?" William asked.

"Oh, you mean like jumping from California to Arizona in a few hours? Oh, how about finding that bar JUST as you were about to go out? Yeah, Billy….it happened, but it didn't happen." Jesus responded.

William looked around, confused. He looked

outside to see Rhonda waiting in the car for him. He didn't know she was waiting. He thought she was working. He remained silent, trying to figure things out, when Mohammed finally pushed his right shoulder to get his attention.

"Yo! Numbnuts. You never left that fucking chair. You figure that shit out yet?" Mohammed barked in his gruff tone. William took a few moments to replay everything that had happened. He went through step by step, moment by moment, and then smiled.

He thought he would be scared at this moment. Everything he was doing before this was to escape death, and here it was. It was the most beautiful thing he had ever imagined, and all he had to do was let go.

"So, Billy. Not bad, huh? A couple of old-school biker gurus as your grim reapers!! HA HA!!!" Mohammed laughed.

"Wait, so that means this is it? I'm done?" William asked. Yet, still not scared. Jesus looked over at him.

"No, Billy. Mo's just fucking with ya. Some deep shit though you're seeing, huh?" Jesus said, smiling at William.

"I'll say. So, is this real? Like right now real?" William asked.

"Yeah. It's real, buddy." Mohammed said, walking over to William in the chair. He looked at the side of William's body, then at his neck.

"Man, you're all fucked up." Mohammed laughed. William stayed in his peaceful feeling, and it didn't even phase him.

"Yeah...I am. That chemo stuff is brutal, especially that last one they gave me." William responded, and the scenery faded back out to the forest.

William's body transformed into a rock, and this time the ocean was in the background. The trees swayed above them, and this time there were sounds of the forest. Rabbits could be seen running through, and the deer there earlier had a whole family with him. A crescent moon behind the trees and the ocean lit the area in a beautiful pale white.

"You outdid yourself on this one, Billy. You know, most people just pull up their house or some random city. Have you ever even been here?" Jesus asked. William shook his head.

"No. This place is just.... where'd I have wanted to go if I could. I wanted to camp and explore the world, but I was always working." William said. Mohammed looked back to see the motorcycles parked behind them, and he pointed at them and nodded in approval.

"Nice!" Mohammed pointed out.

"How long can I stay here?" William asked. He kept adding to the scene. Now there were birds and even a few horses in the background. He took a deep breath and then looked out all around him as he let it out.

"As long as you want, Billy. Time isn't a thing here. It's not like us. We time out and go back. Your rules are different. People usually freak out about now. Suddenly, their whole lives start flashing, and we get to see things we don't want to. Well, that's when it's our turn to host and all. Only the host sees what the guest sees. That's what we've been, hosts. There's so many of us we rarely get to host someone crossing this far out, but usually, when they are where you are, people are freaked out." Mohammed said.

"Yeah, Mo's right. We don't get to see this stuff, but we get a close one every few years, and usually not like this. We usually see every regret a person has, or we get to watch their kids for a while. This place, though…. this is nice, Billy." Jesus said, looking around.

William started to walk around and touch the plants. It had been a long time since he could walk like this. No pain. No fatigue. He kept walking and adding an animal or two. He added an elephant in the middle of the forest at one point. Then the landscape changed to the rain forest with all the animals William could think of. All the animals that he always wanted to see. Jesus and Mohammed followed behind William as he walked. The landscape changed again to the pyramids of Egypt, then again to Paris, France, then again to Antarctica with Polar bears, all with William still walking. It switched back to the forest again, and William stopped walking. He stopped at a cliff to see the ocean and moon with the stars in the backdrop. He looked around again and had forgotten about Mohammed and Jesus behind him. He stood staring off into the moon and the sea.

"Damn, Billy, this is nice. I have to say. I didn't expect this from you. The last one we hosted, we ended up watching an orgy and complete debauchery from a middle-aged homemaker. In the end, though, it switched back to her family. We had to sit there for HOURS watching that damn Spongebob. Over and over and over again with her kids running around the house. This is much better." Mohammed said, walking up and standing next to William.

"Well, didn't help that Mo kept asking what else she wanted to do. Notice he hasn't asked you this time?" Jesus laughed, looking over at Mohammed. William looked out at the ocean and watched the waves hitting a rock.

"Alright fuck it, I'll ask. Anything else you want to do?" Mohammed asked. William shook his head.

"No. I just want to know Rhonda will be alright. I know I can't bring her here, but can I see her?" William asked. Jesus looked over at Mohammed, and the landscape changed.

They were in the parking lot of the clinic. Rhonda was on her phone playing a game waiting for William. She got out of the car and pulled out a cigarette. She lit it and smoked it as she continued her game. William just looked over at her. Usually, he would have been annoyed at the smoking, but that didn't seem to matter. He looked at her for a long time, locking in her image. Rhonda stomped out the cigarette and got back in the car. William watched her through the car window and then looked into the clinic to see his body sitting.

"I'm ready." William said.

"Ready for what?" Mohammed asked.

"I'm ready to go." William said.

"Go where? What the fuck are you talking about?" Jesus asked.

"Isn't that what this is? Like my last moments?" William asked.

"Fuck if I know. You do whatever, but we gotta go, buddy." Mohammed said, nudging Jesus.

"Wait. What? Where are you guys going? What the hell's going on here?" William asked. Jesus motioned over at Mohammed as if to get ready.

"Don't know, Billy. This is where we get off the train. I'd like to say I'll see ya again, but I don't know, buddy. Doesn't happen like that." Jesus said, holding his hand out to shake William's hand. William instinctively shook his hand, confused.

"Wait. Are you leaving? You can't go, what am I supposed to do? What about the whole death thing? Aren't you guys walking me through the gates and all that?" William asked. Mohammed laughed.

"No, dude. We don't do all that. If we could die, we'd have done it already. Damn dude, weren't you listening?" Mohammed said and held out his hand to shake. William shook his hand and still looked confused.

"So what happens next?" William asked.

"No clue, but I'm sure it's fine, buddy. Wish I could tell you." Jesus said, distracting William from Mohammed's handshake. The two of them broke away quickly.

"WAIT! What about Rhonda? She was with Thoth! Is she coming back? How do I get out of here?" William shouted.

"That shit was in your head, Billy! You'll figure it out. Don't count on Thoth either. He's heading back too." Jesus said, walking away.

"Heading back where?" William shouted but got no response. He looked out into the darkness, and both Mohammed and Jesus were gone.

All this time together, they were gone. Yet, that same peaceful feeling remained. He looked around and realized he was alone. He tried to call them back and even imagine them back, but it didn't work. He pulled up the forest again, then the pyramids, and then his house. He pulled up every city he could think of, looking for Jesus and Mohammed. Nothing.

William pulled up the forest again. This time he added people to the background and a few waterfront businesses. He walked down to see the families eating and talking together. He sat at a bench facing the families. He loved hearing the kids' laughter and seeing the families together. Kids. The one thing he didn't have. He thought hard, and the beach became a Boardwalk with rides and games. More people and more kids. Before he knew it, he could hear the crowds screaming on the roller coasters. He walked down the Boardwalk, watching the people playing and the bright lights. The bells would ring, and the kids would scream in delight as William walked by. He stood at the end, watching the roller coasters roll by and all the people going about their business.

"Fake…. it's all fake." William said out loud.

"What's fake?" A voice asked from behind him.

William turned around to see Thoth standing behind him, this time with a cane on his right side.

"All of this. I made it, and it's not real." William responded.

"So, because YOU made this, it's fake? Ask that little girl over there if this is fake." Thoth said, pointing his cane at a girl playing the game where darts are thrown at balloons.

"You know what I mean." William said.

"No. No, I don't know what you mean. You made all this. You can take it down at any time, but it's still here. Why?" Thoth asked. William shrugged his shoulders.

"Hey, I thought you're supposed to be gone too." William said.

"Oh, so that's what those two yahoos told you? Well, no. I'm still here. I don't go anywhere anymore. Funny though, everyone else does. Everyone usually leaves by now, but not you. You're still here. Why are you still here? I mean, you're not the only one, but most people just take a couple of looks at their lives, and poof, they go. I don't know where they go, but they go. You're still here. You have an entire forest and now a city and your bike over there. You could have left at any time, but you're here. Why?" Thoth asked. William thought about it for a minute.

"I don't know. I guess I don't have much to go back to." the scenery switched to the clinic and William's body. William pointed at himself. The scenery switched

back. "Also, I don't know where to go. Jay and Mo....
they didn't tell me what to do." William finished.

"Well...it's not like there's an instruction manual.
They've been doing this a long time, Sir William. They
can only bring you so far. You have to do the rest. The
individual soul. Even the animal souls. The animals
are simple, though. They die, and the lights go out,
except for dogs. Dogs hang out for a while. Anyway,
I'm getting off-topic. You seem to be stuck." Thoth
said, picking up a dart from the game booth. He threw
the dart and popped the balloon. He smiled as the
worker handed him a small stuffed bear.

"I don't know. I don't want to lose this, I guess. I've
been in a lot of pain and just seeing people happy.... I
don't know." William said, looking around. He watched
a small boy about five years old with his family walk by
with a hat with a propeller on it.

"Why the kids and the families? You've never had
one." Thoth asked.

"I remember when I was a kid, my parents....it
wasn't here, but we went to an amusement park. Hell,
it was so long ago, but I remember. I just wanted to
give something back, I guess. Does this stay after I go?"
William asked.

Thoth looked down. "I'm afraid not, Sir William.
You're not God. It's meant to be like a....way to ease you
into the next phase of your journey."

"Well, I said I was ready to Jay and Mo, but I
guess I wasn't. Can I at least ride my bike before I go?"
William asked. Thoth motioned for William towards

his motorcycle parked on the Boardwalk. William took a second and looked around, then walked over to his motorcycle. He threw his leg over with no pain, no sickness, and sat on the seat. He turned the key and smiled as he pushed the ignition button. He looked over at Thoth. Thoth nodded at him. William put the bike in first gear and let out the clutch. He started to move and followed the road out of the boardwalk.

As he accelerated faster and faster, he found himself in the desert again, this time alone, but it wasn't cold. He kept going faster and faster until he just stopped thinking. He was invincible here, so the fear was gone now. He felt the wind running through his hair and realized he wasn't even wearing a helmet. Not here. He kept going and going through the desert landscape with the crescent moon ahead of him. He smiled as he went faster and faster.

He remembered what Jesus and Mohammed had talked about with the bikes, and they were right. Even here, where he controlled things, it was a freedom like no other. One that had no words to it. As he began to accelerate again, he saw the headlight of a semi-truck in front of him. William didn't make that happen. He didn't think that up. Those lights came out of nowhere. His heart jumped, and he tried to brake, but it was too late. Before he could do anything, he collided with the lights head-on.

CHAPTER 13

---◆---

THE CHAIR

William woke up in his chair with the familiar beep of the chemotherapy machines.

"Mr. Tunnicliff, that should do it for today. You did great!" Mary, his nurse, said as she removed the cap from his IV tube.

William looked at her, shocked. Was it a dream? What happened? Everything happened again. Rhonda came in.

"Baby, you're looking good!" She said, holding out her hand as she did for every session. The nausea was back again, but he took a good sniff and could smell the cigarette smoke. He smiled. It wasn't a dream. He pushed as hard as possible, but the sickness overtook him again. Rhonda got him into the car, and they started to head home.

As they pulled up to the traffic light, he could hear the loud sound of the Harley. *Steve....* he thought, awaiting his neighbor to pull up. Then he listened carefully. It wasn't just one, and as he heard this, he looked over to see two very distinctive motorcycles pull up on his side. A distinctive black and a second distinctive white motorcycle that looked like they were from the 1970s pulled up to the red light right next to them. William sat up immediately. He recognized those bikes. He frantically tried to roll down the window.

He looked over to see both bikes and looked at the riders. They both looked over at him. Both African Americans. The one on the white bike had long, straight hair, and the other had very distinctive curly long hair. They looked over at William. He knew them immediately, even with their different skin color. They both held up their left hands with two fingers up in a peace sign as their bikes thundered at the light. William finally got the window down, and the two moved forward, and off they went into the distance, the thunder of the pipes fading as they got further away. He felt something in his right pants pocket that was heavy as he sat up.

William sat with the window down as the car started to pull forward. He felt the object in his pocket and pulled it out. It was the revolver from Bud's place that Jay and Mo had given him. He didn't pull it out of his pocket. Instead, he pushed it back and began to smile.

"You know them, honey?" Rhonda asked, driving. William sat silently and then began to laugh as loud as he could. He laughed so hard he felt tears coming down. Rhonda looked over at him, confused.

"What?" she asked, looking over at him. William looked forward and rolled up the window. He turned and looked at her.

"I need to buy a motorcycle..." he said. Rhonda smiled.

"Aren't you going to wave to Lucy?" Rhonda responded, looking over at the newer model RV with a very pretty African American driver, definitely Lucy. She blew him a kiss and then drove off. William looked over at Rhonda, shocked and wide-eyed. How did SHE know Lucy? Rhonda winked back at him.

The Beginning.

★ ★ ★

CPSIA information can be obtained
at www.ICGtesting.com
Printed in the USA
BVHW041229140822
644510BV00002BA/3

9 781982 277345